"Oh, I think you like
I have many . . .

"Yeah, I can see 'em." He slapped his hat back on his head. "Honey, I wouldn't take it if you were giving it away free."

Legal training had aided her natural inclination to hold her cards close. Her smile actually sparkled under the lights. "Shall we put it to the test?"

His eyes narrowed under the thick lashes. "Oh, I forgot. This is the part where you do your lap dances to make the really big bucks. Thanks, but no thanks. Besides, I tipped you twenty bucks already."

What a jerk. She'd been about to tell him she didn't do lap dances anymore, but now she gave him that little sexy north-south appraisal designed to tickle men right below the belt. And based on the way he shifted his weight from hip to hip, as if his pants felt too tight, it worked whether he liked it or not.

Jasmine said softly, "Tell you what. You follow the rules and avoid touching me and I won't even charge you my usual going rate."

"How much is that?"

"Two hundred bucks."

He almost flinched, but his hard gray eyes delved into hers. "Tell you what. If I don't touch you, you answer two questions for me. Straight on. In more than one syllable."

"You're on, Mr. Policeman."

FOSTER JUSTICE

COLLEEN
SHANNON

KENSINGTON BOOKS
KENSINGTON PUBLISHING CORP.
www.kensingtonbooks.com

KENSINGTON BOOKS are published by

Kensington Publishing Corp.
119 West 40th Street
New York, NY 10018

All Kensington titles, imprints, and distributed lines are available at special quantity discounts for bulk purchases for sales promotion, premiums, fund-raising, educational, or institutional use.

Special book excerpts or customized printings can also be created to fit specific needs. For details, write or phone the office of the Kensington Special Sales Manager: Kensington Publishing Corp., 119 West 40th Street, New York, NY 10018. Attn. Special Sales Department. Phone: 1-800-221-2647.

First Electronic Edition: December 2014
eISBN-13: 978-1-60183-293-1
eISBN-10: 1-60183-293-1

First Print Edition: December 2014
ISBN-13: 978-1-60183-294-8
ISBN-10: 1-60183-294-X

Printed in the United States of America

TEXAS DEPARTMENT OF PUBLIC SAFETY REQUIREMENTS TO APPLY AS A TEXAS RANGER:

"Each applicant must be a citizen of the United States of America, in excellent physical condition, and have an outstanding record of at least eight (8) years experience with a bona fide law enforcement agency, engaged principally in the investigation of major crimes . . . Applicant must have a background subject to a thorough investigation, which would reflect good moral character and habits . . . Little recruiting has ever been necessary and it is not unusual for many officers to apply for only a handful of openings."

Author's notes:

The Texas Rangers are the oldest state law enforcement body in the United States and were established by Stephen F. Austin in 1836 during the formation of the Republic of Texas.

As of 2009, there were 150 commissioned Rangers. They are protected from disbandment by state law. They have statewide jurisdiction and often collaborate with federal law enforcement agencies and agencies in other states.

TEXAS RANGER MOTTO:

"One riot, one ranger."

CHAPTER 1

As rustlers went, they were better'n most, Chad Foster decided, caressing his AR-15 rifle mounted with a night vision scope. The thieves, probably the same ones he'd been chasing all over the Panhandle, had herded his cattle up to this plateau far above the canyon floor, giving the Black Angus little room to escape being forced into the huge trailer. Still, pursuing lawbreakers as part of his job and finding them rustling his own private stock were two different things.

Keeping his spirited stallion, Chester, still with his knees, Chad peeked around the outcropping, gauging distance and angle. If he aimed just right, he should be able to take out enough tires on one side to cripple their rig. Then what? He was one man, on a horse, against three hardened criminals in a huge tractor trailer.

While he contemplated his options, a Texas sunset painted Palo Duro Canyon in golden and red hues of blood and glory. The rays winked off his distinctive Texas Ranger Lone Star badge like a warning light. But the scroungy wannabe cowboys were too busy to notice, zipping around on ATVs, corralling steers toward their cattle trailer. Chad's lip curled. No matter how fancy their rig, likely stolen, too, Chad viewed rustlers on a par with worms and strippers: the only critters too low to fall down.

Cattle prices had finally gone up enough to make it worthwhile for a part-time rancher. Should be just enough profit to catch up on those back taxes Trey had let slide. He wasn't about to lose the cattle now—even if he was outgunned and outnumbered. Hell's bells, the old Ranger motto was still as valid today as it had been when coined over a century ago: "One riot, one ranger." His decision made, in his usual to-hell-with-the-consequences fashion, Chad eased out of hiding while the rustlers were busy with the trailer latch. He reined Chester around the outcropping to take careful aim at a huge rear tire.

A stray steer spooked Chester. The stallion whinnied and reared. Looking up, the rustlers spotted him. In his cowboy hat, chaps, and spurs, with the rearing sorrel quarter horse reddish against a violet sky, Chad was an image right out of the Old West, when retribution was more than a fancy word. Getting the message, they abandoned their ATVs for the truck.

Chad needed both hands to calm Chester, the rifle slung over his shoulder, and by the time he was able to take steady aim, the perps had fired up the huge diesel and stirred up a cloud of dust, leaving him choking in their wake. He squinted, his eyes tearing as he tried to sight, but the scope was useless in all this dust. He shouldered the rifle and kicked Chester into a gallop, moving at an angle that would cut them off at the dirt road leading off the plateau.

Then, to his shock, he realized the huge vehicle, with a screeching of brakes and spitting of dirt and rock, had done a one-eighty, driving back toward the canyon edge. Chad wheeled Chester around to keep pace. The truck's lights pierced the haze of dirt and dusk, blinding spooked and confused cattle. Behind them was the canyon rim; in front loomed that huge mechanical monster.

While Chad stared, trying to figure out what in tarnation the rustlers were trying, the truck lurched forward, Klaxon horn honking, lights blinking, rock chunks spitting as it came, startling several steers. The confused cattle took the path of least resistance and ran away—straight toward the canyon edge, less visible in the growing gloom.

God Almighty, they were forcing the steers over the edge just to spite him! Chad looked frantically around, but he had no backup and little inspiration, only hard choices.

Lose his herd, or risk his life to stop the stampede. On horseback.

In the end, the choice wasn't difficult. He had no wife, no kids, and no girlfriend. In fact, he only had three things he valued in life: one little brother who hated his guts, the fourth-generation Amarillo ranch that had bred them both, and The Job. And if he let these assholes buffalo him, he'd risk all three.

The truck gained speed, horn blaring, and the milling cattle went from a lope to a panicked stampede. At this rate they'd be over the rim in minutes. Spurring Chester into a flat-out gallop, Chad bent low over his stallion's neck, leaping over boulders, down a small gully, back up the other side. But the rough path allowed him to cut in front of the truck and ride alongside the herd, perilously close to the canyon edge.

However, Chester had been a cow pony all his life, and he'd herded panicked cattle before. They wove through the milling herd, slowing some of the laggards a bit more with their diagonal passage. Chad pulled his rifle and fired at boulders above the lead steer's head. Bits of rock sprayed the steer in the face, making him snort and slow a bit, but that damnable horn blared again.

Roaring, the engine revved into a higher gear, brights flashing, and the slowing stampede picked up speed. They were halfway to the edge now, a sheer drop two hundred feet to the canyon floor.

Chad sped up again. He could risk everything and try to get in front far enough to herd them around, or take on the truck now and to hell with the herd. Or he had one shot to do both. Urging Chester to the edge of the stampede again so he could gain speed on the outside, Chad guided Chester with his knees and sighted back over his shoulder as he rode, trusting his horse with his life.

Holding his breath and letting the rhythm take him, Chad became part of Chester, feeling the rise and fall of each step, his hands steady on his rifle. He sighted at the horn as it blew a fresh clarion. *Bam!* The shot landed dead center, killing the horn's bellow with a gush of air.

Next he aimed at the headlights. He hit one before Chester stumbled slightly, and Chad almost went flying. He had to let the rifle sling back over his shoulder while he grabbed the reins. They were galloping even with the lead cattle, and he urged Chester faster, putting distance between him and the head of the herd.

Ten feet, twenty, thirty, fifty . . .

Just before the canyon rim, Chad wheeled Chester like the quarter horse he was, damn near on a dime, sighting again before he stopped. Chester's hooves broke rock off the crumbling edge. One part of Chad registered the rockslide he'd started and how long it took the rocks to hit the canyon floor, but the coolest part of his brain calculated distance and angle.

The other headlight was smack dab in his crosshairs. *Pling!* The last light went out. The truck slowed, downshifting again. Taking advantage of that hesitation, Chad shot repeatedly now at the rocks littering the path of the stampede leader. The steer blinked and bawled as rocks scoured its face, slowing as it shook its head.

Chad shot a scrubby tree into bits, more litter blocking the lead steer's path. It slowed again. The cattle in back, now that they weren't blinded and spooked by the horn and lights, had also slowed. But the truck, idling for an ominous moment, began to speed up again, gears grinding. The cattle in back shied away.

Glad he'd put in his biggest clip, Chad fired at the lead cattle again, grazing hooves. They stumbled. A couple fell, slowing the ones behind.

But they were close, too close, a mere thirty feet away now.

He had one chance to avoid being swept over the canyon rim by his own herd, and he took it, firing at the rig's tires. One blew, two, three on one side, and the truck began to lurch, slowing as the front axle hit the ground.

Chad tried to fire in front of the lead cattle again and cursed when he heard an empty click. They'd slowed a lot, but were still coming. Using the only weapon he had left, Chad cued Chester into a rear and roared at the top of his lungs, wildly waving his rifle over his head, hoping he loomed large and terrifying against the dying sunlight.

Chester whinnied, pawing the air. Ten feet away, the lead steer veered to the side rather than face the angry quarter horse.

The rear cattle milled around again, confused.

Chad was able to whack the last few cattle away from the rim and make his way toward the rig. It lay skewed on one side as Chad quickly put in another loaded clip and reined Chester toward the driver-side door, rifle pointed.

He was expecting it, so when he saw movement in the gloom, he fired. Yelling in pain, the driver dropped the pistol he'd been aiming at Chad's head. Chad fired at the passenger-door side, too, and it slammed shut.

Holding the rifle steady on the driver, Chad appeared at the window, his angular, grimy face as hard as the landscape around them. "Haven't you heard, boys? Beef's bad for you. Especially when it isn't yours." He waved the rifle at them. "Out. This side, all of you."

The driver got out first, cursing a blue streak Chad ignored. His men followed. "Put your hands on the side of the truck." They did so. Still seated on his horse, Chad ignored his handcuffs and pulled his lariat.

"Lean back away from the truck." When they obeyed, Chad neatly hooked the leader around the waist, and got down and tied the hands of the next two men with the same rope, turning them into a cowboy-style chain gang. He cinched the other end of the rope around Chester's saddle horn.

"Hey, mister, what you doing? You don't mean to walk us back all that long way! In the dark?" protested the lead rustler.

Chad kneed Chester, forcing them to stumble along behind. "You put me in a mind to herd something. It's only, say, twenty miles back to headquarters. We'll see how much piss and vinegar you have then." Settling back in his saddle, Chad ignored their bitching and walked them down the road, through peacefully grazing cattle.

He debated calling Trey to let him know he wouldn't be in until morning, but it was a useless courtesy since little brother was probably stone-cold drunk. Like usual. Over a woman not worth a hat tippin', as his daddy would say.

At the Foster homestead, Trey Foster swigged the last of his rum and Coke, swimming in a fog that dulled the enormity of what he was about to do. But it was time, past time, to get the heck out of Dodge, back to LA where he belonged.

Back to the only girl he'd ever loved, ever could love, even if she was someone his big brother would never approve of. Bleary-eyed, Trey looked from the paint on the tips of his fingers to his masterpiece, glistening with wet oil in the bright lights of his studio.

It was some of his best work. A lovely, mysterious woman, her face half shielded by a long fall of deep auburn hair, was depicted from the waist up. She wore only a lace shawl arrayed low over a luxurious bosom. On the lower slope of her right breast was a small but alluring butterfly tattoo, its blue and yellow wings so vivid it looked about to take flight every time she breathed.

He'd painted her from memory, with such lust and longing that the redhead seemed Woman incarnate, the temptress responsible for the downfall of Man since time immemorial. Yet he'd also perfectly captured weariness and longing in her blue eyes . . . as if the hopeful romantic lurking inside the temptress still slumbered, waiting to be awakened by the right man.

Lost in memory, he almost didn't hear the knock until it came a second time, more insistently. He stumbled as he moved off his stool, knocking against his favorite easel with the splintered leg. He'd repaired it so many times it was rickety. He had to catch the wall as he weaved from room to room in the old ranch house. By the time he made it to the front door, the visitor was pounding harder.

"All right, all right," Trey muttered as he flung open the door to Thomas Kinnard's impatient face. As soon as he saw Trey, Kinnard smoothed his scowl into a smile. He pumped Trey's hand.

"Good to see you again, Trey. We've missed you in LA. You ready to finalize the deal?"

Trey stood aside, still clutching the door, but guilt sucker punched him the minute he let into his ancestral home the Beverly Hills businessman Chad would despise. The mere thought of facing Chad after this deal was done made him sick at his stomach. But then Chad belonged here. Trey never had.

Avoiding the stern stares of his ancestors, arrayed in chronological order around the living room walls—most of the severe-faced men garbed in various uniforms and badges—Trey waved Kinnard into a chair and slumped onto the couch. Kinnard pulled a thick sheaf of papers from his pocket and handed them to Trey.

Trey unfolded them and made every pretense of reading, but the truth was, he couldn't even focus past the heading: "Bill of Sale: Transfer of Land and Mineral Rights."

Kinnard stood without being invited and poured them each a drink from the tray. "Mind if I take a look at what you've done since you've been here?"

Trey waved him toward his studio, still trying to concentrate.

It seemed a long time before Kinnard returned. Trey sniffed his drink, confused that all of a sudden it smelled like paint thinner, but then a blur of movement caught his gaze and he realized Kinnard was wiping his paint-smeared fingertips on a rag.

Trey blinked, his voice slurred, but he wasn't too drunk not to be suspicious. Like most artists, he found art gallery owners a necessary evil, but he sure as hell didn't like giving them more than half of every dime he made. "You become a painter all of a sudden?"

"I got a little too close to that portrait you did of Mary. It's stunning. Can I show it after you get to LA?"

"It's not for sale, too private. And I'm not finished with it anyway."

"That's easy to fix. Just give it Jasmine's face instead of Mary's and we'll make a fortune with it. But I like it."

"You're meant to. But I don't want to share her with anyone."

Kinnard scowled, but Trey turned back to the contract, pretending to read. He wished there was some other way . . . but Chad was too damned stubborn, just like their daddy. They were sitting on a gold mine—who the hell cared if it ruined their grazing? Plenty of other ranchers combined cattle and oil. Besides, even though he'd only sold his half, Trey planned to split the income with Chad.

Kinnard wandered the living room, appraising the pictures on the walls. When he came to the picture of a Texas Ranger in full uniform, the last in the line before Chad, in a similar uniform, Kinnard raised his glass.

The movement caught Trey's attention, and through a haze, he saw the businessman in profile staring at Gerald Foster's picture. In twenty years, Chad would look just about like their father. Ever sensitive to emotions, Trey picked up on something not quite right in the way Kinnard stared at Daddy.

The clean shaven, arrogant jaw flexed. Trey saw Kinnard's knuckles grow white as he clutched his highball glass so tightly ice rattled.

His vague sense of unease growing, Trey blinked rapidly, trying to clear his vision. When he looked again, Kinnard was walking back toward him, wearing the smooth smile that complemented his five-thousand-dollar silk suit. "The deal structure's exactly what we discussed. With the price of oil and gas, you and your brother will soon be rich. The preliminary geologicals indicate over a billion metric cubic feet of natural gas and over one hundred million barrels of oil."

Trey hesitated.

"Mary can't wait to see you. And I've already made room on my gallery walls for some of your paintings. We'll schedule the unveiling as soon as we've built up some buzz." Kinnard waited. "Any questions, Trey?"

Yeah, Trey thought glumly. *One. Will Chad ever forgive me?* Trey pulled a gold nugget necklace out of his shirt, worrying at it. He knew he was doing the right thing for both of them, but he also knew Chad would consider him a sellout and a traitor.

Kinnard picked up the necklace and read aloud the inscription on the smooth bottom: "'Family's all that lasts. Mama.' Cute." Kinnard dropped the necklace back. "That and millions in the bank." When Trey still fingered his necklace, Kinnard's voice grew impatient. "Which is worse? Possibly messing up your grazing land or losing everything to foreclosure?"

Taking a deep breath, Trey accepted Kinnard's fancy fountain pen and focused blearily. However, he signed his name with less than his usual flair.

Chad was going to be pissed.

CHAPTER 2

A day late and way more than a dollar short, Chad showed up at the Foster homestead gate just as dawn dew was burning off the scrub. No such thing as a lawn at their place because neither he nor Trey had either time or interest in caring for it. However, the jasmine their mother had planted had taken over one entire side of the porch. Its lush scent aroused visceral memories of home, and happier times, but conversely depressed him more.

Resting his arms on his saddle pommel, Chad sat an equally drooping Chester. He knew he was only avoiding another argument with Trey, but then the sound of a cranky engine roared up the road. Barbed-wire fences lined their ranch. Signs were posted every so often: No Trespassing. No Oil Transport Allowed Across Foster Land.

Chad's hackles lowered as he realized it wasn't a derrick truck from the adjacent oil leases shortcutting across their land as usual, but . . . a moving van. Dread kicked him in the gut as the van passed him and veered into their long, red clay driveway.

Chad kicked Chester into a gallop and drew him to a rearing stop just as the front screen door, rickety on its hinges, slammed open and Trey came out. Chad took one look at him and recognized the signs of a hangover. He was about to tear him a new one when the movers got out of the van and entered the house. Trey spotted him and ducked back inside.

So furious he didn't bother to tie Chester up, Chad stumbled with weariness as he leaped off his still-moving horse and slammed after Trey. It had been a long night, first the grueling trip across the mesa to town, then half a night's worth of paperwork. He'd had no sleep. He was dirty, exhausted, and depressed, and watching Trey flee his obligations snapped the last strand of Chad's frayed patience, which was never strong at the best of times.

Across the width of the hall filled with moving boxes and pictures of their ancestors, Trey and Chad stared at one another. They looked nothing alike, never had, and both knew it.

As Chad scowled at the packed suitcases, a bitter smile curled the edges of Trey's pretty-boy mouth, which had always reminded Chad of their mother. But then, Trey never had much of the grit and determination of the male side of the Foster clan. He was the "sensitive" one. The sight of the easel and painting supplies packed most carefully of all told Chad everything he needed to know.

Trey didn't plan on coming back.

For once, Trey didn't flinch from that accusing, judgmental look. He stared right back. "Big brother's watching."

Chad said evenly, "You know, I figured you for lazy, and maybe even stupid sometimes when your heart's involved, but—"

"At least I have one—"

"But I never figured you for a coward. I taught you better. You gone plumb loco to run out on me when we're facing foreclosure?"

"In loco parentis, big brother. That's what you've always pretended to be since Mama and Daddy died. But you're not my father, you're not my conscience, and you're sure as hell not qualified to be my judge and jury." Trey turned away dismissively and went back into the bedroom he used for a studio on the west side of the house. He moved toward a painting on an easel and stopped dead, staring.

Close on his heels, Chad stared, too.

A bosomy redhead wore only a lacy shawl, and the way the light fell made her alluring form all the more striking because the face was carved away. Chad felt a jolt below the belt, right where he was supposed to, but that only pissed him off. The woman couldn't possibly be that sensual in person. Even decimated, the picture was one of Trey's finest, and he had quite a repertoire. "Your Beverly Hills stripper?" Chad asked. "Why'd you carve her face away?"

Trey grabbed a tossed-aside palette knife and stared down at the same colors he'd used on the face in the portrait, now dried on the knife. "Damn him! He's just trying to teach me who's boss since I wouldn't let him show her. We'll see when I get out there . . ."

Not for the first or last time when Trey was around, Chad was lost. He felt like he'd stepped into *The Twilight Zone* meets *Days of Our Lives*. "Out there? Out where?" He'd assumed Trey was moving into Amarillo, as he'd threatened for years.

Trey carefully rolled up the painting, as if he held the *Mona Lisa*, resolving Chad's last doubt as to the redhead's identity. It was definitely that floozy Trey had talked about one night in a drunken fit. He'd recounted his broken heart, and how the one girl he'd ever loved had visited the ranch while Chad was on assignment, but she hated the isolation and had scurried back to Beverly Hills, leaving Trey a drunken wreck. Chad's cooped-up fury with the girl increased. She'd met Trey when he'd gone to the West Coast to show his art, dangled him like a fish on a hook, then deserted him just as he was about to ask her to marry him. Typical female. The visceral response came before he could stop it. "Dammit, boy, how many times do you have to dip your wick before you learn you can't burn the candle at both ends and run a ranch?"

Trey stopped dead, and the wounded look that flashed across his face took some of the sting out of his retort. "At least I have a date once in a while."

He bent to fiddle with a suitcase, concealing his expression. Chad squelched another remark. No matter how much he deserved it, now was not the time to alienate Trey even more. He was a Foster, belonged here as much as his older brother, even if he was an artist, not a rancher. Chad could almost hear his mother pleading with him to mend fences, to protect what was left of their family.

Chad was about to say something conciliatory when Trey bent to put the rolled painting in a tube he'd obviously left for that purpose. A sheaf of papers fell out of Trey's jacket.

Chad caught one glimpse of the top heading: "Bill of Sale: Transfer of Land and Mineral Rights" before he literally saw red, forgetting everything but Trey's betrayal.

When Trey pocketed the papers, not meeting his eyes, and turned to exit, Chad grabbed his brother's slight shoulder and spun Trey to face him. He shook him for good measure. "How could you? How could you sell out four generations of sweat and toil for an exotic dancer not worth a dime?"

Trey jerked away. "Since she won't come to me, I have to go to her, and I need money to do it. Besides, I have the right to sell my half of this place and go wherever I please. And Beverly Hills is what pleases me."

Torn between two primitive urges, Chad wasn't sure which he wanted to do first: vomit or beat the holy living crap out of his last blood relative.

Fifteen hundred miles away, two women exited the Cheesecake Factory in Beverly Hills. Both were tall and voluptuous, with identical shades of auburn hair. They were laughing, and several men almost careened into other pedestrians as they eyed the pair.

But Mary Baker, the slightly taller of the two, quit laughing as the other girl's purse slipped off her shoulder, disarranging her tailored white blouse enough for a bright yellow-and-blue butterfly tattoo on her breast to peek through the fabric.

Mary stopped dead on the sidewalk and pulled her own blouse aside, revealing an identical tattoo. "I thought you hated tattoos, Jasmine."

"It's temporary," Jasmine replied. "I know it matches yours, but Thomas chose the pattern, said he wanted us to look as much alike as possible for the art show." Jasmine fidgeted her blouse back in place. "Somehow baring so much cleavage in broad daylight, in such a ritzy part of town, seems much cheaper than dancing half naked under bright lights. At least then I can't see all the men watching me."

"Yeah, those rich old farts give me the heebie-jeebies, too," Mary agreed. She pulled her blouse back in place before slowly continuing on. "I'm sorry I ever hooked you up with Thomas, Jasmine."

"At least now I can pay my bills and tuition. Besides, I kind of like the tattoo. I'm using it in my act."

Mary walked in silence, her lovely face grim.

Jasmine eyed her curiously. "What's the big deal? Why do you care if our tattoos match since you don't dance at the club anymore?"

"Let's just say, Thomas Kinnard never does anything without a reason. I'd get rid of the tattoo as soon as possible, if I were you."

Gently, Jasmine caught her friend's arm and pulled her to a stop. "Why don't you admit what you're really worried about?"

Mary's blue eyes met Jasmine's pale green. Mary looked away.

"Trey's coming back out, isn't he?"

Mary shrugged, but then she burst out, "I . . . think so. And when he does, eventually he'll figure out I was never a dancer, and that I worked with Thomas to lure him away from his land." Tears sparkled in her long-lashed eyes.

They were across the street from one of the city's lush parks, so Jasmine drew Mary to a bench shaded by an exotic flowering tree. "Give." She caught her friend's hands.

Outside Amarillo, the subject of the two women's conversation for once in his life stood toe-to-toe with his taller, meaner, and stronger older brother. Trey said quietly, "She's waiting for me at the Beverly Wilshire. The guy who introduced us owns a gallery in Beverly Hills. He's gonna show my paintings."

Chad shoved Trey against the wall. "You ungrateful little shit. Pa'd turn over in his grave if he knew you were willing to sell out his blood and bone for a woman not worth a hoot or a holler—"

The next minute, Chad was lying on the floor, looking up swollen-mouthed as Trey rubbed his sore knuckles. "You won't talk about her like that, got it? You've never even met her. Besides, you're the last man on the planet I'd come to for advice about women." He stepped over his brother and dragged his suitcases outside.

Chad was about to follow when he saw a gleam of gold under the tall bureau in the hall. He picked up a card and read, "Gentleman's Pleasure." And in smaller print, "Jasmine Routh, headliner." Chad pocketed the card and bolted after Trey.

Trey almost knocked him down coming back into the house to get his art supplies. But it was the tube containing the redhead's portrait he valued most. He held it gently under his arm as he stumbled back down the creaky front porch steps to his battered 1998 red Camaro and put the art supplies on top of his suitcases. The tube he set gently in the backseat.

Chad's fingers closed and opened repeatedly. Trey saw, but the sadness in his pale blue eyes only deepened. "How long since you had a date, Chad?"

Chad's fists froze half-formed.

Trey started to get in his car, but he took a few steps to the side of the porch and broke off a twig of jasmine, bringing it to his nose. "This is the only thing I'll miss about this place. I'll always love the scent of jasmine."

What might have been an answering sadness flickered in Chad's hard gray eyes before he said, "It's not too late, Trey. We can find a way to pay off the second lien we had to take when Mama and Daddy died, if we work together on it."

"It was too late for me the day I was born on this godforsaken place. If you have any sense, you'll sell your half and get out, too, before you're as hard as Daddy. Find a woman, Chad. You need one. Bad."

Chad rounded the car to slam the door shut as Trey opened it to get in. "When I take a notion for a stripper, I know who to call. Fine. Get out. But first you have to tell me who you sold to. I'll hock Granddaddy's Peacemaker and everything else I own to buy your half back."

Trey slapped his hand away and opened the car door. "Chad, do you know what happens when you paint everything black and white?"

"Mama would be ashamed of you." When Trey just looked at him, Chad finally gave up and stepped away from the car. "Go on. Be creative. You sure as hell aren't useful."

Trey opened the door and got inside, but he looked up at his brother with a mixture of love, regret, and concern. "Sooner or later, you end up with gray. And gray's a mighty lonely color."

Trey drove out, following the moving van, his words seeming to echo with prophetic wisdom on the West Texas wind, lingering after his passage. The dirt stirred by the wheels danced in a gay eddy around Chad's stunned face. A monarch butterfly fluttered lazily past, landing on his arm. He stared down at it, his hand lifting to squash it, but then he blew on it gently and went inside.

His boot steps echoed on the hardwood floors with lonely finality.

As Trey drove toward California, on Brighton Way in Beverly Hills, a stone's throw from Rodeo Drive, a new art gallery's lights flooded the night. The discreet bronze plaque beside the door glittered with gold lettering: Kinnard's American Masters. Well-heeled guests crowded the spacious gallery, eyeing an interesting blend of contemporary and traditional art, from sculptures to paintings to photos. One entire wall was taken up with acrylic paintings of butterflies unfurled so voluptuously they looked almost pornographic.

Jasmine saw now why Thomas had insisted on the matching tattoos: as usual, he was using business acumen, not some mysterious ulterior motive. The largest, most prominent painting depicted a yellow-and-blue butterfly, spread open in a very suggestive manner, with another butterfly poised above the unfurled wings.

A couple, both dressed in Armani, stood rapt before the painting. The woman enthused, "This artist has done with butterflies what Georgia O'Keefe did with flowers. I must have this, Rupert. The colors are perfect for our salon." But her husband wasn't looking at the painting. He was watching the two voluptuous redheads circulating with discreet price lists.

Jasmine and Mary, dressed identically in black silk gowns that showed too much cleavage as well as their tattoos, seemed living, breathing examples of art themselves.

As a bit of space finally opened up around them, Jasmine whispered, "It's obvious now why Thomas insisted on the tattoos. No dastardly motive except monetary. Thomas is a good guy, Mary. He's been very kind to me. I wouldn't be making my tuition without him."

Mary looked across the gallery at Thomas Kinnard. No rack Armani for him. He wore a handmade silk suit that fit him perfectly. Even when he leaned over to kiss the cheek of an overweight matron dripping in diamonds, not a wrinkle disturbed the expensive fabric. Mary's fingers tightened about the price lists, but her smile was flawless as another couple came up.

Some hours later, as the last guest left carrying a painting, Thomas was in an expansive mood. He kissed Jasmine's cheek, and then Mary's. "My two best masterpieces. Thanks, ladies. It was a smashing success, with your help. When Trey gets here, we'll have an even better exhibition just for him."

Jasmine smiled a bit uncomfortably, but Mary pulled away when he kissed her. Accepting the sizable check Thomas handed her, Jasmine left. Thomas stretched and started to turn off lights, but Mary said, "Thomas, we need to talk."

He eyed her, but shrugged and led the way into his back office. It was like walking into another world. Here Thomas's true self was displayed. The office was paneled with expensive walnut, and a huge Oriental rug in vivid burgundy, green, and blue covered the room from wall to wall, acting as the perfect foil for the Western art displayed in every quarter: paintings, sculptures, including a couple of originals by Remington himself.

He waved her toward a leather chair before the desk and seated himself behind its massive, masculine bulk. "Are you packed yet for the trip to Amarillo?"

"I've changed my mind. I'm not going."

He didn't react with the anger she'd dreaded. He merely lifted one of those silver eyebrows and said calmly, "Why not? We're finally ready to drill. The latest reports indicate the deposit beneath the Foster ranch will yield more than a billion metric cubic feet of natural gas alone. And I never could have convinced Trey to sell without your help. You'll find me very generous when we start collecting checks."

Mary hesitated, and then said reluctantly, "Well, I guess I can finish the preliminary drilling preparation now we have the new seismic equipment available, but I have to see Trey before I go."

"He needs to concentrate on his work, and he can't concentrate on anything when you're around." He shoved a plane ticket and new cell phone, along with a six-figure check, across the desk. "Your share, with a bonus upon signing of the sales contract, as agreed."

Mary didn't pick them up. "Thomas, why did you have Jasmine get a tattoo identical to mine?"

"It worked, didn't it? That old biddy paid an obscene amount for the painting that matched your tattoos, just like I expected."

Twiddling with the ticket, Mary looked as if she wanted to believe him.

Thomas continued smoothly, "Just get the drilling started, and I promise to explain everything to Trey myself after he's settled. By the time you come home, he won't be angry with you. Why on earth should you apologize for helping to make him a millionaire, anyway?"

"Trey deserves to hear the truth from me."

"It's your decision, but he was on the verge of alcoholism when I got him to agree to sell and come back out to LA. If you tell him now, you'll ruin his concentration and he really is a talented artist with a bright future. Keep to the agreement and everything will be fine. He just needs time to adjust to city life."

Reluctantly, Mary rose. "And when Chad Foster finds out?"

The smile playing about Thomas's lips turned cold. "Once he's answered the bugle call to rescue his innocent little brother, we'll have a clear field at the ranch. Get to work."

CHAPTER 3

Three weeks later, beneath the huge Texas Ranger seal in his office, Chad was on the phone, glaring down at a crossed-off list. Stubble shadowed his cheeks and chin. His eyes were bleary and red. "No shit, LA's a big place! But my brother hasn't answered my calls in way over a week and he never does that. I'm telling you, he's a victim of foul play . . . if you send detectives to the art galleries in Beverly Hills—"

A click interrupted him. Chad crossed off the last notation, *LA police*, and shoved the list aside. The flashing computer screen on his desk showed a search engine titled "Corporate Locators." The middle of the screen flashed, "Del Mar Corporation. Nothing found." Chad snapped off his screen in disgust, looking up at his Texas Ranger colleague, Corey Cooper.

Where Chad was living blood and bone representing Texas's ranching heritage, Corey could have posed for a poster advertising the state's new diversity. His name was Irish like his father's, but his lush dark hair and honey-toned skin bore more of the 50 percent heritage of his Mexican mother. While no doubt their immediate ancestors had tried to kill one another, Corey and Chad had turned an armistice into a friendship based on shared beliefs. The Job was better furthered by cooperation rather than the old blood feud between Rangers and Mexicans, going back to 1836 when Texas was a republic and the Rangers were first formed.

"I thought you had a business card to follow up on to find this redhead," Corey said in a soft drawl that bore no trace of a Spanish accent. His mother had forbidden him to speak Spanish at home, but he was still fluent when he wanted to be.

Chad often had to strain to hear Corey, but the way he spoke lent as much weight to what he said as the words themselves. People tended to listen to him. Carefully. "I did. Gentleman's Pleasure won't tell me squat. I hope the whole fucking state falls into the ocean." Chad shoved his hat back and rubbed his forehead.

"Trey's there," Corey reminded him.

"He'll float along with all the other turds." For the first time, Chad realized Corey had an arm behind his back. "You got a trick up your sleeve or an itch to scratch your ass?"

Apparently used to Chad's shortness, Corey merely unveiled the paper he held with a proper flourish. "Since you had the police artist sketch that tattoo you saw, I've done some of my own research. Forget the old motto 'One riot, one ranger.' You're looking in the wrong place to find Trey. Your new motto should be, 'One tattoo, one floozy.' How many tattoo artists do such a distinctive design, even in Hollyweird? Find the artist, you find this Jasmine."

Chad grabbed the drawing as if it were a lifeline. The words were torn from him. "Thanks, Corey. I . . . never shoulda let him leave."

Corey looked at the many medals and award plaques bearing Chad's name on the wall above his desk. "You always take too much responsibility for everything. Trey's an adult. It's not your fault he went off half-cocked and then disappeared as soon as he reached LA." An impish smile curled Corey's sensitive mouth and for a moment he was his Irish father's spitting image. "Women like that keep your peter in the jar beside their beds for special occasions."

"He's just a kid. And the only family I have left. I'm gonna haveta go out there to find him."

Corey was shaking his head before Chad even finished. "Nope. Sinclair won't let you transfer to that FBI task force working in Californio. He wants you after those rustlers in Menard. Since you've had more rustler arrests than anyone on the force, it makes us all look good—"

Chad rose. "We'll see about that."

Corey stared after him, black eyes flaring with alarm as Chad marched to the door stamped "Captain Ross Sinclair, Company C, Texas Rangers."

"Patience, Chad," Corey warned.

Chad repeated the word as if in a Cantonese dialect. "Pa—tience."

Inside his office, Ross Sinclair looked up from paperwork, frowning as Chad entered after a perfunctory knock. "Why are you still here, Foster? They're expecting you in Menard."

Chad had planned to be cool, calm, and collected while he made his case. Instead he burst out, "Dammit, I have to get on that task force investigating this Del Mar Corporation. I got a copy of the closing statement the title company is preparing on the deal Trey signed and tracked them as a suspect in all the mineral-rights land fraud going on in the Panhandle. This I know: They bought Trey's share of my ranch. I'm convinced there's something shady going on that he's probably landed smack dab in the middle of, as usual. He's never gone so long without answering my calls, even when he was pissed." Chad sprawled in the chair before the desk.

"Giving you an obvious conflict of interest. The answer, for the second time, is no. There had better not be a third." Sinclair pulled another form in front of him. "If Trey's set on staying in California, my best piece of advice is simple: Learn to like fruitcakes." Sinclair waved him away. "Now obey your orders or you'll answer to me."

Instead of leaving, Chad leaped to his feet and leaned his palms on the desk, glaring down at his boss.

Sinclair glared right back. He had iron-gray hair, sky-blue eyes meant for laughter, now gleaming with the sharp glint of steel, and a regal bearing as much a legacy of his twenty-five-plus years as a Ranger as due to his daddy's East Coast blue blood. His father had come West with a rich inheritance and bought the Sinclair ranch, now one of the Panhandle's largest, which Sinclair had added to greatly during his tenure at the Rangers. Chad knew even the snootiest of the Hampton Sinclairs moseyed to Texas for the reunions that were chuck wagon gatherings of the rich and famous. Sinclair didn't stay in the Rangers because he had to; he stayed because he wanted to, and Chad admired him for it.

Still, despite their almost friendship, Chad knew Sinclair was ever conscious of his role as Chad's mentor and commanding officer, which was proved with Sinclair's sharp, "Besides, we have a little jurisdiction problem past state lines. Or did you forget that, along with respect for your superior officers?"

"If you transfer me to the task force I'll have jurisdiction."

"Our rights to dispense frontier justice died at our shoot-out with Bonnie and Clyde, Foster. It's high time you learned it."

Chad spoke without emotion. "From where I stand, it looks like it died with you. And your promotion."

The two Rangers locked gazes in the kind of pissing match Texas lawmen invented.

Sinclair took a deep breath. "I'll overlook that, given your stellar career with no insubordination, but you're trying my patience, which grows shorter as my stack of paperwork rises." They both glanced at the towering pile. "You'd stick out in Beverly Hills like a sore-tailed cat at a rocking chair convention, anyway, and probably not get a damned thing done before you got yourself arrested."

Sinclair shoved a file forward. "This is what we have so far on the Menard rustlers. Get to work."

Chad's fingers curled automatically into fists. But he couldn't quite punch his captain, even as a parting gift, no matter how worried he was about Trey. Instead, he removed his badge and gun and set them gently on the desk.

Astounded, Sinclair looked from them to Chad and back, as if he couldn't believe his eyes. "You bullheaded SOB. You worked ten years of car wrecks and speed traps to get here—"

Chad added his handcuffs to the desktop.

"—and you're giving it up over this?"

Chad walked out, proud even without his badge.

Later that day, while he loaded Chester into the horse trailer hooked to his Dodge double-axle diesel dually, Chad watched a geologist take seismic readings from the bluff overlooking his ranch. With her small waist and pleasing hips, she looked feminine even in a hard hat and worn jeans and work boots. Normally Chad would have approached her to warn her away from their boundary line, but she was across the fence on the adjacent property and he was too antsy to get started on his trip to California.

So he drove off, putting her out of his mind the minute he turned onto the highway. As Chad rumbled down the road, Chester's red tail switched from side to side outside the rear of the trailer, as if waving good-bye. Inside, Chad secreted an old but still functional Colt .45 Peacemaker with ivory-handled grips and a fancy *F* engraved in gold, into a compartment beneath his seat.

Just in case . . .

On the land adjacent to the Foster ranch, the woman stared after him and his rig long after he disappeared. A wayward beam of sunlight showed the gleam of red hair beneath the hard hat.

Mary reached for her cell phone and pressed a speed dial button. The phone rang and rang. "Dammit, Trey, pick up. Why haven't you been answering your phone?" For the tenth time, when the phone beeped, she tried leaving a message. "Trey, your brother is on his way to find you. You need to call me right away. Please, give me a chance to explain. I have a new cell phone number." She left the number and hung up, and then went doggedly back to work.

Two days later, Chad arrived in Beverly Hills. With his dually and Chester's trailer attached to the back, he was Sinclair's proverbial sore thumb. The periodic thumps coming from the trailer grew louder. Chester was getting restive and he couldn't blame the stallion. Chad saw a large park on his right and pulled into the half circle street in front. His rig barely fit, blocking the entrance, but he couldn't help that. If he didn't see to Chester, the ornery nag would hurt himself.

Chad unlatched the trailer, haltered Chester and led him out. As soon as they reached the grass, Chester did what horses do. Chad looked around for somewhere to tie him up safely while he fetched a shovel, but he didn't like the looks of the two men eyeing him from a bench. One wore a vest over a beer gut and kilt. Greasy dreadlocks brushed past his shoulders. The other was a bit more respectable but still looked like scum to Chad. Pulling Chester with him, Chad went back to the truck and with one hand got a shovel and blue antiseptic to daub on Chester's hock.

Beer Gut muttered something. Chad straightened from examining Chester's hock and tilted his hat back to eye the guy. "You say something?"

Beer Gut hesitated, and then rose aggressively. "No horse gonna crap in my spot."

"We'll be gone in just a minute." Chad dumped the full shovel into a trash bin and turned back to Chester, daubing bright blue antiseptic on the slightly swollen hock knowing it would bring the swelling down by tomorrow as long as he didn't ride him. At the other guy's hooting, Chad turned back around to see round buttocks mooning him. Encouraged, Beer Gut made a show of his assets, or lack thereof.

Sweaty, tired, and worried about Trey, Chad was in no mood to have all his prejudices about LA proved right the minute he set foot in the place. His temper snapped. Tying Chester's lead over the heavy, anchored trash can, Chad turned and in one fluid motion pushed the guy's jiggling butt with his boot. He went sprawling.

"Why are you complaining? He smells better than you. Get a bath. Better yet, get a job."

Beer Gut scrambled to his feet, his face red. He made fists and started forward, but the sound of a motorcycle drew their attention. Lights flashing, the white motorcycle, a monster of chrome and throaty tailpipes, stopped. An equally impressive cop got off, complete with a starched uniform bearing the famous City of Beverly Hills emblem on his sleeve.

He eyed the tense trio, seemed to recognize the two homeless men. "Ernie, I've told you before, lewd behavior will not be tolerated. Do you always moon the"—the cop paused as he eyed Chad as if he couldn't quite categorize him—"tourists?"

Chad smiled grimly. Good, the local law had seen the whole thing. At that moment, a restive Chester snorted, his head rearing back. The trash can shuddered with a metallic squeal, broke loose from its base and flew straight toward them, spilling its contents as it came.

Chad was able to sidestep in time, but Ernie and the cop, who had their backs to the can, were too slow. An assortment of trash and horse manure was strewn over Ernie's sandaled feet and the cop's shiny boots.

"Stop that, you infernal critter!" Chad grabbed Chester's lead before he could begin to loosen the small concrete stand where the trash can had been secured. Pulling Chester with him, Chad led him back to the trailer, snapped off the lead, and whacked his rump. Chester seemed happy to go back into the trailer, one eyeball rolling back at Chad as if to say, *You've gone and done it now.*

His teeth grinding, Chad turned back to the cop, who was still trying to wipe the mess off his boots.

"I'm sorry, Officer . . ." Chad read the guy's badge. "O'Connor. I'm a Tex—former Texas Ranger on a missing person's case. I had to find an open space to doctor my horse. We just got here . . ." Chad broke off as he watched the cop scribble on his ticket pad. "I'm sure I'm violating some local ordinance, but he's been missing a week and . . ." Chad trailed off again as the cop tore off one ticket and began writing another one. Chad's conciliatory tone grew sarcastic. "Would you believe I'm on my way to a Spielberg shoot?"

"Spielberg isn't working on a Western," came the calm reply. "Good try though."

The snickering from the two homeless men only made Chad angrier. The cop handed him two tickets. Glumly, Chad signed where indicated.

"Illegal parking, no horses in the city limits. I'll forego littering and disturbing the peace as I know these two probably started it." The cop tried one last time to clean the goop off his boots, and then stalked away. "I'll be back this way in a few minutes and if I find that rig parked here, I'll have it towed." He straddled his shiny bike, smiling for the first time. "Welcome to California." He drove off.

The guffaws of the two homeless guys were Chad's musical accompaniment as he collected his shovel and crate of horse supplies, put them back in his truck bed, and rumbled away.

Chad keyed in an address in the GPS on his dash, got back on the 10 East and wished to hell he could head on all the way till sunset. Still, he felt a grim satisfaction as he crumpled the two crisp tickets.

Let them try to enforce them. There was no reciprocity agreement between Texas and California, and since cop courtesy hadn't worked, he'd do what most people did when cited for something that couldn't be enforced: ignore it.

It was late when Chad reached the Los Angeles Equestrian Center in Burbank. He had to admit he was pleasantly surprised by some of the pristine, obviously lovingly restored old homes lining the streets. From exuberant pink bougainvillea flutes to loud tulip trees loaded with throaty trumpets, the entire landscape was a riotous harmony that would never occur in Texas. Still, by the time he had paid for a month's rental of a stall and a place to stake his tent, he was too tired to head for the tattoo parlors as he'd originally planned as his first part of the investigation. Tomorrow, after he'd rested, he'd try the art galleries. Maybe he'd missed one in his phone survey.

The next afternoon, with Chester's trailer safely at the center, but still feeling out of place in his big truck, Chad slammed on his brakes as he coasted Beverly Hills' commercial streets looking at art gallery windows. He'd always thought the name of one of the fanciest shopping districts in the world was a true oxymoron: Rodeo Drive. Yeah, if you like to ramrod two-thousand-dollar shoes and ten-thousand-dollar suits . . .

Chad ignored the honking behind him as he eyed a painting in a large gallery window. It showed Palo Duro Canyon at dusk, mostly shades of gray and black, with a bit of deep blue for contrast. And off center, his back to the world behind him, a man leaned against a sorrel quarter horse that was the spitting image of Chester. His pose was so stark and alone against the larger landscape that Chad felt a visceral recognition.

"Sooner or later, you end up with gray," had been Trey's last comment to him.

This had to be the place. That was his brother's handiwork and his way of moralizing to his big brother. Chad eyed the sign: Kinnard's American Masters. He didn't recall this one on the list he'd investigated from Texas, so it must be a new gallery. Chad looked around for a parking spot.

* * *

Inside Kinnard's gallery, Jasmine lightly touched Roger Larsen's arm. He was Kinnard's attorney and something of her mentor, though he wanted to be much more to her. So far she'd been able to hold him off, but it was becoming difficult.

"This is another one of Trey's paintings." She nodded at a stark but powerful landscape showing blooming prickly pear cactus, long-horn cattle, and a pumpjack. Typical Texas art, but stylized so that its bold strokes became homage to the old and a love song to the new.

While they admired the painting, the door discreetly buzzed. Jasmine looked in that direction, her hand half on, half off Larsen's arm as a tall cowboy entered the gallery, complete with worn Stetson, boots, and a swagger. His hat shaded his face, but she didn't need to see it to know he was no wannabe.

Texas, all right. Jasmine knew the type. Tip to toe all man, and cradle to grave for the women dumb enough to love him.

The cowboy stopped cold when he caught sight of her. Jasmine knew her auburn hair glowed in the sunshine and she stepped aside, turning to go toward the back of the gallery to ask about Trey. Roger trailed behind her.

As Jasmine approached the office, Kinnard exited with that friendly smile on his face that always made her feel welcome. "So what do you think of Trey's work?" he asked.

"It's amazing, but where is Trey? Mary's been trying to reach him, too."

"He told me he was going to drive up the coast for a few days to absorb the sights and smells, wants to try his hand at a seascape next." Kinnard shook his attorney's hand. "So, Roger, see anything you like?" Kinnard's smile deepened when Roger eyed Jasmine's shapely rear end as she wandered away down the gallery walls.

Jasmine had worked her way all the way around and back to the door when she noticed that the cowboy had approached Kinnard. He held out a photo and tipped his hat back, scowling, when Kinnard waved the picture away and said something. She heard Trey's name . . .

Inhaling sharply, Jasmine turned away to hide her shock. She concentrated on the painting in the window; the subject's stance in the painting was so evocative of the man glaring at Kinnard that Jasmine knew she'd just glimpsed the notorious Chad Foster. Trey's brother. They looked nothing alike. She peeked his way again. Trey had perfect, almost effeminate features, but Chad, if it were indeed he, had cold gray eyes, tanned skin stretched over angular facial muscles, and a body long, lean, and muscular, just as Jasmine liked.

The times she'd met Trey when he'd had too much to drink, which was often, he'd talked about his brother with a mixture of resentment and love. A volatile mix Jasmine understood all too well.

So what did it mean that Trey's Texas Ranger brother had dragged himself away from paradise to Sin City? He was looking for his brother, judging by the way he'd displayed that photo and grim attitude. Jasmine frowned, the instinct that said something had happened to Trey now jangling. She'd come here not just because Larsen had invited her but because Mary was out of town and so worried she couldn't reach her boyfriend that Jasmine had promised to see if she could track him down.

As Jasmine pretended to be lost in the painting, the cowboy turned on his booted heel and headed for the door. Behind him, Kinnard glared holes into his back, but his mean expression softened when he saw her looking at him. With a cheery wave, he turned back to his office, Larsen in tow, and closed the door behind them. Jasmine sidestepped away from the door just to be safe, keeping her face turned away, but the firm boot steps paused near the window. She felt Foster looking over her shoulder at the painting. She was tempted to address him by name but resisted.

His voice was as hard and unyielding as the rest of him, though there was a deep, husky timbre beneath the words that made her picture things she shouldn't think of. "So what's a painting of Palo Duro Canyon outside Amarillo, Texas, doing in a Californio art gallery?"

Jasmine turned to look at him. "California has beautiful deserts, too. Western art is big in the Golden State." She didn't know why she felt compelled to defend her adopted state, but everything about this man, from the way he treated Trey, to his attire, to his tone, irritated her. He looked her up and down, thoroughly, and obviously liked what he saw, but she was used to that.

Then his gaze moved to the painting she was convinced he might as well have sat for. "I know that scene, and it's my brother's work, all right."

Vindication should have been sweet. Reading people had always made her good at her job and she hoped it would help her in the practice of law. But her heart sped up instead of slowing down as she felt his gaze wander over her again, head to toe.

"What does it make you think of?" Chad Foster asked. Some of the sternness had gone from his tone.

The words were drawn out of her with more honesty than she expected. "How lucky that man is to be alone."

"You haven't tried it lately."

Arrested, Jasmine couldn't avoid meeting his gaze any longer. She turned on her high heels to look up at him. For an instant, his gray eyes were as cold and bleak as the edges of the painting. Her pale green eyes darkened as she met a long look that had nothing to do with lost brothers and everything to do with loneliness and the hope for someone to fill it. Jasmine's breathing quickened but then Kinnard and Roger exited his office and Kinnard called, "I want to take you to an early dinner, Jasmine."

A shutter snapped down over the desolation in those gray eyes as if Foster knew he'd revealed too much. "Jasmine, huh? Well, imagine that, the famous dancer in the flesh." Pulling his hat low over his face, Chad Foster opened the door and promised softly, "I'll be around to check out your . . . act. Gentleman's Pleasure, isn't it? Great name for a strip club. Fits you." Foster exited, banging the door.

Jasmine peered after him, wondering why the flattery sounded more like a threat than a compliment. And how the heck did he know who she was, anyway?

CHAPTER 4

Chad emerged just in time to see a motorcycle cop, lights flashing, writing him another ticket. Chad hurried over. "I'm sorry, Officer, I'm just moving—" The cop turned. Chad's protest froze in his throat. Great. Riley O'Connor again.

The response was a ticket thrust into his face. "You should have thought of that before you parked there. I suspect you can read." He nodded at the parking sign that forbade parking between the hours of four and six p.m. weekdays.

Chad checked his watch: four fifteen. Crap, he'd been legal when he went in. God, he already hated this place . . .

The handsome young man, not a spot or wrinkle on his uniform, cracked a smile. "Sorry, I don't make the rules, just enforce them. Looks like we're going to be running into one another a lot. Shall we make this official? I'm Riley O'Connor." He held out his hand. Chad shook it. "I have a feeling I'll be citing you again, but in the meantime, try renting a car that fits in LA traffic."

Chad hesitated but couldn't help his reaction to the pucker-assed, by-the-book prick. Even his olive branch felt fake to Chad. "Ever hear the word *reciprocity*?"

That straight back stiffened again. "You saying because we don't have one with Texas, you won't pay the fines?"

Chad shrugged.

O'Connor eyed him. "Well, I guess we know why you left the Rangers. Don't like to follow rules, do you?"

Chad glared. "I follow rules just fine when they make sense."

"Shall I explain why we don't allow parking here at rush hour, or is that too much for you to comprehend, seeing as how you're used to wide-open places and all?"

Chad saw where this was going. This wasn't a pissing match he'd win and before he was done, he might need the help of local law enforcement. It grated on him, but he managed, "Sorry, you're right. I'll move immediately."

O'Connor straddled his bike. "No never-mind to me. At the rate you're going with infractions, you'll hit first-degree felony in a week. No reciprocity needed on that. Have a good day, sir." Off he roared, even his apparent politeness pissing off Chad, as it was supposed to.

"Ha ha," Chad said sourly as he fired up his truck. He'd deserved that maybe, but he still didn't like it. Chad started to toss the crumpled ticket on top of the other two, but he was still a cop in all but badge and gun. He spread the ticket out, along with the others, made a mental note of the monies needed to pay all three fines, and drove away.

A few hours later, Chad exited the showers at the Los Angeles Equestrian Center in Burbank and pushed back his wet hair with both hands as he went to the lockers. His hair was so thick that he usually had to blow-dry it, but he'd left in too much of a hurry to remember such niceties. Now it would curl, and he hated that. Making a mental note to find a barber tomorrow, if such a plebian creature existed in this place, Chad dressed in fresh jeans and a button-down shirt. He wanted to be clean, at least when he saw this Jasmine woman tonight. He hoped his tips might warm her up a bit, get her to be more forthcoming now she was away from that snooty gallery. He was dead level certain Trey had painted those works he'd seen at Kinnard's gallery and that both Kinnard and Jasmine knew Trey.

So what were they hiding? And why hadn't Trey called him back?

* * *

Jasmine pushed her food around her plate. When Roger excused himself to go to the men's room, Jasmine let her fork rattle to her dish. "Thomas, why did you lie to Chad Foster and tell him you don't know his brother?"

Kinnard wiped his mouth and folded his napkin, his smile firmly in place. "That was Trey's request, if Foster came sniffing around looking for him. He wants no further contact with his brother. How did you know Foster asked me about him?"

"I saw him show you a photo. And even more interesting, Foster knew my name and said he'd visit the club to see me dance. I suppose Trey could have mentioned me to him, but it seems more likely he'd have talked about Mary."

As the check came, Thomas tossed down his black American Express card. "Maybe he knows you both danced there. I have no idea what's going on in that redneck's head. Whatever the feud between Trey and his brother, it's none of my business. As for you, well, I imagine his tips will be as good as the next guy's." He was busy scribbling his name so didn't see the hurt in Jasmine's eyes as she looked away. Or the thoughtful way she nibbled her lip as she contemplated his evasive response.

Around eleven that night, music pounded in Chad's ears so loudly he could pretend, at least to himself, he wasn't aroused. Sure, his thumping heartbeat, as the red-haired dancer gyrated around the pole, echoed the primitive drum beat.

Great rhythm. And while he was at it, he could explain that flagpole in his britches as a patriotic salute.

Damn you, Trey . . . He was too humiliated at his own reluctant arousal to get up and leave, even if he had that luxury, which he didn't. While he might be convinced those paintings in Kinnard's gallery were by Trey, they weren't signed—by design, perhaps? And Kinnard denied that Trey had been there, so Chad had no choice but to follow his only other lead. No need now to follow Corey's theory and go to the tattoo parlors, since he'd found Jasmine so easily. So for the first time in his life, he'd entered a strip club.

At least now he knew why they called it Gentleman's Pleasure.

She was a pleasure, all right. To look at, no doubt to smell, and touch. And feel.

He was glad for the long tablecloth and the dark corner, but he kept his face blank as he watched the show. Texas Rangers were good at sitting stony-faced while they grilled their suspects. He wasn't sure if he was angrier with himself or this redhead who'd brought him halfway across the country. Still, his eyes just about popped out of his head as they remained glued to the stage.

She had seemed so classy when he'd met her earlier at the gallery, fully dressed, if a bit frosty. It was an all-fired shame, as his granny would say, that a woman with the perfect features of an angel and the body of a Victoria's Secret model was just a no-'count who danced naked for a living.

Well, almost naked.

She was down to a G-string, a triangle with lacy ties on both sides and a thong up her butt, and a scrap of a bikini top. Imprinted with holographic butterflies that seemed to flutter with her every movement, it was more suggestive—made a man want to catch those butterflies in his hands—than nudity.

She was too beautiful to be a stripper, and she showed some real talent in the rhythm of her moves, but the mere fact she showed her wares off for a price meant to Chad she was capable of fraud, if not worse. She certainly had the right equipment to distract a man to death. At least he finally understood what had drawn Trey away from high-sky Amarillo to smoggy Lost Angeles.

Fascinated—and getting more pissed off by the minute at his own arousal—he watched as The Butterfly crossed both endless legs around the pole. Supporting all her weight, which wasn't much despite her height, she leaned so far backward her long waves of deep auburn hair brushed the stage. Her arms moving Cleopatra style, her upper torso shimmied as she continued to bend farther back until she was a bow of sheer sexual energy, flexed to fly free at a man's touch.

Her large breasts pointed provocatively at the ceiling, the nipples erect. Great boob job, he tried to tell himself scornfully, but his mouth was parched. He licked his lips, watching her lick hers, caught himself and turned tomato red under the weary gaze of a topless waitress.

Well, hell, that's what this was all about, wasn't it? Using a man's baser urges against him to make him part with his hard-earned dollars. Still, the self-lecture couldn't counteract what he saw and heard and, God help him, what he wanted to touch.

One of Trey's parting comments came back to torment him. How long had it been since he'd had a real date, anyway? He tried to remember, but Jasmine Routh made it hard for him to recall what his old girlfriends—either one of them—even looked like.

When would this torture end so he could go to her dressing room and question her?

He'd tried a background check on Jasmine Routh before coming here and found just about zilch. No criminal record, no marriage license on file. She owned one car, a sporty Acura, and lived in an apartment in Beverly Hills near all the other weirdos on the border with West Hollywood.

That was it. Clean as a whistle. She came to work, she danced, she went home to a crappy one bedroom even though, on the money she pulled in every week, she could afford her own house despite LA prices. As for the number of her boyfriends, well, her art obviously didn't stop when she was offstage, given that poor attorney panting over her at the gallery.

Shady ladies naturally made him suspicious, and now he'd seen her, every cop instinct he'd cultivated over the last fifteen years warned that even if she wasn't involved in the land fraud, she was somehow involved in Trey's disappearance. She was just too beautiful to trust.

Most damning, with her auburn hair and lush figure, Jasmine Routh was the spitting image of the girl in that last oil Trey had painted before he'd left Amarillo. Chad vividly recalled the tattoo on the slope of that perfect white breast swaying before him now. However, despite the abbreviated top, he couldn't see a tattoo. That tattoo was the only difference between Jasmine Routh and the portrait without a face. Same length and color of hair, white skin, full bosom, proud tilt of the head. Had to be the same girl. Still, that pissant piece of fabric surely couldn't cover a butterfly tattoo, spread wings and all.

The held breath left his lungs in a whoosh as she pulled herself back up, still attached to the pole only by the strength of her legs, and reached supple arms behind her back to untie the bikini top. It fell, a puddle of sparkles and dreams, to the stage.

Under the brilliant lights, a small yellow-and-blue butterfly tattoo sparkled with glitter on the lower slope of that flawless right breast.

In his pocket, Chad crumpled the card in his hand, wishing it were her throat. He didn't know how, and he didn't know why, but this seductive bitch had somehow contributed to his brother's disappearance. She'd sure as shootin' lured him from Texas to California.

Distastefully, Chad watched her pick up the tens, twenties, even a few hundreds, littering the stage after her dance. She allowed a couple of the guys sitting near the stage to slip large bills into her garter. When he walked up and waved a twenty to add to the little elastic band, she backed away a step, her brilliant smile fading. She crossed her arms over her bosom reflexively, as if embarrassed.

He would have liked her for that, if he believed her act. He folded the bill and set it at her feet. "Talk to you later?"

She hesitated, looking from his blank expression to the twenty, but when a stage hand brought her a robe, she wrapped it around herself, bent and picked up the twenty. Holding his eyes, she stuck one of those long legs outside the robe, folded the bill into her garter, and sashayed offstage. Chad went over to a waitress and asked for the manager.

While he waited, Chad stared blindly at the stage. No matter what it took, if Trey was hurt, or worse, as he feared, no matter if he went to jail in the process, he'd personally take this deceitful, treacherous little bitch back to Texas so the people Trey had introduced her to could positively ID her.

He hadn't given up his badge and The Job he loved for nothing. He didn't care if he had to kidnap her, there would be no Californio-style lenience for the likes of her. Time for some Texas-style justice . . .

Jasmine closed the dressing room door and leaned against it. Even more drained than usual, she stared around her closet-like private dressing room, the only perk she insisted on as a headliner. The minute she walked off that stage, naked but for the G-string and the robe, the vitality and sexuality she oozed on command dissipated with the lights. She was just tired.

Tired of being leered at. Tired of pretending to be something she wasn't, tired of hating herself. Tired of actively disliking men for leaving loving wives and lovers for these few hours to spend more money than they could afford on the lure of the forbidden. In her experience, most of the men who frequented strip clubs fell into three categories.

Some celebrated male freedom for one night at least, running with the wolves, maintaining their atavistic macho right to covet even if they couldn't touch. The second group was as lonely as she was, reaching for the only connection they knew how to offer women and fantasizing she was theirs, the mythical angel in the kitchen and whore in the bedroom.

The last group, well, they were the worst of all. The ones who made her skin crawl and made her glad of all the bouncers. They were the users who saw women as their personal playgrounds and never tarried long after playing.

Someday she'd write a book about all this, when she was married, with her Juris Doctor degree, and had about five kids. She tied the dressing gown more tightly over her G-string, wishing she hadn't promised to fill in for a sick waitress, so she could go home and study. She'd made over five hundred dollars tonight, even without Chad Foster's twenty.

A smile played about her lips as she recalled the look on his face as he stared up at her. He didn't like it, one bit, but he was drawn to her just like all the others. Jasmine suspected he'd never been in a strip club. Still, she hoped his promise to talk to her had been an empty threat; he was a Texas-sized complication she didn't need. Thomas was right about this, as usual: Whatever the conflict between Chad and Trey, it was between the two of them.

Or so she tried to tell herself. She glanced at her message light, but it wasn't blinking. She was worried sick about Trey. Why hadn't he called her back? It had been over a week since she'd left a message on his new cell phone with the California number. She knew he was busy getting ready for the art exhibit, but still . . . this was a cold, lonely place for people like Trey, who looked at a refuse heap and saw only the wildflowers.

She touched up her makeup, staring at the tattoo she still wasn't used to. Maybe Mary had been right, and she should get rid of it. She stroked it with her fingertip. She already felt like she had the word *whore* branded on her forehead because of her job, and this flighty symbol of what she did, not who she was, didn't help.

A knock came at the door. Herman, the club manager, peeked inside. "Jasmine, there's a former cop here who wants to ask you some questions."

"About what?" Jasmine touched up her lipstick but she knew the answer.

"He says a disappearance. Somebody he says you know may have been the subject of foul play."

She froze in capping her mascara.

The door was shoved wide and someone big stepped through. She looked up, way up, at a hard face granite would envy. At her pleading look, the manager stepped inside, too, closing the door. The "cop" glared at him but Herman shrugged.

"Policy. Don't allow my girls to be alone with anyone, even cops."

Cop my Aunt Hattie, she thought. Even if she hadn't met him at the gallery, she suspected she'd have recognized a Texas Ranger when she saw one. Because of her dad, she knew what they went through to become Rangers. They were the elite of the elite special forces in Texas. Known not just throughout the nation, but the world. Jasmine had never understood the mythological sway things Texan held over so many people. This living example of the still vibrant West was in reality only a brass-balled asshole who'd been a harsh surrogate father to his much younger brother. Who made Trey so miserable he'd pulled up stakes and moved to Los Angeles partly to get away from the jury, judge, and executioner eyeing the world from wintry gray eyes.

Chad opened his mouth, looked at the way she crossed her arms over her bosom, closed his mouth. Then he took a long, deep breath, closing his eyes as if to steady himself. She saw how long and dark his lashes were, almost feminine, like Trey's. She would have sworn he whispered something that sounded like "pat—ience" to himself.

He ran his hand around the back of his neck, as if the hair curling about his shirt collar bothered him. And only when that six-feet-plus of male pride exhibited a little-boy charm was her anger disarmed.

Something intrinsically feminine in her, which she normally

quashed, surged in response to his intensity. Her nipples hardened. It had been a long time since she'd been attracted to a man. She tightened her arms across her breasts as the true import of this meeting hit her.

If he'd left the high skies for the smoggy ones, he must have a damn good reason. He obviously viewed strip clubs and LA in general as populated by lowlifes, so he hadn't come by choice. He'd come because he was worried about Trey . . . Jasmine felt her robe gap open as she waved him to an adjacent bench. His eyes were glued to her tattoo. It hit her then—Chad had mistaken her for Mary. Both tall redheads with identical tattoos.

Chad's voice was soft, almost respectful. "I saw you in the gallery today. You looked—different."

She eyed his clean clothes and shining dark hair. "So did you. You clean up well. Did you bring your horse?"

"Yeah."

"I used to have a horse. A long time ago. I miss him."

Chad's head tilted as if he couldn't quite compute her owning a horse.

She'd been about to make an offhand comment indicating yes, she knew Trey but hadn't heard from him in over a week, the truth, but she didn't like the way he apparently thought she was lying to impress him. He slapped that worn Stetson against his thigh, veiling his silvery gray eyes, but contempt behind the empty smile hit Jasmine like a slap to her flushed face.

More importantly, it revived her anger.

He wanted her, but he didn't like it that he wanted her. He was classic type three, a typical macho redneck who had one use for women. She wondered if he wore spurs to bed. She glanced down at the front of his tight jeans at the telltale bulge, her look telling him wordlessly that his mind might find her repulsive but his body sure as heck didn't.

He needed an attitude adjustment. She wouldn't tell him a damn thing about Trey, especially if Trey was avoiding him as Thomas had said.

Pretending indifference, she turned a shoulder on him. She made her voice coarse. "What can I help ya with, mister?" She began adding shadow to her already accented eyes, which were the luminous green color of aspen leaves in spring. So men told her. She saw plain old dishwater green.

"I'm trying to reconstruct the movements of a young man who just moved to Los Angeles," Chad replied. "An artist, with an opening of his work scheduled at that gallery in Beverly Hills I saw you in earlier. Trey Foster."

Slowly, Jasmine put down the mascara tube and met the Texan's eyes in the mirror. "Why have you come to me?"

"I have reason to believe he . . . knows you."

And I know you, too. It wasn't her duty to tell him a thing, especially as Trey obviously didn't want his brother to know where he was. She went back to applying her mascara. "I might have met him a time or two, but I have no idea where he is." Partially true. She knew where Trey was moving, in with Mary when Mary returned from her mysterious business trip, but at this precise moment she truly didn't know where Trey was.

"Oh yeah? Bit strange, isn't it, since he came out here because of you." He slapped a crumpled card before her.

She glanced from it to his hard eyes in the mirror. "So? Lots of men take my card."

"I found it in Texas. That means he already had it on his last trip out here six months ago when he met a redhead. A redhead he wouldn't talk about much because he knew I'd disapprove of her job." He looked at her figure in the thin wrap, his lip curling. "Could be."

Jasmine gave an "OK" look at Herman, who slipped out of the room. She looked back at her accuser, because that was certainly the best term for his attitude.

Mary. He was talking about Mary. She'd pretended to be a dancer, too, when she met Trey. At Thomas's insistence, for a reason Jasmine still didn't understand.

While she had no idea why Trey would have had her card, much less leave it behind in Texas, this explained a lot. But she had no intention of setting this balls-to-the-wall SOB straight. It would be far more fun to lead him astray. For Trey.

For herself and for her momentary weakness. There was a reason why half the dancers she knew hated men, and she was looking at it.

Strong, arrogant, handsome, and a hypocrite big as Dallas, appropriately enough in his case.

She tilted her head to the side as she studied him. And then she gave that slow, sensual, bedroom smile she'd perfected onstage. "Oh, I think you like me more than you'll admit. I have many . . . dimensions."

"Yeah, I can see 'em." He slapped his hat back on his head. "Honey, I wouldn't take it if you were giving it away free."

Legal training had aided her natural inclination to hold her cards close. Her smile actually sparkled under the lights. "Shall we put it to the test?"

His eyes narrowed under the thick lashes. "Oh, I forgot. This is the part where you do your lap dances to make the really big bucks. Thanks, but no thanks. Besides, I tipped you twenty bucks already."

What a jerk. She'd been about to tell him she didn't do lap dances anymore, but now she gave him that little sexy north-south appraisal designed to tickle men right below the belt. And based on the way he shifted his weight from hip to hip, as if his pants felt too tight, it worked whether he liked it or not.

Jasmine said softly, "Tell you what, you follow the rules and avoid touching me and I won't even charge you my usual going rate."

"How much is that?"

"Two hundred bucks."

He almost flinched, but his hard gray eyes delved into hers. "Tell you what, if I don't touch you, you answer two questions for me. Straight on. In more than one syllable."

"You're on, Mr. Policeman. Just give me a half hour to change."

CHAPTER 5

Thirty minutes later, Chad's heart thumped faster than ever, and she was only serving drinks. She hadn't even removed her top, but still, his eyes zeroed in on her over the other topless women, gorgeous though they were.

He'd always had a thing for redheads.

And she knew it, damn her. Worst of all, she was hiding something. She knew Trey better than she let on. Still, his suspicions couldn't stop his libido from running amok. He wiped his sweaty palms on his jeans, vowing he wouldn't touch her no matter what. He'd certainly extracted information in physically painful ways before, but this would be sheer torture.

He didn't remember the last time he'd had such a hard-on. And never in the presence of a suspected perp.

Finally she came over to him and offered her hand. Feeling like a bull led by his balls, he took that dainty hand and followed her to the very back of the club, to a tiny alcove.

Oh hell. He knew what that meant. Now no one could see them. City ordinance forbade men touching the strippers, but that was about as enforceable as the old law still on the books in Texas that you could get arrested for spitting on the sidewalk.

As slow, sensual music began, she shoved him down in the wide, soft chair. It was shadowy behind the curtain, but not shadowy enough. He could smell her, he could feel the warmth of her body, and man oh man, could he see her. She was seductive in the spotlights. In the soft glow cast by the sconces on the wall behind them, she was every man's dream: angel and whore.

She started out slow, dancing in front of him, almost but not quite between his knees. He planted his hands on his thighs and vowed to keep them there, a resolve taxed incrementally more with every move she made.

She didn't just dance, she . . . undulated, upper torso moving in the opposite direction to her gently swaying hips. Her arms reached teasingly toward him, fingers moving as if to weave through his hair, almost but not quite touching him. He held his breath, hoping, but then she backed off a step and did a quick three-hundred-sixty degree turn on one spiked heel before facing him again.

Still perfectly in balance, she started dancing again, eyes half closed as if she heard some mysterious inner rhythm more seductive than the soft jazz tune. Those endless legs, arched to a beautiful shape by the high heels, begged for the touch of his hands. She was supple as silk, he could see it, yet warm, soft, and living. Curved exactly where she should be.

And that silly scrap of a butterfly bodice, well, it was more suggestive than bare skin. Her nipples thrust provocatively at him as she shimmied, moving closer, closer . . . and then she was brushing herself against him. Slowly, in rhythm with the sexy tempo of the music, she nudged his spread legs apart. Then she pressed her entire length against him from his upper chest to his calves. She rubbed herself up and down, front side, then back side.

It took every ounce of willpower he had, not to mention breaking a couple of nails as he clenched his own knees, but he managed not to touch her. She rubbed herself sideways against him, letting him feel the soft warmth of her breasts, and then moved away again, dancing lazily while she watched him in the dim lighting.

He broke out in a sweat, pulling his hat down over his face, hoping she couldn't see his expression. She did another spin, her elbow catching his hat as if by accident. It went flying, leaving his face bare before her. For a moment, he looked at her with a hunger so basic, powered by a loneliness so deep he never let anyone touch it, that she froze mid-step, staring at him.

She looked like a handmaiden on a Greek urn, her arms clasped above her head as she arched toward him. He knew from her expression that she'd caught him at a vulnerable moment.

And he felt naked.

Much more naked than she was. He was embarrassed and infuriated by the pulsing ache below his belt that both proved him human and shamed him. Stumbling to his feet, he brushed past her and shoved the curtain aside.

He was so rattled he didn't realize he'd left his hat until she followed and offered it to him.

He took it, slapping it on his thigh as if to brush away her touch.

She was intuitive about human behavior, he had to give her that, because her half-concerned expression went cold at his gesture. "Good luck with your investigation." She made to turn away

He stopped her with the only defense she'd left him—his voice. "Not hardly. I didn't touch you, did I?" When she turned back to face him, he finished softly, "I'm never led by my appetites. You're beaucoup sugar, honey, but I'm allergic to . . . butterflies." His gaze fixed on her breasts.

There was a moment of silence. When she spoke, her tone was sweet, but he heard anger seething under every nuanced syllable. "Fancy word for a redneck. Then I guess I don't need to define this for you: stalemate. You left before I finished, remember? Or should I say you bolted."

Her implication that he was a coward literally made him see red as her proud auburn mane shone in the lights. His voice remained calm, though his West Texas twang got thick. She aroused damn near every one of the seven deadly sins in him. "Honey, if I'd had one iota of doubt about your guilt, you just ended it. You like plain talkin'?" He smashed his hat onto his head. "I'm gonna get you. I'm gonna see you pay if Trey's been hurt." *Or worse.* He didn't have to say it, but she caught that fear, too. He'd started to turn away when he caught the look on her face.

Shock widened those unusual eyes. "You really think I had something to do with luring him out here, don't you? You think I killed him? Okay, I admit, Trey is my friend!"

Half turned away, he froze, delving deep into her eyes, deeper than he'd dared all night long. Was the pain and shock he read genuine? She swayed on her feet, and with automatic Texas male courtesy, he reached out to steady her.

She slapped his hand away and ran. Through the tables, jostling a waitress who dropped a tray in a patron's lap. Half the place stopped to stare at her, the shock on the faces of the other waitresses proof they'd never seen Jasmine Routh so distraught because of a patron.

As she leaped up on the stage, she even wobbled on one high heel, the only ungraceful move she'd made that night, and dashed behind the curtains.

Chad stood stock still, uncaring of the curious looks and unkind thoughts. What the hell had he just seen? Had she truly been so shocked to hear his worst fears about Trey, or was she as good an actress as she was a dancer? She'd admitted to knowing Trey, but what precisely did that mean?

When he shoved a hand in his pocket and felt that expensive card slice into his finger, he was brought back to his senses. Of course she was a great actress. She was expert at emitting sexual vibes and yet according to everything he'd learned, she didn't even have a lover.

Nope. She was primo, all right. A primo user. She used men like toilet paper, and he wasn't going to fall for her act.

He spun on a booted heel and stalked out.

He had a couple more leads to follow up. He'd give her about a week, long enough to think he'd forgotten her. And then, if he still hadn't found Trey . . .

Maybe next time, he'd let her give him a *real* lap dance. He had no illusions about what happened sometimes behind those curtains. It would cost him a fortune and he'd sure as hell use a condom, but maybe once this wrenching ache was gone from his gut—and lower—he'd be able to think clearly. Face his best lead without all these seething, unseemly emotions.

Chad Foster walked out into the busy LA nightlife, blind to the neon lights that had dazzled him, blind to the tattooed, pierced, and scruffy pedestrians he'd scorned.

All he could see were butterflies.

Dancing over every inch of his body.

The next morning, Chad rubbed his stubbly chin wearily as he sat up in his sleeping bag beneath the tent he'd pitched at the equestrian center. "I'm too old for camp-outs." He wriggled out of the bag and stretched his aching back. He checked his phone for messages and found the one he hoped for from Corey. It was hushed and fast. "Chad, I ran all we have on Thomas Kinnard, Beverly Hills. Seems to be a respected businessman, lots of money he used to open that gallery. Can't find much background on him though; he just appears about ten years ago. I'd dig some more but Sinclair's watching me like I'm the last tank in his pasture—" Corey hit the End button, but Chad had heard enough.

Jasmine wouldn't tell him diddly, Kinnard was denying he knew the artist of the best work in his gallery . . . all in all, LA had pretty much met his very low expectations.

Sighing heavily, Chad put his wrinkled clothes back on and faced the inevitable. Time to spend some of what was left of his last paycheck on a new suit. He couldn't expect to sneak around the Beverly Wilshire looking like this—even he knew that. Trey had said he was meeting Jasmine at the Wilshire, so tonight he'd see if he could surprise them. While his gut told him she was involved in Trey's disappearance, his gut also told him to sweep her into his arms and test her standoffishness to prove it was a lie. His reaction to her was too visceral for it to be one-sided. If he could just see that Trey was all right, he'd try one more time to talk his brother home. If it didn't work, he'd go back to Amarillo and beg for his job.

Or as close as he knew how to beg . . .

The other alternative, he shied away from. That Trey wasn't at the Wilshire. That he hadn't called in so long for one reason. Chad violently shoved away the thought of the lead of last resort: the morgue. Too soon for that.

*   *   *

That night, Jasmine decided to see if she could shrug off her funk along with her stage costume. She'd swapped shifts with another girl and had impulsively accepted a date with Roger Larsen. While she had no interest in him romantically, he'd offered to lend her access to his law books and answer any questions she might have. She had no yen to be a corporate or tax lawyer, his specialties, but she knew he was well respected in Beverly Hills and could be a powerful ally closer to graduation when she was ready to network.

And he was as different as he could be from Chad Foster. In her current state of mind, that was a huge advantage for him.

Still, she'd chosen a conservative black skirt and ruffled white blouse rather than anything revealing. His eyes widened appreciatively when he saw her that night as she met him at the Beverly Wilshire. "How're classes going?" He offered his arm.

She took it. "Good. I especially love my real estate law classes."

"You think you might want to specialize in real estate?"

"I'm not sure yet. I still have a couple of years to decide. So why did you pick the Wilshire?"

"Thomas suggested the restaurant here." Roger pulled out her chair at the table covered with white linen. "He knows the general manager and they just brought in a Michelin chef."

Jasmine managed not to roll her eyes. LA was the most trend-conscious place in which she'd ever lived, and Roger was all about money and power. Like Thomas. They both belonged here, but she was coming to the reluctant conclusion she didn't. A conclusion that had strutted into her life on six feet two inches and boots.

Jasmine twisted her napkin in her hands and forced herself to listen to Roger.

Outside, Chad drove up Wilshire Blvd for the sixth time, looking for a place to park. He hated using valets and knew they didn't much like parking his double-wheeled dually. He was about to give up and turn into the valet line when he noticed a limo pull away about a block down. He wheeled into the spot just in time to beat another limo. The driver glared at him but Chad ignored him, locked his vehicle, and crossed to the hotel.

He went to the front desk. "You have a Trey Foster registered here?"

The froufrou desk clerk had a matching attitude. With an exquisitely manicured hand he pointed at a house phone. "You can try the operator, sir. I'm not allowed to give out names."

Chad dialed zero, eyeing the busy lobby. The operator was taking a while to answer. Chad shifted in his new dress shoes, hating the button-down shirt and dress pants he'd purchased. In anything but jeans, he felt like he was wearing a straitjacket. When the operator came on finally and denied there was a guest registered under that name, Chad gave an irritated sigh. "And what about Jasmine Routh?"

A brief pause, then, "No, sir, no one under that name either."

"Thanks." Chad slammed down the phone. Now what? If Trey had said he'd be at the Beverly Wilshire and wasn't there, he'd already gotten his own place or . . . Chad quashed the thought, but one thing was sure: His few leads were drying up. LA had way too many hotels for him to call them one by one, and Chad had a feeling it would be a useless exercise anyway.

Nope, as much as he hated to have to continue to see her, his best lead stood about five feet six inches, had auburn hair, and knew Trey much better than she admitted. Chad was about to leave and get in his truck to go back to the dance club when he noticed elegantly attired couples entering a doorway. Inside was a black-suited maître d' with a pile of menus in his arms.

Hell, it was worth a shot. Chad walked to the entrance and scanned the packed dining room. His gaze drifted over her the first time. She was laughing at something her companion had said, and looked so classy in the white ruffled blouse, he almost didn't recognize her. But her laugh was very distinctive, musical and husky at the same time, and his gaze zeroed in on the pair. She was with the same man who'd escorted her the first time he'd seen her at the art gallery.

"May I help you, sir?" The maître d' smiled at him with that oily obsequiousness displayed only at the best places, which Chad seldom frequented.

Chad hesitated. The direct approach hadn't gotten him anywhere. Time to try finesse. Chad didn't much like the taste of the little-used word, but the fear in his gut for his brother was a good motivator. "I like that little two-top over there near the window. May I have that?"

"For one?"

"Yes." It was also right behind Jasmine. Careful to pass behind her so she didn't see him, Chad sat down with his back to them but well within earshot and pretended to peruse the menu.

One table over, Jasmine was beginning to think she'd made a mistake in agreeing to have dinner with Roger, but she had her own questions to ask. "So how long have you known Thomas?" Jasmine took a demure taste of her lobster bisque, soup spoon angled away as she'd been taught in fancy schools an eon ago.

"About five years. I've been his attorney for three. I helped him form his various corporate entities." Roger leaned across the table to take her hand. "Jasmine, why won't you go out with me?"

Using the excuse of her napkin to pull away, Jasmine wiped her mouth and said lightly, "I just did."

"You know what I mean. Really date me, not just have dinner with me."

"Despite my occupation, I have to get to know someone, Roger. And I'm too busy right now for complications."

Roger leaned back and blew a breath through his teeth. "So now I'm a complication? I thought you liked me."

"I do. But I'm not in a place right now where I can get involved with anyone. And since you and Thomas are both friends and business partners, that makes things even more difficult."

"How so?"

"Thomas is my employer and a mentor to me and I . . . haven't exactly had the best of luck with men in the past." Jasmine searched for a way to defuse the situation and was glad when their meal arrived.

As soon as the waiter left, Roger meticulously folded his napkin over his lap, his every movement controlled. "I get it. I'm good enough to use for my knowledge and my library, but anything serious, no."

"That's not it, Roger. I'm just not ready right now . . ." Jasmine trailed off when she saw the precise but vicious way he dissected his steak.

She smiled and mimicked a cultured male voice, "Would you like a nice Chianti with that?"

This surprised a laugh from him. "I've been compared to many things, but Hannibal Lecter isn't one of them." He cut another bite, less viciously this time. "All right, you win. I'm a lawyer, I know how to play the waiting game. What would you like to talk about?"

Chad had ordered the least expensive thing on the menu, a sirloin in the mere thirty-dollar range, as he listened to their conversation. Man, she was good. Lead a man by the ring in his nose like a prize bull. Then slam the door to the breeding pasture just as he scented the cow. Chad wondered if she'd used the same tactics on Trey. Likely.

Sexual artifice like that could only partially be instinctive; most of it was learned through much practice. His instincts about her from the time he'd seen her name on that card had been right, confirmed in the seductive tease of her lap dance, and now by the way she dangled a poor bastard who was all but panting for her.

Chad half listened to them talk about legal issues and the Lakers until he finally tuned them out. A waste of time and money coming here. He'd pushed his half-eaten meal away and signaled for the check when the conversation got interesting again.

"Has Thomas mentioned his newest artist from Texas?" Jasmine asked.

"You mean the guy who painted the landscapes we liked the other day?"

"Yes. Trey Foster. I'm friends with him and have left him a lot of messages he hasn't returned, so I'm a bit worried."

"Never met the guy. I don't recall Thomas mentioning him. Why don't you ask him?"

"I did. But he only tells me Trey went up the coast to work on his art. The other thing that's weird is, don't you think it's strange he didn't have Trey sign his paintings?"

"You know, he creates mystique as he builds a new artist, then he plans to have Trey personalize them when they sell. Adds even more value."

Blindly, Chad signed his credit card receipt, still listening. What game was she playing? Had she seen him sit down behind her? Or could it be she really didn't know where Trey was? And was really worried about him . . .

Then his ears literally started burning . . .

"His brother is here looking for him. He came to see me at the club and acts like I'm involved in Trey's disappearance. He . . . scares me a little."

"Has he threatened you?"

"No, not really."

"Give me his name and I'll do a background search on him—"

"I already did. I know someone at USC who has access to all the databases. He's a Texas Ranger. And Trey even talked about him, so I know it's him."

"Oh. Well, hopefully he's not dangerous. He's probably out of his depth here, and also out of his jurisdiction. I wouldn't worry about him. Trey will turn up."

When Larsen changed the subject to movies, Chad stalked out. As he exited the hotel, he smiled grimly. A bit afraid of him? She was smarter than she looked . . .

CHAPTER 6

Chad came to a dead stop when he saw a gleaming limo where his truck should have been. He went to remove his hat and smack it against his leg before he remembered he'd left his Stetson at camp since it didn't exactly match the dress pants and shirt.

Chad took a deep breath to calm himself. He was about to go back into the hotel to ask about the tow yard when he noticed a motorcycle idling half a block away. Chad's eyes narrowed. Was this prick stalking him?

He strode over. "You the one who called the tow truck driver?"

Riley took off his sun shades and rubbed them against his pristine, starched uniform shirt. "Yep."

"You got a hard-on for me, or are you just an asshole?"

"Actually, you were in a commercial zone. You know, hazard to commerce and traffic, all that."

"Hazard my eye. You might as well piss around the perimeter of this fancy little city. You know, protecting your turf, all that." Chad imitated the kid's perfect diction.

"You're pretty aggressive for a guy working his own case with no authority."

Chad's hand reached for the place where he kept his badge and then fell.

The sunglasses were folded neatly and inserted into Riley's shirt pocket. "I admit I am a bit curious. Why did a Texas Ranger come to Lost Angeles—"

"I prefer the land of fruits and nuts myself—"

"Or should I say former Texas Ranger?"

Chad realized this Riley O'Connor must have called Sinclair to assess his status. Since he'd only resigned a week ago, it was doubtful his resignation was showing up in the databases when the cop ran the plates. The kid was more thorough than he gave him credit for.

But all Chad said was, "Well, feature that. Even pucker-assed Beverly Hills cops know how to run plates." He turned on his heel and went back into the hotel to get the tow yard address, smiling grimly as he felt Riley's glare boring between his shoulder blades. Four tickets, two days. Must be some kind of record.

A few days later, at the Los Angeles Equestrian Center in Burbank, Chad debated how much good it would do that he'd filed a missing persons report with the LA police and the City of Beverly Hills. They'd barely paid him any nevermind because he lived in Texas, not LA, but they said they'd get back to him. It was a formality he knew he had to take care of, but that didn't help his frustration level.

Then he caught a break, blessing the fact he'd brought his old police band radio. Listening, he stood up so fast he knocked his coffeepot into the campfire. Sizzling, the fire went out but ignited all his nerve endings as the radio blared, "Nineteen ninety-eight red Camaro abandoned on Sixth and Alameda, downtown Los Angeles, Texas plates. Owner reported missing. Tow truck driver saw signs of foul play."

Chad was slamming the door on his truck before the dispatcher finished asking for officers to meet the driver at the scene. Normally he'd have tidied his campsite before leaving, but he knew he had to be fast to make it downtown from Burbank while the trail was hot.

Over an hour later, Chad had navigated his rig through heavy traffic to see a driver in overalls hooking Trey's car to his tow truck. Slamming on his brakes, Chad left his dually double-parked because there was no time to look for a space on the crowded street. He turned on his flashers and bolted out to meet four cops. Two wore uniforms, probably the ones manning the black-and-white, but one was in a suit and tie and the other, likely the crime scene investigator, wore a lab coat as he packed a large bag. Chad recognized a sampling kit, though this one was definitely a bit more high-tech than what he was used to.

The detective held several plastic bags in his hand, peering down at them. Chad had one flashing glance of what looked like a smashed piece of pink bubble gum before the detective pushed all the evidence bags in a yellow envelope and handed it back to the technician.

Chad tried to be patient, he really did, but all that came out was, "Can I see that?"

The detective looked at him and scowled. "This is a police investigation—"

"The owner of this vehicle is my brother. I'm . . . a former Texas Ranger. I came to LA to look for him. He's been missing over a week."

The detective gave him that cop once-over, boots to hat, and shook his head, obviously not impressed by Chad's current credentials. "Sorry. You'll have to go through channels. Have you filed a missing persons report?"

"Yes." For all the good that would do him. LA's backlog of missing persons was in the thousands.

"Then you'll be contacted when we know something. This isn't Texas, it's California. We respect the law. Now run along."

The two uniformed cops snickered but looked away at Chad's expression.

To hide his anger, Chad pulled his hat low. "Is that bubble gum you found?"

The detective turned back to him. "Could be. So?"

"So Trey hates bubble gum. Never chews it. So sample it for DNA."

Grudging respect pushed a bit of the knee-jerk dislike out of the detective's face, but he still blustered, "We don't even know for sure if this Trey Foster is really missing or just abandoned his vehicle—"

"Trey loves that car. If there were signs of a struggle, it would save your department some time and budget to let me do a quick search before the evidence is tainted. I know what to look for."

The detective sighed heavily, eyeing Chad again. Then he said curtly, "Captain won't like this, it's not proper procedure, but what the hell, I'd want to do the same if it was my brother. Let me see your ID." Using an iPad, the detective took a screenshot of Chad's Texas driver's license, made a notation on the digital case file, then handed Chad's ID back. "You have five minutes."

Pulling on disposable gloves a tech handed him, Chad started in the trunk, the detective hovering. "You have a swab kit?" Chad took the swabs and baggies the technician handed him and carefully scraped the dark red streak on the trunk liner. He bagged it.

The tow truck driver said, "I found the same blood on the back-seat."

"It's not blood. It's paint. Trey is an artist." Chad slammed the trunk and handed the bagged swab to the technician. "I think that particular shade is called Indian Red."

Ignoring the detective's obvious surprise, Chad opened the rear car door. He took another sample of the dark red streaks the tow truck driver had mentioned. He found nothing else of interest in the back so moved to the front. He immediately froze, staring at a long gash in the leather. That wasn't there when Trey left, Chad was sure of it.

Chad ran another swab along the deep cut in the driver's seat. It was long and straight, as if cut by a knife, but the edges were frayed in a jagged pattern. Using the tweezers the detective handed him, Chad pulled at the foam, looking for particles of something, anything that would give them a clue to what someone had been searching for. Stuck to the side of the foam Chad saw something flaky, a bit darker than the cream foam. Very carefully he used the tweezers to pull at the flake, dropping it into another evidence bag. He straightened and held the bag to the light.

The detective peered at it, too. "Looks like yellowed paper."

"Yes. An old newspaper clipping—you can see part of a date at the bottom." Chad turned the bag to a better angle. "Looks like the number nineteen—the rest is gone, but it may be a 1990s date. Can your techs see if they can get a paper match?"

The detective took the bag. "I'll insist on it. Thanks."

A chill ran up Chad's spine as he considered the mounting evidence that Trey had been nosing into something that might have got him kidnapped, but he only handed over the sample and carefully moved the seat backward and forward, taking off his hat so he could eyeball under the seat as it moved. Using the long tweezers again, he removed a crumpled piece of blue, white, and pink paper. He sniffed it. "Bazooka."

"That's standard street issue for you Texas Rangers, right?" One of the hovering uniformed cops snickered at his wit, but his smile faded under Chad's glare. He backed up a step as Chad straightened.

"I told you, Trey hates bubble gum. I'd wager my mama's best china the DNA on this wrapper matches the gum. How good are your CODIS files?" Chad knew the LA police had to have a port to the FBI's Combined DNA Index System, CODIS for short, that allowed law enforcement nationwide to access national files on prior convictions and samplings.

"The latest, if we can get a sampling through the backlog." The detective had relaxed further and even offered a cop to cop look of amused frustration, which Chad returned. From Maine to California and points south and north, there wasn't a cop alive who didn't hate the red tape that went along with the job.

Chad went back to his search, shoving his gloved hand up under the seat springs on the driver's side. He felt something and pulled out a crumpled but familiar card. "Gentleman's Pleasure. Jasmine Routh, headliner." Without a word, Chad shoved the card into a bag, handed it over to the technician, and then went to the other side, but he found nothing else of interest.

Lastly, he knelt and examined the tire treads. "You sampled this mud?"

"Yes," the technician answered.

"And you took a scraping of the gash on the driver's seat, looking for metal particles?"

"No, it didn't look recent."

"It wasn't there when Trey left Amarillo. Long knife, jagged edge. Could be a Ka-Bar. Trey's never used a knife like that in his life.

Someone searched his car, even ripped open his seat. It's usually full of trash, but it's clean except for what we found. So yes, signs of foul play."

Chad pulled off the gloves and tossed them into the trash bag at the scene. "Thanks for the look-see."

The detective slowly, with obvious reluctance, held out his hand. "Impressive police work. Sorry we missed a few things."

"Thanks." Chad shook his hand, took the proffered card. "I'll be in touch if I find out anything else."

"I guess it wouldn't do any good to tell you not to interfere in a police investigation."

Tilting his hat to the right angle, Chad said, "Nope," and turned on his heel. He was still close enough to hear part of the reaming the detective gave his technician for shoddy work. He smiled, glad he'd at least made these big-city assholes have a modicum of respect for his breed. His smile faded as he saw his dually tail lights receding up the street, the front end hooked to a big tow truck. Chad ripped off his hat and slammed it against his leg. "Aw hell . . ." As he looked up the street, he saw a green lowrider skid around a corner.

The car registered with him somewhere, but resigned, and at this point more worried about Trey than the inconvenience, he went into the adjacent shop to get the name of the tow yard. He wondered if any of these tow truck guys had stock he could buy into . . .

Every time a man in boots and a hat entered the club, Jasmine felt an urge to flee. And every time, it turned out to be a wannabe cowboy instead of the real thing. Maybe he'd given up. Maybe he'd found another lead to follow. Or hopefully, maybe Trey had finally broken his silence and phoned his brother, so she'd never have to see Chad again. Mary had left a message telling Trey that Chad was in LA looking for him.

Jasmine did her best, but she knew she was jumpy and it was showing in her dancing. Before, she'd been able to pretend under the blinding lights that she was dancing for her one and only, but Chad had a way of making the entire place feel seedy. No matter her goals—to better herself and help others defend themselves against an overreaching, cold legal system—it was wrong to use her natural gifts to coax so much money from men who could oftentimes ill afford it. Yes, there was always another, younger girl to take her place, but at least she'd not be complicit in propagating this horrid, wrong stereotype that all strippers were loose women.

Conversely, Jasmine knew she'd have to shoulder enormous student loans if she quit this job. She'd lived hand to mouth so long after coming out here, she couldn't bear the thought of yet another new beginning loaded down with so much debt. She'd never be able to afford to hang out her own shingle if she didn't pay as she learned.

So despite her qualms, she stayed. And she danced. Hoping Chad was gone forever.

She was just starting to relax a bit into her old self when he showed up as she was serving drinks while another headliner performed. Praising her lucky stars she'd insisted on wearing her top, she stopped at his table far in the back and deadpanned, "What's yer poison?"

He tilted his hat back but didn't remove it. "When you talk like that, you only remind me what a good actress you are."

She snatched his hat off and tossed it on the chair next to him. "And when you act like this, you remind me you never listened to your mama. Mind your manners."

The rueful smile playing about his lips loosened some of the starch in her spine. At least he could laugh at himself . . .

"You sure you're not from Texas?"

As if she were deaf, she pointed at the sign that was prominent on every wall: Three Drink Minimum. "You drinking or leaving?"

"Michelob. On tap."

She walked off, hoping he'd leave before her number.

When she came back a few minutes later with his beer in a frosty mug, she couldn't help herself—she looked at his crotch. But apparently despite the other girl's crescendo, where she even took off her G-string against code, Chad's posture was relaxed and there was no lump in his jeans.

"I'm for hire, if you make the offer enticing enough," he drawled. "Want a lap dance?"

Embarrassed he'd caught her looking, Jasmine turned to leave so quickly she stumbled on one of her stilettos. She would have fallen into his lap if he hadn't steadied her with a surprisingly gentle touch on her arm. When she tried to pull away, he turned her to face him.

"No, I don't find her attractive the way I do you. Wouldn't it be easier if you just asked?"

"Nothing is easy with you." She jerked away but stood her ground. "You not only like it that way, you thrive on it."

"I admit I like a challenge. So how about a different deal?" He rubbed his chin as if contemplating. "I need someone to help me navigate the shark-infested waters of LA. I keep getting tickets or my rig towed, so obviously I no speako the lingo."

She laughed, flinging her long ponytail over her shoulder to tease, "Have they cited you yet for being outside the hash marks? I got a two hundred dollar one for that."

"No, but I got the one for being fifteen minutes late." He laughed. too, and the moment was so intimate and warm as they shared a common experience that Jasmine was startled when a man at a nearby table banged the tabletop.

He was wearing a very expensive suit and a very cheap attitude. "Hey, you bitch, I've been signaling you for five minutes. We need some service."

Chad made to rise but Jasmine shook her head, pinned on a blank smile, and went to take their orders. When it was time for her to go get dressed for her act, she decided to take the bull by the horns and see what Chad had been going to say to her. She wanted, no, needed, to get him out of here before her performance. Why he unsettled her so, she didn't know, or at least couldn't admit, not yet, but this place felt two sizes too small when he was present.

He was playing with an untouched third Michelob when she walked up. "We got interrupted and I have to go backstage, but I wanted to see what you were about to propose."

"Curious?"

"My eyes are green."

"I noticed." Chad put a generous tip on the table and caught her elbow. "Can you walk me to my car so we can chat in private?"

"I can't leave the club dressed like this. This way." She walked him to a private meeting room and snapped on the light. He closed the door.

"Would you be willing to spend a few hours with me several times a week if I pay you, say, fifty bucks an hour?"

That was chicken feed compared to what she earned in a night. "Why? Why me?"

He hesitated then admitted, "You know the city, you know Trey, and I'm hoping you might help me track him down, show me some of the places y'all hung out."

She relaxed a bit when he confirmed her suspicions. If he'd lied, she'd have told him no. "I honestly don't know where he is. His gir—" She broke off, about to mention Mary, but she knew he'd just think she was making her up. Why not? It would give her a chance to introduce him to Trey's real girlfriend when Mary returned from her mysterious mission. When he saw the two of them together, he'd have to admit he'd zeroed in on the wrong redhead. The fact that she wanted to get to know him better, whether it was good for either of them or not, she would keep to the secret confines of hopes and dreams . . .

"You have a deal." She held out her hand. He shook it. He held the door wide for her with his Texas courtesy.

"Should I stay for your act? Anything new?"

"No, same old same old."

He nodded, but the words seemed hauled out of him. "Why do you cheapen yourself like this?"

She backed away several steps and the distance allowed her to say honestly, "When I moved out here, I worked three jobs while I tried my hand at acting. I still couldn't make my bills. When I finally faced reality—" She broke off, not quite ready to tell him about her studies. "Let's just say I do my best to make it a craft, not just a slutty act. You can tell me when you want to get together. My number's on that card you keep flashing at me." She stalked off, wishing she'd told him no.

The next morning, Jasmine dragged herself out of bed after a few hours of sleep. She listened to her voice messages. Nothing of import except another message from Mary.

Her friend sounded as if she were battling tears. "Jasmine, I'm sorry to keep bugging you about this, but I'm stuck on a job and can't pursue it myself. I . . . have a feeling something awful might have happened to Trey. I just don't think he'd go this long without calling me, especially after coming back to LA. Would you do me a huge favor and slip into Thomas's office sometime when he's gone and check his computer contact list for a different cell number for Trey? He gave me this new one and I'm beginning to think he deliberately gave me the wrong number. This one keeps going straight to voice mail. Thanks, talk soon, hope work is going well."

Jasmine hung up, pouring herself a cup of coffee. She had an early class, but she wasn't bleary eyed just because she'd worked into the wee hours. She was having trouble sleeping because of worrying about Trey. Sure, Chad was getting to her, too, but she'd honestly liked Trey and she knew that though he might ignore big brother for a while, he'd never ignore Mary.

But why on earth would Thomas give both of them a wrong number? Behind his affable smiles and helping hand, always with conditions, Thomas was about two things: money and power. She'd assumed his interest in Trey was because of his talent, but if Thomas had deliberately kept Trey and Mary apart, he had a reason not related to art.

Idly, staring into space, Jasmine stirred cream into her cup. She touched the cup to her lips, almost burned her tongue, and spit the sip back as she recalled an offhand remark Trey had made about his homestead.

"Enough oil and gas under it to make us rich, but Chad, like my daddy, won't let them explore because he wants to keep the land safe for ranching. We'll just see about that." And he'd moodily ordered another drink.

Jasmine knew the source of Thomas's money was oil and gas. The gallery was a sideline, and not very profitable at that, at least not yet. Mary was a geologist, and Jasmine suspected her trip was related to oil and gas. Could that be the connection?

A priori, as they were teaching her in law school, if Trey wasn't up the coast painting as Thomas claimed, and his disappearance had nothing to do with art, then it had to do with Thomas's true interests . . .

Jasmine set her cup down almost untouched and turned off the coffeepot, hurrying to dress. After class, she'd make a trip to the gallery and search Thomas's contact list as Mary had requested. She had to help find Trey, not because Chad had asked for her help, but because she loved Mary, liked Trey, and had to know the truth about Thomas.

Or so she convinced herself. The fact that she'd also be working to prove herself to Chad didn't enter into her decision to snoop . . .

CHAPTER 7

Chad parked his dually the closest he could to the gallery. This time, when he got out, he didn't just glance at the parking sign. He walked over to it and read it carefully. Two hours, nine to five, except for, he read the small print, street sweeping day. Tuesday. This was Wednesday. Clear.

Chad wore a snap-button shirt today. He felt for the tiny imprint in his pocket, satisfied when he felt it still there where he'd put it after leaving the electronics store. Since he wasn't a Ranger anymore, what he was about to do could get him arrested, just as Sinclair had predicted, but somehow Chad knew Kinnard wouldn't call the cops under any circumstances.

Closing the gallery door gently as the chime sounded, Chad paused at the window display, once again admiring the black-and-white painting of the lonely man on the bluff. The discreet price tag on the back, five thousand dollars, was darn near a month's take-home pay and had to come from his dwindling retirement account, but it would still be cheap if buying it elicited the reaction he suspected would come from Kinnard. It was also very strange Trey hadn't signed the painting, and Chad knew that must be because Kinnard had told him not to.

Besides, it was the only way he could figure out how to get into the man's office.

Kinnard entered from a side door, that too-smooth smile Chad detested on his face. It faltered a bit when he saw his customer, but Kinnard offered his hand. "Welcome back. What can I do for you?"

"I can't get this painting out of my mind. It would be perfect for over my couch." *If I had one*, he amended to himself. . . Trey had taken it.

"Yes, it's one of my current favorites. Shall I have it wrapped for you?"

"Would you mind if I used your landline to check my account balance and move my funds from a holding account so I can write you a check? I don't like using a cell phone for a sensitive transaction like that." All true enough.

Kinnard hesitated a bit too long.

Which only whetted Chad's instinct that the man was hiding something. "If it's an inconvenience, I can drive back to my hotel and do it from there, but I won't be able to come back until tomorrow." Close the sale was every true salesman's basic credo. Chad smiled slightly as he waited for Kinnard's response.

True to form, Kinnard stepped aside and waved a hand before him. "No problem, you can use the phone in my office."

Chad stopped so abruptly as he entered the office that Kinnard stepped on his heel. Chad barely noticed. The office was a complete contrast to the spare modernity of the showroom. From the huge oak desk to the original Western bronzes and the enormous buffalo painting over the studded leather couch, this office spoke of a man who loved the West. How did this jibe with the slick Beverly Hills businessman? This office might have been on the front of *Texas Oilman* magazine.

He only said, "Nice office. Is this the phone you want me to use?"

Nodding, Kinnard moved a stack of papers onto a credenza to leave the desk clear.

Chad walked behind the desk and pulled a checkbook from his rear pocket. He waited, but Kinnard hovered at the edge of the rug. "Do you mind if I have some privacy?"

Reluctantly, Kinnard exited, leaving the door slightly ajar.

Eyeing all the corners for surveillance devices, Chad walked to the door and closed it firmly. No cameras that he could see. Besides, Kinnard wasn't likely to record his own dirty dealing.

Chad pulled the tiny bug from his shirt pocket, quickly went to the desk phone, pried apart the receiver end with his smallest knife blade, and wired the bug inside. With all the news about prying ears on cell phones, Chad was hoping Kinnard did indeed have a lot to hide and would use his landline whenever possible. It could still be bugged, of course, but wasn't as easy to trace. Chad put the receiver cap back on and then used the phone to call his bank.

A minute later, a discreet knock came at the door.

"I'll be out in a minute. I'm on hold," he called through the door.

While he waited, wondering why every bank on earth used the same elevator-type music, Chad quietly pilfered Kinnard's desk. He found nothing more suspicious than a stack of cream-colored stationery—with a Dallas, Texas, address. Chad folded one of the sheets into fourths and snapped it into his pocket.

A representative finally came on the line. Chad's transaction was short and sweet, and he didn't even have the heart to ask for his account balance; he knew it was pathetic. He memorized the confirmation number simultaneous with another knock, this one less discreet. Chad called, "Come in." As Kinnard entered, Chad thanked the banking rep and hung up the phone.

Kinnard offered an expensive pen. Nodding his thanks, Chad wrote out the check for five grand. He was signing with a flourish when he sensed someone entering the open office door.

He looked up. A burly young man who couldn't have been more than legal age by much, hovered there, but he had the attitude to match his muscles. His face was pocked with acne scars. He wore a baseball cap backward, had tattoos from bicep to wrist on both arms, wore baggy jeans, and his underwear showed. If he'd carried a sign marked South Sider, his gang affiliation couldn't have been clearer. Even in Texas, the Los Angeles Latino gang that spanned lots of Southland geographies, was notorious. Chad couldn't help it. His eyebrows rose as he looked at Kinnard.

Looking flustered for the first time since Chad had met him, Kinnard caught the guy's arm. "I told you never to come here."

"I had to. We got trouble." Cold black eyes glanced at Chad, then quickly away.

With an apologetic look at Chad, Kinnard shoved the guy out the door and closed it, blocking Chad's view.

Chad left the check in the middle of the spotless desk pad and hurried to a wooden file cabinet. He bent down to appraise the lock to see what type of tool kit he'd need when he opened it later.

Satisfied, Chad wandered the office, appraising the art, when Thomas reentered. "Sorry about that." He scribbled out a receipt.

The rumbling sound of a loud engine caught Chad's attention. Still acting casual, he sauntered to the side window, twitched the heavy curtain aside and looked out. A green lowrider leveled itself with hydraulics over the rough alley pavement and screeched out of view before Chad could read the rear plate. He frowned. He'd glimpsed that car before . . . Where was it?

It came to him and his hand clenched so hard on the curtain he heard the stitching tear slightly. Oh, the green lowrider was familiar, all right, and with that flame decal flowing over the hood, probably one of a kind.

The same car had hovered a half block away as the driver had watched him search Trey's car. He'd only noticed it because of its loud engine, paint job, and flashy hubs, but he was certain it was the same car. A gangbanger's car at the site of his brother's abandoned vehicle in a rough area downtown, now showing up at the Beverly Hills gallery where Trey's work was displayed? *Coincidence my ass*, Chad thought.

Blindly, Chad let the curtain fall and turned. Despite the gallery owner's protests to the contrary, Kinnard was connected to Trey's disappearance, and Chad was pretty damn sure he'd just met the coconspirator. So angry he couldn't meet the man's eyes, Chad pulled his hat low over his face. So far evidence linking Kinnard to Trey's disappearance was circumstantial at best; he still had to bide his time.

He accepted the receipt, looked down at it, and gave it back. "You mind signing it? Just to make it official and all, from the owner of the gallery."

Kinnard's eyes narrowed as they met Chad's, but when Chad

smiled blandly, Kinnard could hardly say no after a man had written him a five-thousand-dollar check. He signed it. This time, Chad folded it and put it in his other shirt pocket. "Pleasure doing business, Mr. Kinnard."

"Same here, Mr. Foster. My artist will be pleased at your recognition of his talent."

"Surely would enjoy meeting the feller."

"I'll tell him when we talk that you asked about him."

"Any chance I can get his number?"

"That's against my contractual agreement with my artists. But again, I'll ask his permission next time we speak."

"And when might that be?"

"He's up the coast painting, mostly in solitude, so I never know when he'll call. He leaves his phone off, but I assure you when he comes back to town he'll personalize his signature on the painting for you."

Convenient. And not like Trey, who hated solitude and didn't much care if he left his name behind. Some of his best work had been produced in a painting class. But Chad only shrugged and exited the office. He lifted the wrapped, bulky painting under one arm, nodded his thanks, and moved to the front door.

It opened before he reached it and in stepped Jasmine. She was dressed casually today in tight jeans and a long T-shirt over her hips, and never had she been more appealing to Chad. She was even wearing cowboy boots. His favorite color. Red.

She arched her eyebrows at the painting in his arms, glanced at the bare window display, and smiled at him as she held the door. "You two were made for each other."

"That's more like my line, isn't it?"

"I don't think you could use a line if your life depended on it."

The words were out before he could stop them because they came from deep in his gut, where he lived. "I bet you've heard every last line there is."

Her smile faded and she pointedly stepped aside so he didn't brush against her as he exited. "Better an honest attempt to get me into bed than a hypocrite who thinks he's too good for it."

Chad turned so fast the bulky painting caught his hip. "No one calls me a hypocrite!" The Fosters, even Trey, had always prided themselves on honesty.

She hesitated, and then, as if goaded, snapped, "Well, there's only one way to find out. I owe you a lap dance." She gave him that north-south look. "I dare you. I double dog dare you. Show me you don't want me right down to your big ol' pointy-toed boots and I'll believe you." She closed the door so hard it brushed him in the butt, leaving him half in the doorway, half on the sidewalk.

But then the little witch, or maybe she fit the other rhyming word better, always left him off balance.

He stomped off in his big ol' pointy-toed boots to his truck.

Inside the gallery, Jasmine steadied her shaking hands by gripping her satchel purse more tightly. She didn't want Thomas to see how much Chad Foster could rile her. However, Thomas came rushing out of his office, his hair a bit mussed, which was unusual for him, his expression grim.

He lightened up a bit when he saw her. He gave her a distracted kiss on the cheek as she passed him. "You here for your check? I think I just sold the last painting that was in the show, but your bonus should be pretty good. I told Roger to leave it in my desk. I'll get it for you, but then I've got to run—"

"I can get it, Thomas. I know where you keep them."

He tossed her his keys. "Lock the door and my desk and leave the keys behind the counter in the gallery when you're finished. Gotta go." He bolted out.

She stared after him. She didn't recall ever seeing him so frazzled. And Chad hadn't been exactly bubbly either, but then he never was. She suspected they'd had some type of confrontation.

She unlocked his office door, closed it behind her, and appraised the dim, elegant room. When her schedule allowed, she'd even used his password and his computer to help him with his accounts, so he was comfortable giving her free rein in his private space.

Clicking on the desk lamp, she sat down in his desk chair and powered up his computer. However, when she tried the password he'd given her, she got an error message. Well, she was only supposed to pick up a check, so he'd have no reason to give her a new password.

Still, that he'd changed it without telling her was a bit worrisome. And while she was a bit squeamish about sneaking around like this in the office of a man who'd been kind to her, worry about Trey and concern for Mary overrode her scruples. This had nothing to do with Chad.

Absolutely nothing. She didn't care what he thought of her . . .

Not at all.

Did Thomas not trust her? Or was he hiding something? Or was it both?

She stared into space for a minute, trying to think what password he might have used. None of the usual, kids, pets, of which he had neither. Despite all the warnings from Internet gurus, just about everyone she knew used the same password or variant of something easy to remember, and Thomas was not that computer literate. She thought of the things most important to him and a memory popped into her head of the time he'd told her of his first big oil discovery.

His eyes had lit up as they shared wine in his office one night and she'd asked about his oil activities. "Everyone said that field was played out, but the geologicals showed substrata that broke off on a diagonal and angled downward. It was obvious to me they just drilled in the wrong place. It was called the Dorado field, West Texas."

Dorado. She typed it in the password box and the computer came to life. Feeling like an intruder, she went straight to his contacts list and scrolled through to the *F*s. She must have missed it. She scrolled through more slowly, but sure enough, Trey wasn't listed. She was there, here was Chad's cell phone listing. Jasmine seriously thought about entering Chad's number into her phone but felt that would violate his privacy since he hadn't offered it. She looked once more, but found nothing for Trey . . . or a new number for Mary. That was very odd because she was sure Mary was working for Kinnard.

She leaned back in the chair, her mind racing. What did this mean? How could Thomas be promoting Trey's paintings and saying he was one of his top artists when he didn't even have a cell number for him?

The answer was obvious: He couldn't. Trey was missing, at best, and quite possibly dead. And Thomas was involved.

Alarmed and dismayed, Jasmine rose so abruptly she knocked

over the heavy executive-style chair. As she bent to raise it upright, the arm of the chair knocked into the side of the desk. She heard a strange, hollow clicking sound emanating from the bottom of the desk. She bent down and looked under the heavy piece of furniture. A hidden compartment built into the side of the panel supporting the file drawers on the right of the desk had popped open. It was the exact dimensions of the panel and so cleverly concealed, she'd never have seen it even if she'd been looking. She crawled all the way under the desk because she couldn't see inside the drawer and realized it had a spring catch. She popped it and the long, deep sideways drawer came loose in her hands.

Scooting out, she emptied the contents onto the top of the desk.

Just some contracts, including the one for Trey's land. She opened the document and scanned it, her nerves jangling when she read the legal plat description. Mineral rights, section so-and-so of the Dorado field. Next she fingered through yellowing old newspaper articles, one showing Thomas riding a pumpjack, a cowboy hat in his hand as if he rode a bucking bronco. She checked the date: 1995.

There were torn bits from a couple other articles. The paper had yellowed about the same so she concluded they were from about the same era. She carefully spread the tiny scraps on the desk pad, wondering who had taken them and why. She saw only "Thomas Hopper . . . land fraud." And the second one showed a caption but no picture: "Lead investigator Texas Ranger Gerald Foster testifies in Hopper trial."

Jasmine didn't need a picture to complete the vivid one in her head. She knew Chad and Trey's dad had been named Gerald. Everything snapped into place, and the image was not pretty.

Why Mary was away, why she felt so guilty. She must be helping Thomas in whatever land scheme he was working on. Trey probably took these articles when he saw his father's name mentioned. That also explained why Thomas had reacted so strongly to Chad. Perhaps even why he'd invited Trey out here. If Chad and Trey were sole owners of the last parcels of a big new claim in the Dorado field, Thomas would do anything to get them out of the way. Especially if they were the sons of the man he blamed for his prison sentence years ago. He'd told her about his time in jail, made light of it, saying it was the making of him and so on, but from this perspective it was obvious he was up to his old tricks and hadn't learned a thing. Changing his name from Hopper to Kinnard didn't change his stripes.

The only question was—What did she do now? If she told Chad what she'd found, he'd go on a tear and haul Thomas back to Texas, procedure or not. She knew he was working without jurisdiction, that he'd quit the Rangers to find out what had happened to his brother. Besides, these scraps were not real evidence, not enough to convict Thomas of murder anyway. Thomas would hire the best criminal lawyer in the country and Chad would be the one under fire. No authority, wrong arrest, lack of jurisdiction, the string of infractions just kept scrolling across her mind's eye.

The only viable option, legally anyway, was to collect more evidence.

Feeling very old and in need of a shower, she put everything back the way it was, carefully attached the drawer into its hiding place, grabbed her check out of the desk, turned off the lights and powered down the computer, being sure she closed out of all the menus she'd used. She also deleted her browsing history, and then she locked the office door. She put the keys behind the counter as Thomas had asked, threw the lock catch on the front door as she exited, and walked out.

She was opening the door to her sporty little car when she sensed someone watching her. She looked up and saw a hooded Hispanic kid, tattoos on his arms, wearing a backward baseball cap, watching her from behind a light post.

Thinking nothing of it because men of all ages stared at her, she got into her car and started it.

So she didn't see the kid pull out a cell phone and make a call. "She just left. Want me to follow her?"

CHAPTER 8

Chad waited for Corey to come on the line, looking down at the fax confirmation in his hand. He'd just come from a copy store where he sent the fax to Corey's machine. His partner should have had time to see it by now.

"Corey Cooper."

"Hey, Corey, it's Chad. You get the fax I just sent?"

"I figured that was you, with the CA area code. Why on earth did you send me the signature page of an invoice for some work of art?"

"That work of art is by Trey, and I think the man who signed the receipt is involved in his disappearance. If you can access the Del Mar files, I want you to cross-check the signature and handwriting with any of the deeds we have copies of from the land grab task force. This Kinnard guy might not be using his real name if he's head of the Del Mar corporation, but he can't change his handwriting."

"Chad, I'd be pissing in the wind. I'm no handwriting expert. Besides, I'd have to sneak in after hours since I'm not on the case, and if Sinclair caught me . . ."

Chad could see the shudder even across the miles. He whacked his hat against his thigh. "Then give the fax to the head of the division working the Del Mar case with the FBI, not sure who that is—"

"Uh, Chad, guess you haven't heard. Sinclair said he was getting stale, so he asked to head the case. Right after you left."

Crap! Chad smashed his hat back on his head, half wishing he'd punched his old boss and erstwhile friend. He was close, he could smell it, and this Kinnard was not only hiding what he knew about Trey, he was hip deep in the Del Mar muddy waters. There was Texas in his office, Texas in his attitude, and too many connections between him and Trey. His gut told him this asshole was head of the Del Mar Corporation that had signed the contract to buy Trey's half of the land. Now all he had to do was prove it.

Chad said wearily, "All right, well, just hang on to it for now. You got the name of that FBI fella leading the task force on the Feds side? Maybe I can't go through official channels, but I still own a ranch acquired in a questionable land deal by our prime land fraud suspect. Just say I'm doing due diligence on this Del Mar Corporation."

While he waited, still standing under the exterior awning by the Beverly Hills copy store using his cell phone, Chad heard a distinctive roar. He looked up in time to see that suspicious green lowrider prowl around a corner—two car lengths behind Jasmine. He recognized her sporty little Acura exiting the alley behind the gallery. When she turned, the lowrider turned after her. He punched the End button on his phone, glaring up the long blocks to where he'd been forced to park his dually. They'd be gone by the time he reached it . . .

He bit off a curse and scanned the street in time to see a cab disgorge a passenger directly across from him. He ran to the driver. "Follow that green car."

"Off duty. Sorry."

The two cars had already rounded the corner. Never had he wished more for his badge than now, but he did the next best thing—flashed one of his dwindling hundreds. "How about now?"

The cabby grabbed the bill and opened the rear door. Chad climbed in. "Catch up to that green lowrider that made a left, but keep your distance. I don't want him to know we're following him."

Starting his meter, the cabby did as directed. He was a grizzled old pro with a graying ponytail. He knew how to trail a suspect, staying several cars back in the next lane over so he could always see his target.

They wound up Wilshire slowly as rush hour was starting, and when they reached West Hollywood, snaked through less crowded side streets. The cabby dropped so far back they could barely see the bright green tail end, but then the car stopped. The cabby stopped, too, pulling to the side as if parking.

Chad used the zoom feature on his cell phone to take a picture of the vehicle's rear license plate. Inside the car he made out the driver, wearing a baseball cap. Using the zoom on his phone again he tried to get a picture of the driver but only caught the back of his head. "Drive forward," he instructed the cabby. "Slowly. I'm going to duck down in the seat so he won't see me. Stop at that stop sign two blocks up. I should be able to get a good shot of his face from there."

While the cabby complied, Chad tossed his hat on the seat and ducked behind the rear seat. When the cabby stopped again, Chad inched above the rear windshield and snapped a pic. This time he got a clear shot of the driver's face. He was on a cell phone and frowned as if he didn't agree with what were obviously instructions, but he shrugged and tossed the phone down.

"You want I should drive on?" the cabby asked.

"Circle the block and come down that street he's stopped on, but pull up before he sees us."

Sure enough, when they'd circled the block and he could see the street sign, Chad recognized the name. This was Jasmine's street. He glanced up at the historic looking fourplex, old but still impressive, knowing Jasmine lived in a one-bedroom on the top floor. He'd run her sheet before he came out here and he recalled the address though it was nicer than it had sounded on paper.

The outside stair landing was empty, the ornate wrought-iron gate closed, but her car was parked in a tiny slot next to the building. So this asshole was definitely following her. However, for now she seemed safe because the lowrider had rumbled back to life. "Can you cut behind this building up the alley and come in behind him again? I need to see where he goes next."

"Yes, but it's gonna cost you."

"So what else is new in this damn place?"

The cabby glared over his shoulder. "You don't like it here, git. Just so's you understand, cowboy. You don't like us, we don't like you."

"Well, lookee here, someone else speaks the lingo." Chad waited until they were moving again, following the same gangbanger he'd seen in Kinnard's office. The kid had driven south on La Cienega Boulevard to pick up the 10—toward downtown. He kept his tone conversational. "I thought you Californios were all the liberal, live-and-let live type. I can't walk down the street without someone calling me a cowboy and I haven't ridden a bronco in fifteen years. I love fine wines and expensive art. So who's stereotyping?"

The cabby growled something to himself but subsided and went with the flow of traffic several cars behind the lowrider. Chad sighed, thinking he needed access to a blackboard and his old English teacher, what was her name? Oh yes, Miss Gorne. She'd make him write his favorite word five hundred times, the same one she'd made him write whenever he acted up. Oh, he could spell it just fine. Funny how he'd never learned its meaning. . . .

Patience.

As soon as she walked into her apartment, Jasmine saw the flashing light on her answering machine. She listened to her messages. Junk call, sales call . . . she caught her breath as she recognized the voice. Trey . . . Husky, quiet, panicked.

"Jasmine, no time, they took my phone, can't reach Mary, someone else has her number, she must have a new one. They're holding me out near City of Industry, I think. Some kind of deserted warehouse. Cars everywhere. Think it's a chop shop. Can you call my brother in Amarillo at the DPS offices, don't remember his work number, he didn't answer his cell—" The call cut off abruptly.

Jasmine flew to her cell phone before she remembered she and Chad had never actually spoken on the phone. He seemed to know all about her, but she didn't even have his number as she'd been too conscientious to record it from Thomas's files. She tossed the phone on the couch, took a deep breath to steady herself, then, her fingers shaking only slightly, she paged through the digital messages until she found the time stamp. She glanced at her watch—three hours ago. Damn, what if they'd caught him and that was why he'd hung up abruptly? Jasmine looked down at the caller ID but the number Trey was using must have been unlisted because it showed "unavailable."

No time to waste.

Holding her phone close so it would record as she replayed Trey's message, she tried to remember what little Chad had said about where he was staying. Just "farther east up the 5." Big help. Time to make another stop at the gallery, and this time she wouldn't be invading Chad's privacy because he'd be desperate to hear this tip. She grabbed up her purse, stuffed in her cell phone, locked her door, and flew down the stairs to her car.

Fifteen minutes later she snuck into Thomas's office, greatly relieved he wasn't there, and turned on his system. Using the Dorado password, she brought up his digital contact list. She paged through the screens until she found Foster, Chad. Using her cell phone so she'd have the number, she dialed the unfamiliar area code.

All it did was ring . . . a few times only, as if he'd turned the phone off in the middle of the rings. His curt message came on, name only. She spoke softly, "Chad, I just got a message from Trey. He's being held somewhere in the City of Industry he thinks. I know where that is if you'll meet me. Here's my number in case it doesn't appear on your screen." She recited it and turned off her cell phone. She was about to power off the computer when she noticed another notation below his cell number.

Thomas was nothing if not efficient. Address in LA: Los Angeles Equestrian Center, Burbank. Good, that was on the way to City of Industry. She turned off the computer and bolted out.

Chad tapped the cabby's shoulder. "Pull in behind that truck so he doesn't see us." The cabby complied without a word.

The lowrider had pulled up to a grungy diner downtown, but a brand-spanking-new Mercedes C63 AMG was parked a few spaces down. Not exactly typical wheels for this demographic but exactly what Kinnard would drive. Every instinct he possessed told Chad he needed to hear what these two unlikely allies said. No way Kinnard would even come here unless he didn't want to be seen.

Chad's cell phone rang as he was getting out, and irritably he shut it off and tossed it on the seat, along with his hat so he'd be less conspicuous. He'd gotten another missed call earlier, but when he looked at the contact it said "unavailable," so he'd not paid it much attention.

From his window, the cabby watched him trying to blend in, and shrugged as if to say, *Doesn't help. You're still a sore-tailed cat.*

Chad glared at him. "I'll be back."

"You have the wrong accent for that line." The cabby smirked.

Did everyone out here reference the whole world with movie lines? Biting back something more pungently Texan, Chad peered around the big cargo truck that was double-parked, the rear ramp down, still idling. He couldn't see a damn thing from here; he'd have to move closer. He had to move almost into the doorway to see inside the diner's grimy plate glass window, but sure enough, he recognized the punk, facing him, and Kinnard's fancy-suited but perfectly straight back and five-hundred-dollar haircut.

When the punk glanced up, Chad ducked to the side. What he'd give for some of that fancy audio equipment they sometimes used on stakeouts. No way could he slip in and out of this joint without their seeing him. He debated the wisdom of his next move, but it was the only thing he could think of at the moment. He went back to the car and opened the cabbie's door. He pulled his last hundred from his wallet and dangled it in front of the scowling face. "Another tip for you plus full fare if you'll slip into that diner and play little pitcher."

The cabby snatched the hundred. "Little pitcher?" He got out.

"You know, little pitchers have big ears." When he got a blank look, Chad stood back and waved his hand impatiently toward the diner. "Never mind. Eavesdrop." Must be another Texas saying Mama had cursed him with.

Chad pulled the cabby to the side of the door. "See those two huddled together near the back? Can you slip into that booth behind them and see if you can hear what they're saying?"

The cabby eyed him up and down. "You a cop?"

"Not anymore. I'm looking for my brother, that's it. I promise it's nothing illegal."

The cabby sighed heavily but walked into the diner and seated himself as Chad had requested. He pretended to read a menu but from Chad's perspective he did indeed have big ears. Chad also suspected this wasn't the first time this grizzled veteran of the LA freeway wars had listened in on people. However, he'd barely sat down before Kinnard rose abruptly. Not offering his hand to the kid, he turned on his heel and strode arrogantly toward the door.

Chad barely had time to duck out of sight behind the idling truck. Kinnard stalked toward his vehicle, anger in every abrupt move. Usually he was smooth as owl shit even in the way he moved, but not this time. What had they been arguing about?

The punk exited on his heels and went to his lowrider, firing it up. He screeched off before the cabby could make it to the door. Chad gestured impatiently, *come on!* But by the time the cabby had started his engine, the lowrider's rumble had faded. They drove around the block, searching, but it was gone.

"You catch anything?" Chad asked

"Not much. Something about how the gangbanger could clean up his own mess from the old dude. That he'd come out and check the new merchandise himself sometime tonight. Then he got up and left."

A chill slithered down Chad's spine. Mess? Had time already run out for Trey? And he'd lost his best lead . . .

When he arrived back at his truck after paying the astronomical cab fare with his credit card, Chad was just in time to see a tow truck driver hooking up his dually. Chad bolted out of the cab and ran to the driver.

Only then did he see Riley sitting astride his bike, idling his engine as he talked to the driver. Chad took his hat off and whacked it on his thigh. While he didn't technically have to respond to any of these stupid tickets because he'd be heading home soon, this was getting ridiculous. Not to mention expensive. He forced a grin. "Did you call this guy, Riley?"

Riley smiled back, sunglasses shining along with his white teeth in the late afternoon sunlight. "Yep."

"Can you call him off? I'm working a case. I'll move the truck now."

Riley's grin deepened. "Working a case without authorization, you mean?"

Chad's temper snapped. He whacked his hat so hard on his thigh that it stung him. Trying to collect his wits, Chad looked up the street for inspiration and saw the famous Art Deco–style sign that read: You Are Entering Beverly Hills.

For the first time, he realized he must have parked just outside the city limits. He'd given up long ago trying to figure out which city he was driving through, but for once he was glad of this confusing megalopolis. Chad put his hat back on and adjusted the brim just so. Calmly, he went to the rear of his truck and unhooked the tow chain. Both Riley and the driver protested, but Chad merely went around to the driver side of his truck and looked over the roof at Riley.

"Seeing as how you're such a big shot in Beverly Hills and all, not good for your image to work without jurisdiction." Chad got in his truck and pulled away from the curb.

Riley shouted after him, "You can teach me that, too!"

Chad grinned, so happy to have won this one that he barely, for once, noted the traffic.

A good hour later, Chad parked his dually in the huge parking lot of the equestrian center, locked it, and walked toward his campground. He'd wash up a bit and then head over to Chester to feed and groom him. Maybe that would help with the ache in his gut that was turning into a knot of fear for Trey. He'd been here over a week, followed every lead he could think of, tailed a suspect, searched Trey's car, grilled his girlfriend, bugged the likely mastermind, and he was no closer to tracking down his brother. Again, he wondered if he should contact the morgue, but he felt, deep in his gut, that Trey was in trouble but still alive. He'd act on that presumption for another couple days, and if nothing turned up he'd start contacting all the various morgues in LA and give them Trey's description. In his tent, Chad put on some washing overalls and an older pair of boots and walked toward the stalls. He was so distracted, he'd tossed his cell phone on his sleeping bag without remembering he'd turned it off.

As he neared the barn, he heard splashing along with a feminine voice that sounded familiar. "Stop that! Who's bathing who?"

He rounded the barn and came to the washing stalls. His heart skipped a beat when he saw Jasmine, in the same T-shirt and red boots she'd worn earlier, but now the T-shirt clung to beautiful breasts and taut nipples as she gave Chester a bath. The ends of her long red hair were wet and curly, her boots muddy as Chester butted her again with his head so she'd rub his nose. Based on the marks on her shirt, this had been going on for a while. She complied, one hand rubbing the horse while the other guided the spray hose over his back, suds flowing down into the drain beneath them.

She was giving his horse a very thorough washing and getting one in return.

Chad wanted to yell at her.

He wanted to demand what the hell she thought she was doing.

He even wanted to whack his horse on the rump and call him a traitor, as Chester usually didn't like strangers touching him. How dare he be Mary's little lamb with this woman who tormented him day and night . . . Any minute now he'd literally fall down in adoration at her feet, the ornery critter.

Like owner, like stallion, came the traitorous thought. Weary in body and soul, Chad wanted nothing more than to kneel before this wicked woman and bury his face in her bosom, pull her across his lap and . . .

However, Chad's iron-willed discipline, far more his guiding star than his wants, came to the fore. And his needs? Well, he couldn't think about those even if she brought them to blazing life in a manner hard to ignore, despite his fears for Trey.

Holding himself in, he crossed his arms over his chest, leaned against the side of the barn, and appraised her. He kept waiting for her to look up and see him, but she was intent on her task. She pulled the straps of the rubbery grooming comb over her hand and began brushing the water away from Chester's sleek red hide.

And Chester, the turncoat, literally groaned at her rhythmic stroking and soft whispering. "Big, tough old stallion, you're just a big baby. One of us might as well feel good while we wait for Chad. I'd love to ride you. You think he'd let me? How about that, boy?"

"Sounds good, but me first." The words were ripped out of Chad, deep and guttural, before he could stop them. He walked around the barn so she'd see him.

She started so hard she almost lost her footing on the slick grate. He reached out to steady her but she caught herself on Chester.

"You said something?"

Thank God she hadn't heard him. "What in tarnation are you doing with my horse?" Chad growled, glaring between the two of them. Jasmine looked a bit guilty, but Chester was happier and more docile than Chad could ever remember seeing him, which only made him angrier. This was the same mettlesome nag who sometimes nipped at his master when he didn't like the way things were going? Chester arched his long neck for her to stroke it. He swiveled an eyeball sideways to appraise Chad's glare, gave a disdainful *whuff*, and preened under Jasmine's stroking.

"I—I was just trying to help while I waited for you. They gave me your campsite number and it matched the number on his stall, plus they confirmed he was yours. He kept pawing at the ground and pushing against his gate, and I could see he was . . . restless."

Restless? Was that what this was called? What a sorry term for all the physical and emotional feelings she roused in him by loving on his horse. There was no other word for it, and the practiced ease in her movements said she'd performed this task many times before. How could it be she was so comfortable around horses, high-spirited stallions at that, if she was an LA party girl?

Not for the first time, he couldn't compute properly when it came to her, but one thing he was sure of: Chad was sorry he'd put on his overalls as they complicated his current state. Luckily Jasmine was beet red and hurrying to finish her task, so this time she didn't notice. "Why are you here? How'd you know where I was staying?" He was pretty sure he'd never told her.

She picked up a grooming towel and smoothed it down Chester's hindquarters, his back, his legs as she responded, "I needed to talk to you, and you didn't answer your phone. Didn't you get my message?"

Oh crap, Chad forgot he'd shut off his phone outside the diner. "Why were you calling? My phone's back at the tent."

Jasmine hooked a gleaming Chester back to his lead and tied him up, coming over to face Chad. He had to force his gaze to stay fixed on her face, and she seemed to finally realize the state of her shirt because she hastily crossed her arms over her chest. That only pushed her breasts higher. "I got a message from Trey."

That got his attention. His gaze zeroed in on her face. "When? What did he say? Where is he? Is he OK?" Part of him heaved a huge sigh of relief—

Until she said, "He's in trouble. I left my phone in your tent so I could let you listen first thing as soon as you got back. I didn't want it to get wet. I knew if you came back you'd come looking for Chester. I recorded Trey's message for you." She untied Chester and took him to his stall, putting him back in. He balked, turning his long, beautifully arched neck to look at her soulfully.

She smiled. "I'll bring carrots next time." She patted him on the rump and he reluctantly entered the stall. When she locked it and walked off, he whickered mournfully after her.

Chad moved from foot to foot, biting back a plea for her to hurry, and he half ran, half walked back to his tent, which was close by. She had to run to keep up.

Inside his tent, she knelt and pulled her phone out of her purse, which she'd buried under his sleeping bag, bringing up her functions list and hitting Play on her record button. The familiar voice at first gave Chad a huge sense of relief, but by the time the message ended, Chad's face was grim again.

"How many warehouses in this City of Industry?" he asked, fearing he knew the answer.

"Hundreds, probably. It's one of the most industrial areas in Los Angeles."

"Did you get the number?"

"I checked my caller ID but it read unavailable. It must be unlisted."

Chad wanted to scream. Crap, that call he'd missed had been from Trey, but his brother had obviously been too rushed to leave a message so he'd called his girlfriend instead. Dammit, now he really missed the badge. If he hadn't quit, he could fix this problem with one phone call, just trace the unlisted number with the phone company. He debated asking Corey to do it, but he couldn't keep putting his partner's job in jeopardy. Sinclair would crucify him.

Chad ducked under the tent flap and strode up and down, so antsy he couldn't be still. Jasmine followed, nibbling her lower lip as she watched him with obvious concern.

He barely noticed. Okay, on his cell phone he still had some of the databases he'd used as a Ranger. He hadn't tried to use them since coming out to LA, but he was dead-level certain that the green lowrider and its driver could lead him to Trey, especially if his brother was being held at a chop shop. That pimpmobile screamed custom.

Ducking inside the tent again to grab his phone, Chad brought up his link to the FBI vehicle registration network. The FBI cross-referenced all state DPS databases for exactly this reason, so cops working multi-state jurisdictions could trace license plates. However, the access required was high level and the user codes limited. He'd only been granted access himself recently because he was working multi-state rustling cases. Chad held his breath, wondering if his PIN still worked or if Sinclair had him locked out.

The little screen flashed. "Access granted." Chad pulled the scrap of paper from his pocket and texted in the lowrider's license plate number he'd photographed and then written down. His fingers were shaking slightly, so it took him a second to get the numbers right. It took a bit, but finally an address flashed on the screen.

He showed it to Jasmine. "Do you know where this is?"

"Yes. That's the address for the Beverly Hills Police Department. Where'd you get that?"

Chad's jaw dropped. Ballsy move, and it sounded like something Kinnard would orchestrate. "Unbelievable. Phony plates. They must have stolen them from the police parking lot." Chad started striding up and down again, pausing only to toss off the constraining overalls.

"You know, there's an easier way," Jasmine offered. "I know someone who works at the police department. Maybe he can help us trace the call. Y'all can do that, right, even when it's unlisted? My provider is AT&T and I know they have a deal with the Feds."

Even with all the stink in the media about privacy, he was impressed she knew that. Most people didn't. She was pretty smart for a stripper. "Who is it?"

"Riley O'Connor. He sometimes works on the side in security at the gallery—" She broke off at the look on his face. "You know him?"

"Kinda. He a pucker-assed whey-faced motorcycle cop?"

"I wouldn't put it that way, but yes."

Chad thrust the scrap of paper into her hand. "It's a green lowrider with a flame decal wrapping the hood, fancy chrome rims. You call him. I'm going to City of Industry. And be careful, because the driver's also been following you."

"But Chad, there are hundreds of warehouses there. I thought you wanted my help navigating the city. I won't even charge you at the going rate of fifty dollars an hour."

In other circumstances he might have smiled at the gibe, but not now, with his best lead since he got here. "Maybe I'll get lucky. Besides, this could be dangerous."

"I'm coming with you." She stuffed the paper in her jeans pocket. "I can call him on the way."

He blocked her path, eyeing her up and down. "You'd be real popular in a gangbanger area dressed like that."

The T-shirt still clung to her nipples and her hair was a riot of damp curls. She looked exactly like a woman ready for bed. But not for sleep. But then she mostly looked like that. He turned sharply away and broke into a jog toward his truck, ignoring her plea to wait.

For once, he could put her out of his mind easily enough. He drove off, tires popping gravel, and punched the Play button again on his phone. The message was a bit degraded, having been copied twice, but Trey's panicked voice was clear enough. That scared him, for he'd only heard that tone once before. Shortly after their parents died, Trey had fallen into a rattlesnake den.

He'd called until he was hoarse, but Chad hadn't heard him until he went looking for his little brother because supper was ready. He'd never realized that limestone outcropping on the edge of the bluff hid a small cave until Trey's trembling voice reached him faintly on the wind.

Chad called back, "Trey! Where are you? Call to me again."

"On the bluff. Hurry, Chad, there's snakes everywhere and two of them bit me. Bring a rope . . ."

Chad stopped cold and ran back to the house at top speed for the antivenin kit. He pulled Chester out of the pasture and jumped on him bareback, just taking time to halter him and grab a rope.

A few minutes later, when he finally found his brother, Trey was unconscious. Chad barely fit into the narrow opening as he climbed down the rope he'd anchored to a tree. He was glad he was wearing his chaps because the minute his boots touched down, he felt rattlers striking at him, and there was so much rattling going on his blood ran cold.

He stomped at the head of one curled next to Trey and felt it go limp. He kicked others away. He felt one bite him, but the sharp fangs didn't quite pierce his heavy rawhide chaps. He grabbed the snake's tail and pulled it away so hard the fangs tore out of the snake's mouth. He threw it against the limestone wall. It spewed blood as its head burst open.

Maybe the other snakes were spooked by the scent of one of their own dying, or maybe they were just tired, but they crawled away to the back of the cave. Chad grabbed up his brother, put the slight weight over his shoulder, and pulled them both out of the god-awful maw of venom and darkness. He immediately laid Trey flat and administered the antivenin, then propped Trey before him on Chester and kicked the stallion into a gallop. He calculated thirty minutes to the hospital once he reached the truck.

"Hold on, little brother," he whispered over and over, but Trey never woke up until the next day.

The doctors told him later that if he hadn't administered the antivenin when he did, Trey would have died. Chad had the shallow cave filled in with concrete, snakes and all. And for a while, he and Trey had gotten along much better. Chad took an interest in Trey's art, and Trey actually asked a few questions about Chad's cases as Chad took his first job with the Rangers.

The recollection ended as abruptly as his trip up the 5 when traffic snarled. Chad wanted to scream, wondering why every time Trey's life was truly in danger, he was missing in action.

But he took the opportunity to pull the Peacemaker from the seat compartment to confirm yet again it was loaded.

CHAPTER 9

Waiting for Riley to answer, Jasmine tapped her foot impatiently. She was still at the equestrian center, and it was growing dark. She was worried, now not just about Trey but about Chad, too. He might be fearless, he might even be a Texas Ranger accustomed to violence, but no one really understood how cold and treacherous LA could be until they'd lived here. It was not unusual at all for people to walk right past others in distress. He'd stick out like a sore thumb in a bad part of LA in that big truck with Texas plates, and whether he'd admit it or not, he needed help.

Jasmine herself had rescued a disabled African-American woman stuck in a wheelchair on Sunset Boulevard in the middle of four lanes of zipping traffic. The woman had the old-fashioned push-type wheelchair, and she'd only managed to cross half the street when the light changed, leaving her stranded on a yellow line. Cars whooshed past her on both sides with just a foot to spare. Jasmine had had to park and run out into the intersection, waving her arms to stop the drivers, to wheel the woman to safety.

No, driving by himself in a bad part of LA wasn't smart even for a former Texas Ranger. . . .

Finally Riley came on the line. She cut into his greeting. "Sorry, Riley, but I need your help." She explained what was going on.

There was a rattling noise in the background, but dead silence from Riley. Finally he protested, "Jasmine, I can't do this. I'm a traffic cop, and if I start poking my nose into gangbangers and grand theft auto without authorization, I could lose my job."

"But, Riley, he's gone out there on his own. Isn't it our responsibility to help him, especially since we have proof Trey is being held against his will? And he did call me. Isn't it my duty as a citizen to report this? If Trey was snatched, it probably happened in Beverly Hills." She started to mention the gallery, but bit back the urge. She didn't know for sure yet if Thomas was involved, so it was best to let the facts speak for themselves.

Still, Jasmine knew enough about the law and lawmen to understand how protective they felt about their turf. And few jurisdictions were more discriminating than Beverly Hills.

Dead silence again. Then a heavy sigh. "Bring in the message and I'll play it for my boss, see what he says."

Jasmine bolted to her car.

When Chad reached the outskirts of City of Industry some time later, it was dark. He looked around at the greasy, pocked asphalt streets, the huddle of long, low buildings surrounded by huge lots studded with big rigs, and the railroad track bifurcating the road like an accusatory finger. If Chad had his way, the entire city would be leveled and rebuilt from the ground up, but even he knew the importance of modes of transportation when it came to warehouses and commerce.

The railroad . . . Chad turned the message volume up on his cell phone to its max. He'd heard the slightest noise in the background earlier but hadn't paid it much heed given his concern over Trey. Now he tuned out his brother's voice to listen to the slight rattling sound.

A train rattling over tracks. So wherever Trey was being held, he had to be close to these tracks.

Letting his gut instinct take over, Chad paralleled the tracks as best he could, keeping a grim eye peeled for a green lowrider. The phone on the seat beside him kept vibrating, but he eyed the ID and left it where it lay. He knew the 310 number. Jasmine had no business out here with him; he might have to do something illegal.

Come out shooting . . . like the Rangers of old. And he was just in the mood for a riot.

At about the same time, Jasmine squirmed on the seat next to Riley. He and his captain had both listened to Trey's frantic message and agreed he was likely being held against his will. The captain had given Riley one-time authority to go after Chad and see what evidence was readily available. Then the LA police, who had instigated an investigation because of Trey's deserted car, would have to take over. But if Trey had been snatched from Beverly Hills, that did give them some authority to at least investigate, if not lead, the inquiry. The captain told Jasmine in no uncertain terms to go home, that she had no business riding along on a potentially dangerous assignment.

To which she responded that she was the only one who knew what the gangbanger looked like and that Trey had called her, which made her a witness already. And since the gangbanger who drove the lowrider had brazenly stolen an unmarked car's plates from the Beverly Hills Police Department, and since she and Chad had given them the plate number, they were already involved in the case. The captain had glared, but Jasmine had been paying attention in her criminal law class.

So now, as Riley drove an unmarked car down congested freeways, Jasmine dialed Chad's number for the third time, but he never picked up. "Drat the man. Doesn't he know how to use a cell phone?"

"From my short acquaintance with him, I'd guess he's got his nose so close to the ground, his ears have pavement burns," Riley observed dryly. "I have a suspicion he won't welcome my help."

Chad had worked his way all the way through the City of Industry, mostly following the tracks, without seeing anything resembling a green lowrider. But, hell, it could be parked inside one of these massive warehouses.

And it might already be too late for Trey while he literally blundered in the dark. When his phone vibrated again, he slammed on his brakes, snatched up the phone, and growled, "Quit calling me. Can't you see I'm busy?"

"Hey, it's not my idea to be here, but if you look behind you, you'll see a beige unmarked car on your ass."

The male voice sounded slightly familiar. Was that O'Connor? On Jasmine's phone?

Chad looked in his rearview mirror. He couldn't see a lot until the bright headlights shut off; then, under the street lights, he could make out Riley O'Connor, for once without the helmet, sitting in the driver's seat, and next to him, Jasmine. She waved tentatively, as if knowing he wasn't happy to see them.

Chad bit off a groan and stuffed the pistol back in its compartment. Just what he needed. A by-the-book asshole who'd slow him down and a party-girl stripper airhead who'd be cocaine to these gangbangers. Well, maybe she wasn't an airhead . . . but the rest was right.

Chad parked and strode aggressively to their window. "How the hell did you two find me?"

"How many double-axled trucks with Texas plates are there in this city in the warehouse district?" Riley rejoined. "Cruising at about ten miles an hour. I can always put out an APB on you if you want me to." At Chad's scowl, Riley softened a bit. "Why here?"

Chad played the message again at its loudest volume. "Hear the train?"

Riley did. He jerked his head toward the backseat. "Get in. I'll see what I can do to help."

"You can use your federal connections to get me the address of that unlisted number."

"It's not as easy as people think. I can't just call up AT&T. Getting access to an unlisted number will require a warrant, and what's the probable cause?"

"How about fucking kidnapping?" Chad growled.

"We don't know that yet. All we have is Trey's call—"

"And a missing person's report, which I filed a few days ago; his deserted car, his only means of transportation; a new knife gash in the seat; over a week without other contact with any of his usual relationships; no response to repeated phone messages. What do you need, a map?"

"And the most important piece of evidence?" Jasmine interjected. "I know for a fact Thomas has sold several of Trey's paintings in the last week, but Trey hasn't been in to pick up his cut. And since he just moved here, I know he needs the money."

Riley sighed heavily and shut off his engine. "All right, when you put it like that . . ." He picked up his own cell phone and dialed rapidly. "Get me the duty officer in communications." He took the piece of paper Chad handed him. "I need a trace on an unlisted number. No, I don't have a warrant but there's no time. A crime could be in progress. It's a landline, we think, so it should pull up an address." Riley listened and then bit off, "I don't care if you have to dig up Mother Teresa and get blessed, get authorization!"

Chad looked at Riley, impressed for the first time with more than Riley's hygiene.

Inside a deserted-looking warehouse several miles away, on the border between City of Industry and South El Monte but close to the railroad tracks, Trey glared at the man he'd literally entrusted with his life and assets.

"My brother will never stop until he finds me. He keeps on a-comin', in Texas parlance, but then you know all about that, don't you, being Texan yourself?" Trey glared at Thomas Kinnard, but knew his bruised and bloody face made him less than threatening. Trey wished now he'd never let Chad's paranoia rub off on him. Having second thoughts about the contract and the fact that Kinnard insisted he not sign his own paintings, he'd told himself it was okay to look for Mary's new number since Kinnard was obviously keeping them apart. Instead, he'd found something totally unexpected. Something that finally explained Kinnard's fixation on the Fosters and their land. The old clippings detailed Kinnard's prior identity as an aggressive young wildcatter, cut down in his prime for his shyster land deals by Texas Ranger Gerald Foster. Kinnard had gone to prison. Obviously it had taken him years, and a change of venue to a state more forgiving of prior misdeeds, to overcome his past.

Trey had taken the articles with him and hidden them inside his car seat, then pulled a block away from the gallery to call Chad. Before he could complete the call, the world went black.

To make matters worse, a few hours earlier Kinnard's car-thief hoods had caught him on the phone and beat the living daylights out of him. The one they called Montoya, whom he'd seen at the gallery skulking around the alley a time or two, used a tire iron but, thankfully, stayed away from Trey's head. Trey assumed he was still alive only because they were waiting to see what the big boss wanted to do with him. His ribs hurt like the devil when he moved and he suspected one or two must be cracked.

The big boss had arrived a few minutes ago. Kinnard's gleaming Mercedes and Montoya's green lowrider somehow looked quite at home next to one another in the chop shop populated with cars of every type and age in various stages of construction or de-construction. Everything from Ferraris to plain old Ford F-150s. Trey had known the minute he made it out of that storage room where he'd been held for over a week that he was in the chop shop of a highly successful auto theft ring. He'd been confused as to why anyone would bang him over the head in his own car, toss him in a trunk, and then take him to some oily-smelling warehouse, but when he got a clear look at Montoya a few days later and recognized him, everything fell into place. Now Trey assumed Kinnard had searched his secret drawer, found the clippings gone, and sent his partner in crime after Trey.

Watching Kinnard pace up and down in agitation, Trey heard again that lecture from Chad he'd always hated: "Boy, don't you know you can't dip your wick at both ends and still run a ranch?" *Shut up, Chad.* Mary had been his next thought. *Please, God, don't let Mary be involved.*

Now, as he looked around with more calm than he felt, Trey shoved away thoughts of his girlfriend and brother. The last puzzle piece about Thomas Kinnard fell into place as he recognized a Ferrari that he knew the owner had reported stolen from the art gallery.

"I always wondered why you opened an art gallery," Trey said. "You never have seemed to know that much about art. But it's the access to the cars you wanted—"

Kinnard spun on him, a flush on his high cheekbones, but this time there was nothing charming about his smile. "And the people. You'd be surprised how many of them jumped at a risky investment like a Texas oil deal. Your art was the perfect icebreaker. Homegrown

Texas talent who grew up on a ranch sitting on a pool of black gold. They ate it up."

Trey's heart sank. No way would Kinnard be so forthcoming unless he knew his bragging would never leave this warehouse. Still, while Trey believed Kinnard would do anything, cheat anyone for money, murder was a bit extreme even for him—which was probably the only reason he was still alive.

Trey glanced at Montoya, who was supervising his chop shop crew as they crated up the more valuable parts. Trey squinted down the huge bay and thought he saw cars being loaded onto transports. They were moving their operation. He felt a brief surge of satisfaction that his phone call had spooked them.

But then he caught Montoya's eyes. Trey backed away a step, but he was slow and could barely move because he was so sore. Montoya had always creeped him out, for he seemed so expressionless and hard for a guy in his early twenties. Montoya's black eyes were not just cold and expressionless. They were a void, like deep space where even a scream made no sound . . .

Trey tried to guess how long it had been since he'd left that message for Jasmine, but the warehouse had no windows so he had no idea of the time of day. Still, it had to be hours by now. Keep Kinnard talking. "I sent my contract to the best oil and gas attorney in Amarillo," Trey lied. "I barely read the damn thing, but then you know that, because I was out of my head about Mary. Just like I know you've screwed me somehow out of my oil royalties, because that's your true calling. Not art, not even stealing high-dollar cars. Shyster land deals, just like years ago when my dad nailed you."

Trey leaned forward. "But Daddy was a pussycat compared to Chad. He'll lock you away for good this time."

In any other man, Kinnard's rude noise would have been impolite, but somehow even that sounded cultured. Kinnard smiled. "If I believed you, which I don't because you came out here too fast to contact any lawyer, I might be a bit concerned. That's the thing about good attorneys. They can bury you to your neck in paperwork and you still don't know a damn thing. There's only one document in existence that ties me to the Del Mar Corporation, and neither you nor your brother will ever get your hands on it."

Montoya whispered something in Kinnard's ear. Thomas looked genuinely pained as he eyed his protégé, saw the calculating fury in Trey's blue eyes. "You should have stayed in the storage area, Trey. And not made that phone call."

"Do you really think getting rid of me will stop my brother?" Trey smiled this time. "As Chad would say, not hardly."

"Your brother doesn't scare me. He's alone with no jurisdiction, he quit the Rangers—" Kinnard broke off at the shock in Trey's eyes. "You didn't know that, did you? You're mighty important to your brother, apparently. Important enough to quit his job to come a-huntin'. He's so broke he's living in a tent at the equestrian center and he's barking up the wrong tree. Damn shame there are so many gorgeous redheads with butterfly tattoos out here."

Trey inhaled sharply. "Jasmine. You're using Jasmine as a decoy to keep him on the wrong trail."

Clicking his tongue, Kinnard made a shooting motion with his forefinger. "You're smarter than I thought. Turns out your brother has a real hard-on for our lovely stripper Jasmine, and he doesn't like it one bit because he blames her for luring you away from home."

Now Trey wasn't even listening. His eyes closed as he whispered, "Mary. Mary, how could you?"

"Right again. She's in Amarillo setting up the fracking rig to come in at a horizontal under your land. Turns out the biggest deposit may be under Chad's half, but Chad's busy, isn't he?" He looked at Montoya and shrugged. "I tried, but this peckerwood has become a real liability."

Tears burned behind Trey's eyes. Montoya and two of his gang came at him in a blur. He turned to run, but it was too late.

For him. And for Mary . . .

Trey whirled just as Montoya and his men grabbed him roughly. One of the gang members pulled out a switchblade and with a lethal *snick*, opened it. Trey stood still, knowing of only one chance. As the knife moved to his jugular, Trey looked at Kinnard. "If you kill me, Mary won't help you anymore. Whatever she may have done, she still loves me."

Kinnard made a stop motion with his upraised palm. Montoya scowled but glared a command. His attack dog backed off enough that only a dot of blood came out to decorate the gleaming blade. They still held Trey between them.

"She'll never connect me to your disappearance," Kinnard blustered.

"She's been suspicious of you for a long time, especially when you had Jasmine get that identical tattoo. We talked about it before I even came out here. And if she's the one supervising the horizontal, you going to put your entire deal at risk? Who am I going to blab to anyway? I'm sure you won't let me near a phone again."

Trey stared back as coolly as he could manage with his pounding heart and sweaty palms. He could see he'd given Kinnard pause by attacking the bastard's one weakness. Nothing would get in his way of being the next oil baron.

Kinnard pulled out his phone. "Time to call her, let her know you're all right."

"No." Trey slapped Kinnard's phone away when they held it to his ear. A fist in his gut made him double over, but he still didn't take the phone.

When Kinnard gave a grim nod, the blows came fast and steady, but for once in his life, Trey took them without complaint.

The choice between a beating and death was no choice at all.

Hurry, Chad, he thought as the lights began to dim. *Time to keep on a-comin'.*

CHAPTER 10

Several miles away deeper into City of Industry, the unmarked car idled far more patiently than Chad. "For God's sake," he burst out after they'd waited an hour, "let's cruise around and see what we can find while we wait."

"You don't do stakeouts very well, do you?" Riley asked. "Let's look at this logically, shall we? City of Industry has some of the highest percentage of industrial footage in Los Angeles County. The odds of us just blundering across Trey—" He broke off and yanked up his bleating phone. "What was it again?" Riley went to his phone notes and texted in the address the caller had given him. "Got it, thanks." He keyed the address into his GPS and wheeled out of the parking lot.

Jasmine looked out the window and noted they'd almost passed the border into South El Monte. But the railroad tracks abutted this thoroughfare, so that fit, at least. Jasmine turned to Chad. "Why are you so sure Thomas is involved in this?" she asked, wanting to find out how much he knew.

"His background is too clean." Chad never even turned his head from scanning outside the window as he answered shortly. "No record of him at all until he moved to California about ten years ago. And if he's a Californio, I'm a dyed-in-the-wool Ivy Leaguer. He doesn't always hide his Texas accent, and his office shouts Neiman

Marcus, not Saks. Besides, he's making his bucks in something besides art. And whatever it is, I'd bet my half of the ranch it's illegal and Trey is smack dab in the middle of it."

Jasmine had speculated that herself, so she nodded and looked pointedly at Riley. "Thomas isn't making much money at the gallery, Riley. I can confirm that from both him and Roger Larsen. Thomas has also told me himself he used to work oil deals before he moved to California. I'm pretty sure he's still working them." She could hardly admit how she'd illegally searched Thomas's computer and files, so she only added logically, "So where's the big bucks coming from and why is one of the guys who does his dirty work following me and stealing plates from the Beverly Hills Police Department?"

Riley scoffed, "Supposition about one of the richest men in Beverly Hills." He threw on his brakes to avoid an eighteen-wheeler coming off a side street. When the intersection was clear, he turned down the same street. It was lined with a row of warehouses. The vast, dark buildings had the occasional truck parked in huge lots, but no other signs of life.

Riley slowed the unmarked car to a creep. "Help me find an address. This should be the block."

They couldn't see any addresses but as they watched, another eighteen-wheeler exited an open bay. Quickly, Riley killed the engine and cut the lights. "Duck." They all ducked down but as soon as the huge rig exited the lot, Chad popped back up to snap the license plate with his cell phone. He threw open the car door and ran toward the bay, which was being closed behind a last vehicle.

A green lowrider. It idled, lights off, but the yard floodlight was bright enough for Chad to ID the vehicle. The hood hadn't seen him yet, and appeared to be waiting for his pal to lock the bay door and get in the car.

Shielded behind a Dumpster next to the corrugated steel building, Chad slid to a stop, his hand automatically going to his hip for the pistol that wasn't there. He'd left it in the truck rather than take it into Riley's unmarked car, fearing if Riley saw it he'd confiscate it. Now what? If they followed the lowrider, they couldn't search the building. Chad's heart was pounding and the mere thought of losing his brother now, when he was so close, made him break into a cold sweat.

Only one way to do this.

Chad waited until the lowrider had turned to drive toward the exit and then he came out in the open so Riley and Jasmine could see him under the yard light. He waved his arms over his head frantically to get their attention, then pointed toward the vehicle.

They got the message because Riley waited until the lowrider had turned up the street before easing out of the lot after it, his lights still off. Chad went straight to the bay door and pulled out his knife to pry at the sturdy lock. He had but one thought, to get to Trey, so his reaction time wasn't as quick as usual.

By the time he realized someone was behind him and began to turn, his knife raised, the tire iron came down on his skull with a dull thud. He collapsed, his hat flying as his head hit the ground first. Blood seeped onto the greasy pavement, coating it with a brackish pool that slowly widened from his head wound.

Cursing in Spanish, Montoya opened his cell phone and made a call, tossing the tire iron into the backseat of the spiffy little truck he'd kept to drive while the lowrider, pristine of any evidence, led the unmarked car away. He'd made the vehicle the minute it turned into the vacant lot, but the cops were too late. The last truck had loaded up and exited, full of car parts and one damaged piece of highly incriminating evidence . . .

Chad opened his eyes to a blinding light and the sickening smell of antiseptic and bleach. His head hurt like a sonofabitch. He felt the aching spot but it was covered with bandages. Only then did he realize he was in a hospital, wearing one of those ridiculous smocks with no backside.

Trey . . . what about Trey? Chad forced himself to sit up and almost vomited as the room swam around him. He sank back, closing his eyes. He felt a presence and cocked a wary eye on Jasmine's sympathetic face.

"You need rest and quiet for a few days," she said. "Mild concussion, according to the doctor, but no long-term effects. Apparently you have a very solid skull."

The teasing lilt might have pleased him under other circumstances, but he could only manage a hoarse, "Did the lowrider lead you to Trey?"

"No. The driver wasn't Montoya. Would you believe he actually pulled over and cooperated?"

Chad groaned and closed his eyes again. "He let you search the vehicle and you didn't find diddly."

"Right again. The vehicle isn't even registered to Montoya, it's in the name of some LLC."

"And the plates? That's enough to warrant an arrest and impound the vehicle."

"Uh, they must have switched them again. These came up as I said, legal under the name of some LLC. It matched the insurance card. So we swung back around for you and . . . and . . ." Jasmine trailed off.

She didn't need to paint a rosy picture because Chad had a good idea of how much blood he'd lost by how he felt. He turned his head away, embarrassed both at the way they'd caught him unprepared and at how weak and hopeless he felt now. He had to swallow back or choke on his growing fears for Trey. "Did Riley search the warehouse?"

"Yes. With the very tangible evidence of you bleeding at his feet, even Riley had to admit there were signs enough of foul play. He got the El Monte police to assist. They brought a warrant while I rode in the ambulance with you to the hospital, but other than the few remnants of a highly sophisticated chop shop, they found no evidence of Trey. It was the right place, though. They matched the phone number Trey used to the landline in the warehouse. We did a search on the company that pays the phone bill and it's been there for years. The owner of the building pays the bill for the tenants. The latest tenants had a short-term lease that just ended. They always paid in cash. He gave us what he had, a copy of the lease and a credit check, but it wasn't much. It led to a dummy LLC. They're still searching for a connection to the Del Mar Corporation."

Chad summed up the situation in his usual blunt way. "Square one." Infuriated, worried sick about Trey, Chad tossed back the thin blanket and put his bare feet on the floor. He moved to sit up, so frustrated he didn't care what he bared to Jasmine, but somehow the floor didn't stay under his feet where it belonged. It seemed to want to rise up to meet him . . . Damn floor. Chad felt surprisingly strong, limber arms catch him before he made intimate acquaintance with the linoleum. Jasmine staggered a bit beneath his weight and they both fell back on the bed, half on it, half off, in a tangle of arms and legs.

Chad hadn't been so close to her since the night she gave him the lap dance. His head swam again, but not because of the concussion. She felt so good, she smelled so good, and she looked . . . Half lying on top of him, she looked at him with those lucid green eyes that riled him in ways he'd never believed he could be touched.

Even slightly nauseous and with a pounding headache, Chad couldn't resist pushing himself back onto the bed and taking her with him so that she lay atop him. She tried to rear away but only succeeded in pushing her lower body into the vee of his sprawled legs. The thin gown had twisted. He was decent, barely, but he felt the sheet against his backside and knew if she moved just right, they'd both be embarrassed. In fact, he felt a growing . . . embarrassment that neither the aseptic setting nor the clinical garb could quell. Her eyes widened and darkened as she looked into his, so she felt it, too.

"You really want to make me feel better?" he asked huskily. All of a sudden, he wanted to kiss her, bad. Not all of a sudden, actually. It had been coming on him like a West Texas thunderstorm. Sometimes they built slow, but when they broke, nothing could contain their gale-force winds and lightning.

When she bit her lip he groaned and caught her head in his hands, pulling her lips down to his, running the very tip of his tongue over the slight depression her teeth had made in her soft upper lip. She gasped, her heart leaping against his rib cage, but he knew she wasn't afraid. He caught the emotion in his mouth and gave it back to her in a deep breath, opening them both to the tingling charge arcing between them like static electricity before a storm. The hairs on his body stood on end as every dormant scintilla of his male being came alive.

He shouldn't do this.

She made him weak when he had to be strong.

He was alone, had been alone for a long time, but her soft warmth and curves brought home to him how acutely he missed the touch and taste of a woman.

Trey, he reminded himself . . . this woman had bewitched Trey into deserting his birthright. This wicked woman used sex against men like a howitzer.

But for the moment, his body won, especially in this vulnerable moment under the feel of her soft warmth. When she sighed a deep, shuddering breath into his mouth and slanted her lips over his in a brazen invitation, he wrapped his arms around her back and kissed her like he'd been longing to. *Kiss* was a weak word for this seminal event of his spotty romantic life, for he'd never felt so hungry and so fulfilled at the same time. The taste of her on his tongue was honey—edible, pure sustenance.

And in the purest sense, they fed one another in that moment. Here was a feast in a dreary world of famine. Both had starved for this nurturing, the male and the female, the yin and the yang, the angles and the curves.

They fit. Perfectly. Only in this way could two halves make a whole.

Jasmine muttered something and squirmed closer to him, unafraid, apparently, of the hard male need thrusting into her stomach as she lay atop him. She brought her hands to the sides of his head and tenderly caressed him under the bandages, as if wanting to take his pain away.

And somehow, she did. Her lips softened in their desperate connection, confident enough now to whisper against his, yet increasing their tingling sensation by her very gentleness. Chad went limp, letting her feed all the lonely, hungry places he let no one see, much less touch. He kissed her back, caressing the long flow of her back into her hips, alive finally with the feel and taste of female.

Their play of lips moving in sync segued into tongues, Jasmine gently offering, Chad accepting as his male due the darting invitation to deeper intimacy. He'd never been very good at French kissing, but

Jasmine brought out both his best and his worst . . . It was his turn to groan when she reciprocated passionately, thrusting into his mouth to test his tongue and teeth. He moved to pull her harder between his legs, lifting them around her hips, when a strange sound invaded their intimate feast.

Footsteps? A genteel cough. "It's good to see you're feeling better, Mr. Foster," the doctor said drily. "I'm not sure if it's the drug or your potency that gives you such . . . energy, but in any case, if the two of you want a shared suite, you have to go one floor up."

Reluctantly, Chad relaxed his tight hold. Jasmine moved to scramble off the bed so quickly he had to grab her arm to keep her from sliding to the floor. She was almost as red as her boots. Chad glared at the intruder as best he could under the thick bandages, but the doctor only eyed the lump under the covers. Chad dared him with his scowl to make another smart remark and he relented. He helped Jasmine situate Chad in bed properly, head on the pillow, sheet and blanket folded under his arms, and then he checked the chart and glanced at the vitals on the monitors. He shined his scope into Chad's eyes, nodding in satisfaction when Chad's pupils contracted.

"All in all, you're a lucky man," the doctor said, sneaking a glance at Jasmine.

Chad noticed his interest but pretended not to. "When can I get the hell out of here? Hospitals give me the creeps."

"You have to have rest and close observation for at least three days," the doctor stated. Softly, but adamantly. "Bed rest. Total."

"Three days? I have a case to work—"

"The Beverly Hills Police Department is working it now," Jasmine inserted, safely two feet away, her flush slowly fading. "Riley has always wanted to get away from the streets and work the bigger cases, so really, we've done him a favor."

"He's a wet-behind-the-ears, prissy little prick," Chad stated, "and—"

"Don't mind him, Doctor, he's just cranky," Jasmine said with a wry smile. When the doctor's lips twitched as if he knew why, she added hastily, "What about if you release him to my recognizance? I'm certified in CPR and I know what to look for in a concussion. Dilated pupils, nausea, cold sweat—"

"Why, have you slipped down that pole one too many times and bumped your head?" Chad growled, squirming as if he couldn't get comfortable.

Jasmine's smile stayed fixed. "If he gets out of line, I'll just give him a matched set."

Chad closed his mouth on the next protest. Anywhere was better than here. At least at her place he could work the Internet, call Corey. She probably had a nice, soft bed, too, along with other nice, soft things she'd given him a taste for a few minutes ago.

She obviously read his mind. "I have a great, comfortable couch."

His smile faded.

"I'll even let you have the remote."

He narrowed his eyes at her cheeky little grin, promising retribution.

The doctor scribbled something in the chart. "If he relapses, call an ambulance. And no . . . strenuous activity. Clear?"

Jasmine nodded vigorously, but under Chad's gaze, she blushed again. When the doctor leveled a stern stare on Chad, he shrugged. "Clear."

"I'll send a nurse in for your exit interview and to help you dress. Be good." And with that admonition, the doctor walked out, already thinking about his next patient.

Chad looked at Jasmine. He wondered what to say, if anything, about what had happened between them, but he wasn't sure he understood it himself. How could a woman who riled him up so much with her lack of morals feel like hope and heaven in his arms? As the last of the heady passion faded, his usual cold feet made his toes curl under the covers. Maybe it wasn't such a good idea for him to go to her place. "I can go back to the equestrian center, Jasmine. I'll be fine. I still have a couple of leads to follow up on—"

"You can do that from my place. You don't need to be sleeping on cold, hard ground and you need observation. Who else will do it?"

"Your Christian duty is noted, but not necessary. The ladies in the Baptist church around the corner from our ranch gave up on me years ago."

"Well, maybe a sinner will have more luck." At his look, she started backing toward the door. "Uh, I'll bring the car around and wait in the patient pickup area." She bolted.

Chad smiled slowly, happy that for the first time since he'd met her, Jasmine seemed off balance. Well, at least the confusing storm of feelings wasn't one-sided. Chad swung his legs to the side of the bed to look for his clothes. Strange, his head barely twinged and his dizziness had subsided. Maybe she was more of a tonic than a poison, and he was just too stubborn to see it . . .

He began to dress as he waited for the nurse. One thing was certain: The next few days would be real interesting. Either they'd help him get close enough to her for her to admit she'd been Trey's girlfriend, or she'd keep lying to him and he could use her as ruthlessly as need be to find his brother.

Chad recalled the ease with which that asshole had bushwhacked him. He hadn't heard a thing. Maybe he'd been too worried about Trey, maybe all the city noise had disguised the footsteps coming up behind him, but by any estimation he'd been caught napping. and the gangbangers had whisked his brother away for the second time.

To where? And in what condition?

He'd have to use the time at Jasmine's to methodically check all his leads again because concussion or not, he couldn't afford to take three days off when Trey's life hung in the balance. Chad bent to pull on his boots, but his head swam so much that nausea filled his throat. He had to sink back and shut his eyes. Lights danced behind his closed lids, and he saw himself standing alone over a fresh grave on the homestead. Next to Mama and Daddy.

About to throw up, Chad opened his eyes and took several deep breaths. No. He was just weak from the concussion. Trey was still alive. He had to be. Chad waited until the nausea subsided and pulled his foot up on the bed to put the boot on it so he didn't have to lean down.

As she waited for Chad at the curb, Jasmine tried to make sense of that kiss that was more than a kiss. She'd kissed many men, though far fewer had ever gotten to first base with her, but never had a kiss affected her like this. If she'd doubted Chad's awkwardness around women, she believed it now because even so vulnerable and ill, she'd read the hunger that drove every awkward touch. This was a man who was not comfortable around women. He put up a good show, all right, with all that arrogance, but when you peeled away the layers, he was at heart as much of a romantic as his little brother. She remembered that nugget necklace Trey always wore and wondered what kind of woman had reared two such unusual sons, especially for Texas. Jasmine said softly, "Ride 'er hard, put 'er up wet!" She smiled. The Texas saying seemed to be the credo of most of the Texas men she knew, but not Chad and Trey. They seemed genuinely hungry for a connection.

That kiss had supplied it, on both sides . . . Their embrace had begun tentatively, but by the time the doctor interrupted, thank the Lord, enthusiasm and curiosity were mutual. Jasmine felt her cheeks flush at the recollection, and she knew it was a bad idea to take six-plus feet of male temptation into her sanctuary. She'd never slept with a man in her place, which she kept sacrosanct, one of her few inviolable rules. She'd had fewer than ten partners since she'd moved to LA, which for a woman in her profession, was pretty damn choosy. And part of that was because she wouldn't sleep with anyone at her place.

She wouldn't violate that rule now, especially with a man who'd been directed by his doctor to avoid strenuous activity. As uncertain as she felt about many things, Jasmine knew if they ever laid hands on one another, the activity would be a marathon.

CHAPTER 11

Trey awoke to a burning pain in his side, his head, and his arms, which were pulled behind his back and tied. He'd fallen over long ago, and even in the dark he recognized the smell of oily car parts overlaid by the scent of diesel exhaust. He bounced over hard planking as he was jostled; the burning in his extremities became a blessed numbness.

He was in one of the big rigs, headed God knew where. Almost certainly out of LA, but at least he was still alive. His ruse about Mary had worked. They'd beaten the living tar out of him for the second time in a week, and he retched but had nothing to vomit. When the nausea slowly passed, he couldn't avoid the hot flow of tears. Mary . . . For a moment he allowed himself the luxury of emotional pain and somehow it was worse than the physical.

She'd led him on like a prize bull into the glare of the arena, tempting him as a dancer and then giving him those sultry looks and long kisses to sucker him back out to LA. The couple of times they'd had sex had been the highlights of his romantic life. The brief time she'd spent with him in Texas made him miss her all the more, until he'd signed away his heritage to trail her back to LA. Now he understood why she'd been so curious about the lay of their land, had even bent several times to examine the rock strata and shaded her eyes to look at the pumpjacks adjacent to the homestead.

She'd been working with Kinnard all along. And Jasmine? Was she involved, too? He knew Jasmine had worked longer at the club than Mary had, but now he suspected Mary had been planted there as a guest act just for his benefit. She'd certainly given it up quickly enough when he asked.

So Kinnard had adroitly used two red-haired floozies like bait to lead the Foster brothers away from their land, if he hadn't been lying during their confrontation at the warehouse about how Chad was attracted to Jasmine. And knowing Chad, who'd been too long without a woman, how could Jasmine not be to his taste, stripper or not? And they'd fallen for it, hook, line, and sinker.

He blinked, forcing the tears back, but in the crack at the rollup door, which allowed in a few rays of sunlight, he could see shadows. Night was coming or his vision was getting blurry. Probably a bit of both.

Ignoring the pain in his wrists, he forced himself to sit upright. Using his feet to push his weight against the side of the truck, he levered his upper back slowly up until he could get his feet beneath him. His arms were almost wrenched from their sockets as they took the brunt of his weight. They settled back into blessed numbness as he staggered against a car, bending over the hood to hold himself upright over a bad road bump. Pain knifed into his side, but he only braced himself as best he could.

When the rig's tires hummed again, he wound like a drunkard through the packed cargo until he brushed against something sharp. A car part of some kind, half out of its canvas cover. It snagged on his shirt, ripping it. He turned around and sawed at the duct tape holding his wrists together, feeling blood seep over his fingers, but he was so angry at his gullibility that he didn't care. Served him right.

Then he was free. He rubbed his wrists for a few minutes, and slowly feeling came back into them, the tips of his fingers on fire as if he'd had frostbite. He opened and closed his hands to keep his circulation going, as Chad had taught him years ago during a blue norther.

Chad. . . . if he knew his big brother, Chad was already in LA tearing the city apart looking for him. At least that taunt to Kinnard hadn't been an empty one. And Kinnard hadn't scoffed at him. In fact a very subtle flicker of his eyes at the gibe made Trey feel as if Chad had already made Kinnard understand that the Foster brand of justice—keep on a-comin'—had passed from father to son.

If Chad was here, Trey had to get a message to him somehow.

When the burning faded to a dull ache, he used his fingers to feel around every part of the cargo bay. Flashlight, paper, pen, in that order. He had a plan, such as it was.

He pushed Mary to the back of his mind. Right now he just had to stay alive long enough to confront her . . .

In the nicest hotel Amarillo, Texas, offered, Mary paced her spacious room from one side to the other. It had been almost two weeks now since she'd spoken to Trey. Jasmine had told her several of Trey's paintings had sold, but he hadn't been in to pick up his check.

Something was wrong. It didn't do any good to talk to Thomas because he was lying. Trey had stumbled on something he shouldn't, and Thomas would have his own private little Latino gang shut him up. The question was—how?

Mary's circuit brought her to the mirror. She looked at her reflection, and for a moment, her lovely face wavered, becoming a ghastly caricature with a long, beaked nose and pointy chin. She blinked the tears away, only then realizing they'd distorted her vision. It had been a long time since she'd cried, and she certainly hadn't counted on falling in love with her mark. She'd been alone so long since she hit the streets at sixteen that she'd forgotten what it felt like to need another human being. People scared her for the most part, especially men. Oh, she knew how to use her looks to her advantage, but the two times she'd had sex with Trey had been different. He was so . . . sweet. As creative and generous in bed as out of it.

When he left to go back to Amarillo, she'd been devastated.

Jasmine and her unquestioning friendship had put the first crack in her armor. She didn't care that Mary had walked the streets at one time. Until she got a grant to go to junior college, and from there scholarships to USC to work on her geology degree. The two redheads turned out to have a lot in common.

So when Thomas had approached Mary and asked her to be a guest star at the strip joint where Jasmine danced, offering her a handsome sum to do so, Mary had accepted without a second thought. It wasn't until Thomas promised to sweeten the pot if she could get Trey Foster interested, that she began to realize Thomas, as usual, had some grand plan that typically involved fleecing someone.

And now here she was in Amarillo, using the newfound geology skills she'd been so proud of to complete his plan. He needed someone compliant, someone who would look the other way if he had to bend the law a bit, so he'd taken an interest in her schooling and gotten her an internship at a big firm to learn the ropes of assessing new deposits. It was a lousy economy and she'd welcomed his connections. At first. Now she wore golden handcuffs linking her to him, despite his likely involvement in Trey's disappearance. One percent of the gross revenue produced by the wells was a helluva lot of money. Enough to keep her safe for a very long time.

But what would that mean in the end if she lost the only man she'd ever met who made her believe in love? Mary blinked and wiped her tears on her sleeve until her own face stared back at her in the mirror. The darkness in her blue eyes was nothing new, but that hatred had never been self-directed before.

The rig was almost set up. She knew now she wasn't going to reach Trey. She was on her own, and she had a very big decision to make.

Chad tossed and turned on Jasmine's plush couch, unable to get comfortable. She'd insisted on tucking sheets over the soft leather, a bottom one and another one on top along with a homey quilt his mother might have used. He'd fingered the scalloped edge and lifted an eyebrow at her. "You quilt, too?"

Her lips twitched. "No, it was my mother's." At his doubtful look she said grimly, "Strippers have mothers, too. Kinda like Texas Rangers, I imagine, unless you sprang full blown from "Lone Wolf" Gonzaullas like Athena from Zeus. Of course your head's big enough to do that."

Arrested, Chad looked up from the quilt to her face. How the hell did a Californio big city girl know about one of the most famous

Texas Rangers? Or, for that matter, did all strippers know so much about Greek mythology?

She must have read his expression because she hustled to the kitchen, as if fearful she'd revealed too much. "Sandwiches for supper?"

"You don't need to wait on me." He moved to get up but his head swam and he had to sink back.

She peeked around the corner. "Today only, full restaurant open and turn-down services at night. If you're a good guest I may even put a chocolate by your pillow." She disappeared again.

He settled back, but he still felt uncomfortable. He had to get to his rig. The bug he'd planted on Kinnard's office phone had been active long enough that he might find something revealing on it. Jasmine had told him they'd towed his rig to the Beverly Hills impound lot, this time, one and only, on the house. He also wasn't comfortable leaving the Peacemaker there, even hidden.

While he waited, he looked around her small but comfortable living room. Lone Star map reproduction, Western Remington-style statues, a book on Texas history. Either she was a big Western buff or she knew a lot more about Texas than she let on. Chad rubbed his tender head, but the worst of the aching had subsided. Not for the first time, he'd observed the duality of a personality that troubled him.

Bottom line, whether he was using the Ranger instincts honed by ten years of interviewing various law breakers, or his questionable instincts as a man, this woman did not add up. She didn't fit his preconceived notions of a stripper or anyone else.

Which left . . . what? Him confused as hell and worried about his brother. Right where he started.

Jasmine carried a tray in. It bore a steaming soup tureen, a neatly halved grilled cheese and a bag of potato chips. She set it on the coffee table in front of the couch. "We can have fresh fruit for dessert, if you like. Nowhere has better fresh fruit than California."

"Umm, yeah. Fruity out here." He took a big bite of the sandwich at her glare. "I'm just saying . . ."

"Why is it that even when you're complimentary, every other word out of your mouth sounds like an insult?" When he didn't answer, she ripped open the packet of chips. A few went flying. She bent to pick them up. He knew she intended to toss them in the trash.

On impulse, he caught her hand and brought them to his mouth. He lipped them from her hand and then licked the salt residue away. He looked at her as he did so.

Her eyes widened, going that clear green that was like sun on a prairie. The thought was so fanciful and unlike him that when she jerked away and got to her feet, fleeing to the kitchen, he let her go. That's all he needed, to wax poetic over a woman he didn't, couldn't trust.

She was Kinnard's little sex-kitten pet he put on display, and that was proof enough of her morals. He forced the delicious supper down, leaning back against the couch, listening to her banging pots and pans. Slowly the warmth and sustenance steadied him until he almost felt normal.

Hearing his Mama's chiding voice in his head, he went to the kitchen, grabbed a towel, and began to dry the skillet she'd washed and put into the dish drainer. She opened her mouth to protest, gave a little shrug, and handed him the clean spatula to dry.

And so it went for his first evening at her place. Little domestic chores, shared, as if they'd been longtime roomies. When she brought out the vacuum, he lifted the coffee table to let her vacuum beneath, then the legs of the heavy couch. Each time, she bit back a protest because she seemed to sense his need to help. He winced once as he straightened. She reached out to feel his forehead, but when he glared and straightened, her hand dropped.

He flopped back on the couch. "Thanks. I can only stand so much mothering."

"I'm not your mother, I just have a natural sympathy for pain. Sue me."

While she was busy, he'd been eyeing the legal books on her shelf. "I have a feeling you could defend a lawsuit pretty handily."

She followed his gaze. "Oh. That."

He waited.

Her voice was so soft, he had to strain to hear. "Maybe there's more to me than meets the eye. Maybe I grew up around lawyers and maybe stripping isn't my long-term career goal."

"Maybe you should quit pussyfootin' around and tell me if you're going to law school or not."

She shrugged. "Think what you like. You always do." She wheeled the vacuum back to the closet and closed the door firmly. "You need anything else? I'm going to bed. I'm tired and I have to work tonight." She didn't look at him as she spoke.

He felt her need to be alone and shared it. "I'm good. Sleep well." When she reached her door, he added in a gravelly tone, "Hey, Jasmine."

She paused with her hand on the door knob. "Yes?"

"Thanks."

She nodded and fled into her room.

For he knew that's what she was doing. Fleeing from him. And perhaps from her own feelings? Chad picked up the remote but stared unseeingly at the map on the wall. If he was smart, he'd flee, too, right back to Texas where he belonged.

But the memory of a freckle-faced kid shadowing his every step overpowered even the gut-wrenching emotions Jasmine incited in him.

As if it were yesterday, Chad could visualize Trey. "Chad, why does the sky smell so funny after it rains?" And through the progression of years, "Chad, why can't I take the truck? You never drive it." Or "Chad, I'm leaving for California for a while." And lastly, "Chad, when you paint everything in black and white, sooner or later you end up with gray. And gray's a mighty lonely color." And then he'd disappeared in a cloud of dust.

Would that be his last memory of his brother?

Tossing aside the remote, Chad picked up his cell phone and dialed the saved number for the cabbie who'd driven him earlier. He had to get his truck and check the surveillance on Kinnard's phone. Jasmine would never even know he was gone. Using the key she'd loaned him, he locked her door and went down the steps. He plopped down on the bottom step to wait, wondering if he should kill two birds with one stone and stop at the Beverly Hills station to talk to Pucker Ass. He glanced at his watch, thinking Riley had told him he was working long hours. Seven p.m. Would he still be there?

An hour later, Pucker Ass, AKA Riley O'Connor, glanced up when the Beverly Hills duty officer appeared at his desk, looking agitated. "There's a cowboy asking for you. He looks a bit green around the gills and mean enough to spit venom. Says he's helping with an investigation, and he's going at it now with Captain Barnes. He's going to get himself arrested."

"Damn the man, he's supposed to be in the hospital." Riley hurried out to the entry desk and sure enough, Foster towered over Captain Barnes, who made up for his lack of height in lofty diction and soaring intellect.

Foster stabbed a finger in the air at chest height, almost hitting the little officer in the nose. "He's my brother, and I don't give a flying f—"

Just in time to make Chad swallow the obscenity, Riley banged on the glass divider. "Foster, I'm ready to discuss the file with you. You're late."

Barnes turned on him. "You actually made an appointment with this . . . this . . ."

Chad ripped off his Stetson before he could finish and looked like he wanted to throw it against the wall. "If one more guy calls me a cowboy I'm going to rake him with my spurs just to prove him right."

Riley kept his smile pasted on. "This way, Foster." He buzzed the door open. "Sorry, Captain, but he's already aided the LA police in their part of the investigation into his brother's disappearance, and he's a former Texas Ranger with forensic training, so the chief said he could assist. He has a slight concussion but insisted on coming in today." Riley gave Chad a look.

Chad paused long enough to mutter to Barnes, "Sorry, my head aches like blue blazes, but I shouldn't have taken it out on you."

Captain Barnes relented. He nodded at Riley, though he still refused to look at Chad. "Very well. Since you went through proper channels, I presume my protestations are immaterial." He swiveled on his heel and marched out the front door.

Frozen, Chad stared after him. "That guy come from the Precambrian or the primordial soup?"

When the duty officer smirked and retook his seat, Riley hustled Chad inside the office, to the chair facing his desk. "He's got an eidetic memory and is the only one who can soothe all the rich old ladies when they come into the station. He's raised millions in funding for the department's charities."

"Perfect. Honorary title. I hope you don't let him near a gun."

"Never mind him. Just thank me for stopping him from arresting your ass." At Chad's glare, Riley sighed. "Why the hell aren't you in the hospital?"

"You think I'm going to lie flat on my back while my brother is missing and probably in extreme danger?"

"Does your Ranger captain, Sinclair I think his name is, know you're in LA going off half-cocked?"

Chad shrugged.

"Does Jasmine know you're here?"

Chad shrugged.

"You really expect me to share the entire file with you?"

This time, Chad didn't shrug. For a moment, Riley read in his eyes a fear for his brother so deep that Riley was surprised it didn't take life and grab the file. Which would be tough, since most of their investigations these days were digital. Riley wheeled his chair over. "I give up. It will take less time and resources to keep you in the loop than it would to shut you out. Not to mention the uproar if we actually took a decorated Texas Ranger into custody."

"Former Texas Ranger. Now I'm just a guy from Amarillo who can't get laid." Chad reddened, obviously regretting his frankness as Riley burst into laughter.

"You're honest, I give you that, Foster. If it makes you feel better, in that way, at least, you're just like Beverly Hills lawyers. I know more than one who can't get laid, either. Jasmine's actually pretty choosy."

Chad just whacked his hat on his thigh, which Riley recognized as the Ranger's body language when he was begging to change the subject. Riley pretended to study his computer, recalling his conversation with Sinclair about Chad. Sinclair had told him, without saying it, to do what he could to help Chad's investigation. "He won't stop unless you shoot him. And he's one of the best men in my company when it comes to tracking down missing persons. Not that I'd intrude. It's your department's call, of course, whether to involve him."

So with Jasmine's pleading, Riley had gone to the chief to ask for the unusual arrangement, but that didn't mean Riley was happy with the way Chad had barged in here, when he should be in bed. Chad stood up and wheeled his own chair around, bent his head briefly, and then fell into it. Riley bit back another caustic remark, handed Chad the hard copy of the file for docs they hadn't scanned, and opened the digital portion on his computer.

Jasmine finally tired of tossing and turning and got out of bed. She dressed for work and then slammed out, not surprised to find Chad gone. Nothing would interfere with his investigation. She was glad she'd be gone when Chad got back. Having him here was just as hard as she'd feared. She was so drawn to this man, more than any other, and if she wasn't real careful, she'd fall in love with a man who hated her.

Or at least hated what she did. It wasn't like she'd chosen to be a stripper, no one did. But if the options were that or forgoing law school, well, the choice seemed pretty straightforward. And she hadn't slept with as many men as Chad apparently assumed. No, the real way to get past his defenses, other than the obvious one, was to help him get evidence against Thomas. If Thomas Kinnard was really the mastermind behind a land fraud in the Texas Panhandle, using an entity that was, according to Chad, a dummy shell called the Del Mar Corporation, based in California and the Grand Caymans, only one man would have access to the records. Because he'd drawn them up.

If she brought Chad proof of Thomas's involvement in the Del Mar Corporation, he'd have to believe she wasn't part of the scheme. And it might be leverage to save Trey. Still thinking, Jasmine wasn't quite as luminous that night on stage.

Two hours later, Chad exited the Beverly Hills police station, more frustrated than ever. At the snail's pace of the BHPD's investigation, he'd never find Trey in time. He was usually a stickler for the legalities in a case, but he wasn't a Ranger now. He was a brother.

Chad fired up his truck after checking it for damage from being in the impound lot. But if anything, it was cleaner, which didn't surprise him anymore. Everything this city did was as picky as its residents. His nausea had faded and the residual dizziness only troubled him when he stood up too fast. Still, he sat with the giant engine idling, debating what he was about to do. Riley wouldn't like it. Hell, Sinclair wouldn't like it either, but that was too bad. He was out of options. Legal ones, anyway.

Chad's truck seemed to drive the short route all by itself. Chad circled the dark gallery twice to be sure, but he saw no light or any sign of occupation. It was past ten, so that wasn't surprising. The tiny parking lot in front was empty, and when he passed the alley and looked down it, there were no vehicles. Chad parked in the alley behind the Dumpster, eyeing the security camera trained on the back door of the gallery.

Avoiding the camera's eye, he circled the building to the window he'd noticed when he was transferring the funds for the painting. It was a heavy dual-paned window, no doubt wired to the gallery's security alarm. Taking the glass cutter he'd selected from the small case of tools he carried, he carefully cut the first pane of glass at the very edges next to the window frame. It was a big-paned window, so if he cut just right, he should barely fit inside without having to raise the window and break the security alarm contacts. With the first layer of glass cut, he put on his gloves and tapped gently, breaking the bond between the two layers. Part of the glass cracked, making it easier to remove. The second layer was thinner and cut easily. Chad propped both almost intact pieces of glass against the side of the building, tossed his case over the sill, and boosted himself through the window. He felt a few slivers of glass pierce his heavy work shirt, but then he was up and over.

Chad pulled the small flashlight from his case and appraised the room. He started at the desk, but found only bills, art receipts, meeting agendas, nothing interesting. He eyed the computer, which was off, and moved to the drawers, knowing there was no way he'd be able to break the password. He searched each drawer thoroughly, but again found nothing of interest beyond the stationery he'd seen before. In frustration, he slammed the drawer closed. It made an odd, hollow sound, not quite closing properly.

Chad knelt and looked at the drawer bottom, seeing that it didn't shut correctly because it had a panel behind it. He tapped and played with the panel and suddenly it sprang outward, leaving a deep cavity. Chad shined his light inside and saw some yellowing newspaper articles. He pulled them out carefully, stiffening at the sight of a familiar, but much younger, face.

Thomas Hopper had discovered a brand-new pool of oil called the Dorado field. Some of the largest deposits were around Amarillo, Texas. A later article hinted that exploration was in progress and the Texas Ranger land division was investigating the partnership. Chad remembered the tiny scrap he'd found in Trey's car seat. He held up the paper to the light, trying to recall the color of that scrap. They seemed to match. Then he saw, cut off but still legible, his father's name as arresting officer. Chad knew Trey must have taken these articles, which was why a scrap had been left in his seat.

Everything fell into place.

Why Kinnard had left Texas and assumed a new identity. Why he'd opened an art gallery in one of the world's richest cities. His interest in Trey had nothing to do with art and everything to do with their land. He'd wanted them out of the way so he could drill, illegally if need be, because he'd had a hard-on for the vast pool of oil under the Amarillo plains since he'd struck his first well in it over twenty years ago. He'd known Chad would come running to rescue his brother, leaving him clear to drill.

Must have been a great bonus to the bastard that they were Gerald Foster's sons. The next leap was a short one: Thomas Kinnard had to be the head of the Del Mar Corporation. If he and the California agencies could prove that, they'd have enough evidence to put the bastard away for land fraud. For good this time. And a charge of kidnapping would sweeten the sentence.

And Jasmine? What was her role? The dull headache began again at that thought, so he shoved it away instead.

Chad hesitated, badly wanting to take the articles, but instead he made a mental note of the dates, knowing he could pull them from archives, and put everything back as it was. Best if Kinnard just thought there'd been a break-in until Chad could convince Riley to get a warrant. He dumped out the desk drawers, found a bank bag holding what seemed to be petty cash, and had no choice but to take the money to perpetuate the MO of a theft.

He next circled his light over the closet. He opened it, and inside saw art supplies, brushes, paints, easels. He was about to close the door when he saw a splintered leg on one of the easels. Something jarred his memory. He turned the easel around, seeking a tag of some kind. There it was, on the back: Lubbock Art Supplies. This easel was Trey's. Using his cell phone to take a wide shot of the easel and its location in the closet, along with a close-up of the label, Chad deliberately disarranged everything to make it look like thieves had searched the closet. Chad started on the file cabinet, but he stiffened as he heard a car pulling up in the front. Lights slashed across the lobby floor at the same time, and then the sound of a smooth engine turned off. Voices, one that was Kinnard's and a second one with Hispanic overtones.

With one last scan to be sure he'd taken all his tools, Chad tossed some files on the floor, vaulted over the window feet first, his broad shoulders almost getting stuck as he dangled, his feet a foot from the ground. But he wriggled from side to side and managed to get free. Safely on the ground, he still had a dilemma to face. If he started his big engine, Kinnard would hear it for sure. If he didn't, it would be a dead giveaway that he'd been there because it was highly unlikely they wouldn't see the missing glass, look outside, and notice the truck.

Chad got in his truck and fired it up, backing up a short distance, and then, as a head poked out the broken window, Chad put the truck in gear and drove forward as if entering the alley. He parked, got out and lifted a hand. "Howdy, Mr. Kinnard."

"We're closed." Kinnard scowled at the broken glass on the ground.

"I just came by to see if you still had that painting of the pumpjack and cactus, couldn't get it out of my head, but I see you have bigger problems." Chad made his voice sympathetic. "Looks like you had a break-in. Want me to call the police?"

"No, thank you, I can handle my own security. Why'd you come by so late?"

"Can't sleep, I know you work late sometimes—" Chad broke off.

Another head poked out the window, and Chad recognized the driver of the green lowrider. They shared a look. Chad pulled his hat down low, but it was too late. Lawman and criminal had an instinctual recognition of an adversary.

Kinnard saw it, and his lip curled. "Cut the crap, Foster. You just broke into my office and when I can prove it, I'll see you in jail."

Chad debated lying, but he shrugged. "Maybe we'll be cell mates."

"Find what you're looking for?"

"Not yet. But I will."

"Little brother run away from home? Can't find him, huh? Pity."

Chad took a long stride forward before he realized he'd moved. "I know who you are and what you're doing, Mr. President of the Del Mar Corporation." Chad was tempted to mention the easel but knew Kinnard would only destroy it.

Kinnard's smile only deepened. "Ask Jasmine. I hear she's helping with the legal work. She might be able to point you in the right direction if you want to meet the president."

Chad recoiled at the implication that confirmed his fears about her, but he caught himself. He knew Kinnard was yanking his chain. His voice came, long, low, and more Texan than usual. "We exterminate vermin in Texas. No mercy. But then you know all about Texas, don't you?" Chad went to his rig. He gave both men an equal share of his rage, looking from one to the other. "Time you learned about justice, Foster style. If my brother is hurt, I'll kill you." Chad drove away.

When he got back to Jasmine's, he slipped inside and went straight to the couch, but despite the late hour, all he could do was stare up at the ceiling. He really should listen to the surveillance recordings, but he was literally sick at his stomach and his head was aching again. Tomorrow.

Besides, both of his main suspects were back in Beverly Hills, and wherever they'd taken Trey, he'd bet it was outside the city. For a moment he wondered if he should try to follow Montoya, but his truck would be a dead giveaway and he didn't have any more hundreds to bribe cabbies. Besides, if he went off half-cocked he might make a conviction even harder in this nanny state.

As tough as it was, Corey was right. He'd talk to Riley about the easel and see what he could stir up. "Patience," Chad whispered to himself. The word came a bit easier than usual . . .

But unable to sleep and unable to lie still, Chad got up and powered on Jasmine's computer. She'd told him he was welcome to it. Chad spent the rest of the night searching for Thomas Hopper, the Dorado field, and the Del Mar Corporation.

CHAPTER 12

The next day, when Jasmine arose after her late shift, it was noon. By the time she exited the shower some time later, she heard rattling in the kitchen as she dressed hurriedly in street clothes. Jeans, T-shirt, and boots seemed to be her favored attire these days. She'd given up boots long ago, BC. Before Chad.

When she went into the living room she found the tray she'd given him for a late lunch the previous day, reset for two. He'd found a box of macaroni and cheese in her pantry and added some frozen mixed veggies and a can of tuna. He topped off the meal with whole wheat garlic toast, all cooked perfectly. Not bad for an impromptu meal in a strange place. Jasmine was touched and surprised at yet another example of his domesticity and kindness.

Still, she had to make light of it or break into tears. For the first time in a long time, she didn't feel totally alone . . . "Wow, do I get a flower?"

Chad uncorked the bottle of white wine he'd pilfered from her fridge. He poured a finger into a wine glass, whirled it around, and offered it to her to smell. "Bouquet—a hint of sunflower mixed with woody pieces of oak."

Jasmine sniffed. "I'm not sure those two go together in the sommelier world."

"Lady, I'm just making this up as I go. How am I doing?" He poured his own glass.

She laughed at his honesty. "Not bad for a guy from West Texas."

"Why don't you just say it like everyone else? *Cowboy*."

Jasmine tilted her head as she studied him. "I have a feeling there's much more to you than that."

They sat down before the tray and ate. Again, the companionable way they broke bread, he sensing her need for pepper and handing it to her, she picking up his napkin when it slipped to the floor, gave her deeper food for thought. But she'd think about it later; she could never keep her head when he was so close. She debated bringing up the articles she'd found, but hated to spoil their rare amity.

When they finished, she insisted on taking the tray to the kitchen. "You cooked, so it's my turn to wash."

"That the way your Mama raised you?"

"Yes. In that way, I suspect, we had a similar upbringing."

When she came back out, Chad was standing at her bookcase holding the only picture she had of her father. She'd ripped it apart, intending to throw it away, but she couldn't bear to and taped it back together, putting it in a beat-up, rickety frame that was almost coming apart, telling herself that's all he deserved.

"I can glue this back together for you if you want."

She snatched it out of his hands and set it back in the shelf, not needing to see the tall, stern figure in judge's robes because her father was still a living memory to her.

He looked at the patrician bone structure of her face, back to the picture. "You have his chin and cheekbones. It's your father, isn't it?"

"Yes. Why do you think I left Texas?"

He nodded, apparently not surprised. "Whereabouts?"

"Houston. I ran away when I was sixteen."

"Why?"

She hesitated. Even after ten years, the tears still rose up to choke her and her voice was husky when she said, "He made me have an abortion. He wanted me to live his idea of the perfect debutante daughter, wedding one of the oil and gas heirs of Houston."

His gaze remained averted, ostensibly scanning her bookcases, but she saw his white knuckles as he gripped the edge of the shelf and knew he was acutely aware of every word.

The story tumbled out then in a way she hadn't shared before, even with Mary. "He didn't approve of my boyfriend. I know now one reason I became so wild was because he was so strict."

Chad nodded, still not looking at her. "Ponies and kids need a light touch. I had to learn that the hard way myself with Trey."

She stared at the stern figure. After the abortion, Judge Routh had lifted a hand to slap her for the spiteful things she'd said, but when she shrank away, his hand fell. As soon as he hurried out to his Mercedes and screeched away, she packed one bag, took her mother's jewelry and quilt, and ran before he ever came home. She'd already broken up with her boyfriend, and she was the perfect misfit in her elite private school, so she had no ties to keep her in Houston. It wasn't hard to figure out where to go. Her mother had been born in Huntington Beach and her stories of growing up with a surf board in the golden years of the Golden State had made Jasmine's destination the only easy choice.

California. A new life. In the land of dreamers and misfits. She'd fit right in.

"I'd always thought it would be fun to try my hand at acting, and California was as far away from Texas as I could get." She kept the remark as light as she could, but he was good at reading between the lines. To her knowledge, her father had never tried to track her down, and she had never called. Texas? It stopped being home to her with the loss of her child. Jasmine started when Chad's big hand took the picture out of her trembling fingers. Only then did Jasmine realize she'd picked up the photo again and had been stroking her father's severe face with a compulsive finger.

She tried to turn away but he was there, his broad chest and strong arms a refuge. She leaned into them, unable to help herself. The tears ran then, for the first time in many years. Tears for the girl she'd lost, the baby who never had a chance at life because of her foolishness, and the father who lost his only child to his own rigid sense of right and wrong.

"At least now I understand why you have a thing against Texas males."

Jasmine sniffed and pulled away. "Why do you have a thing against strippers?"

Chad hesitated, and then said baldly, "It's wrong to use a man's male instincts against him like a weapon and fleece him in the process."

She couldn't disagree. On the other hand—"No one forces them to come."

"Some men, that's all they have. Poor suckers."

Jasmine had to know. "Had you ever been in a strip club before you came to see me dance?"

"Nope." He flung himself back on the couch and picked up the remote. She wouldn't allow him to barricade himself behind that male avoidance, especially after he'd been so empathetic to her history.

Compelled despite the risks to all she'd struggled to become, Jasmine knelt in front of him and dared what they might be, together. She put her hands on his knees. Immediately he tensed up. Expecting it? Or longing for it? Was there a difference? They were very alike in this regard, at least, afraid of emotion. Not because they didn't care enough.

Because they cared too much . . . She tugged the remote from his hand and turned off the TV, knowing she was playing with fire but too agitated to let things lie. "Chad, I'm not what you think."

"You're exactly what I think . . . a gorgeous, sexy woman. And I guess, if I were in your shoes, I might use that, too, to get what I wanted out of life."

"No, you wouldn't. You'd go hell-bent for leather in one direction. Yours."

That impossibly strong but sensual male mouth quirked into an appreciative smile. "You are beginning to know me." When she lightly moved her fingers up his thighs, he caught her hand on its journey and brought it to his mouth, switching the torment of touch given but not fulfilled right back to her. "You want to know why men come to strip clubs? You want to know what we think, what we feel?"

Holding her eyes, he brought her fingers to his mouth and sucked them one by one.

Oh God, finally she had a measure of the torment she'd wielded so uncaringly for the last few years since she took up stripping. Was that what men felt and imagined when women gave them a lap dance? The long, moist slide of hardness into softness, warmth into a clutching hold that led to pleasures all the more enticing because they were forbidden. Since she didn't dare jerk away as she longed to, her body took the only protective measures possible; her toes curled inside her boots until they were compressed in the narrow tips and the pain snapped her back to her senses. "Stop it!" She pulled her hand from his mouth.

"You stop it." He firmly removed her other hand from his thigh and made to rise. "You started it."

She said, softly this time, "Stop it."

Under the intensity of her green eyes, he sank back to the couch. "Why?"

"Because we've played games long enough."

He barked a harsh laugh. "Games? Not hardly. I'm trying to find my brother."

"If you stopped being so judgmental, so caught in a black-and-white world—" She wondered at the way his long, dark lashes went down like lights-out. "I know you'd see I'm trying to help, not stop, your investigation."

When he rigidly looked over her shoulder, evading both her and his own feelings, she scooted up on her knees, pushed his legs apart, and scooted between them. She didn't care about the hard lump in his pants, she didn't care about the moistness creeping out from the secret places she seldom heeded, no matter how she used them to pay her bills. In a very strange way she neither understood nor questioned, she only cared about truth. Without that, they had no future and all that had gone between them was a botched symphony: a prelude with no crescendo.

The words came of their own accord. "Stop pretending you hate me, stop pretending I don't affect you, and I'll stop pretending I'm not attracted to you. I'll admit that if not for too many bad relationships, I'd have you pinned to my bed while I tried every weird position I've ever heard of in the *Kama Sutra*. How's that for honesty?"

His gray eyes darkened as they latched on to her passionate face with an intensity she could literally feel. "Stop. Don't take this any further unless you want to go where it leads."

She was so tempted to test him further, but she felt the tremor in his strong thighs, took the prudent if cowardly path, and leaned back on her heels, outside the vee of his legs.

He swung his legs to the side and stood to put distance between them. Staring at her father's picture on the shelf, he said, his tone going that gravelly texture that betrayed his own stifled emotions, "How did you end up stripping?"

"I couldn't make my bills and when I met Thomas, he suggested it."

"Of course he did."

"He's the only reason I've been able to afford law school. I owe a lot to Thomas."

"And if he's behind Trey's disappearance?"

"Then I'll do all I can to help you bring him to justice."

He nodded, but she could see he still doubted her. For a minute, she contemplated giving him that matched set of knots on his head that she'd threatened in the hospital. He was under her roof, she'd fed him, doctored him, and gone on a police ride to help him, even committing a possible felony by searching her boss's private office and computer. And still he distrusted her? She debated telling him about the articles but before she could he shut her out. Chad picked up a book to scan it. "I know you have to go to work today, so we'll talk more later."

He was dismissing her? In her own place? She tried one last time, the knowledge driving her that until he saw her as she really was, a woman on the verge of loving him, doing all she could to help him find his brother, they'd never bridge the gap of distrust between them. "Trey was never my boyfriend! He was only here once. He never left the living room."

He just looked at her. "How many redheads are there in this town with butterfly tattoos? Who just happen to be strippers? I saw your card at my house, in Trey's car. Trey even told me he loves your scent, the scent of Jasmine—"

"My tattoo is temporary, you know. Thomas suggested it."

"I bet he did, but that doesn't change the facts. The tattoo implies you're working with him. How much money have you really earned through him?"

With an *ooh!* of frustration, Jasmine hurried into her room and slammed the door to finish getting ready. Or at least that was what she was supposed to be doing. Every nerve in her body felt on fire and she knew she wouldn't be able to lose herself in the dance. Almost without her volition, she saw her hand reach out for her cell phone. After she got a coworker to cover her late shift, she shut off her phone and began to remove her clothes. She debated telling Chad about the newspaper remnants she'd found in Kinnard's hidden drawer, but Riley was on the case now and Chad would just break in to look at them himself, possibly getting into more trouble. Besides, they had more volatile unfinished business first. They'd work together much more effectively once he admitted how much he wanted her. For now, the physical would have to do.

Smiling grimly, she pulled on her favorite bustier and fishnet stockings. She owed him a lap dance, and he owed her the raw honesty of sexual attraction. Men bonded to women through sex. There was no bolder truth they could share as a basis for a real relationship. And she needed it, too. With this step she was banishing her own demons and taking a first step toward going home . . . And somehow, she knew Trey would approve.

When she came back out of her room, she was calm. Contained. He couldn't see what she was wearing beneath the coat, but she had on fishnet stockings. For her act, no doubt. For an instant he felt an urge to cover her in the quilt and lock her in her room. Other men had no right to see her so scantily attired . . . He squelched the primitive male instinct, and told himself she only had him so fired up because of her talk of the *Kama Sutra* and such.

She stopped directly in front of him. "I got someone to cover my shift. I think you shouldn't be left alone. You're kinda in a tizzy, aren't you?"

He waved a hand. "I'm fine. Better by the minute." To prove it he stood up quickly from where he sat and smiled. "Not dizzy anymore."

"That's good. Because you owe me."

Chad was confused. She wanted him to pay her rent? He sat back down, getting a feeling he'd need the support for whatever was brewing between them. Whatever it was, he didn't recognize the taste but he knew it was going to be volatile.

"You never let me finish that lap dance."

His breath caught as her gaze raked him from his toes to the top of his head. His voice was husky. "I don't have much cash on me."

"I don't want your money."

"What do you want?"

"Not much. A comeuppance first. Then an apology. And finally, honest emotions. No more games."

The coat dropped to the floor. Beneath it she wore a lacy corset that barely reached her waist, panties topped with a garter belt, and black fishnet stockings. "We'll never see eye to eye on anything, even finding Trey, until we settle this between us. You despise me, right? You hate strippers because we use our looks to manipulate men."

His hands curled into fists. He stuffed them beneath his thighs on the couch to stop the instinct to grab her. He compulsively eyed her breasts, straining against their black lace confinement. Since he was sitting and she stood over him, they were so conveniently near his mouth. He licked his lips.

All thoughts went out of his head. Even Trey . . .

She leaned down to whisper in his ear, her minty breath setting fire to his lobe. "Prove it. Sit still without touching me for one entire dance and I'll believe you find me distasteful. I'll tell you anything you want to know about Kinnard. And I won't ever bother you again.

"Time to go the full eight seconds, cowboy, or quit the rodeo." Jasmine went to her stereo and turned on a soulful blues song by Nina Simone.

Chad wanted to get up and flee. He had to listen to the phone tap, he had to follow up on all his leads, he had to . . .

When she lifted her arms above her head and began to sway, his list of to-dos became a list of why-nots.

Why not let her dance for him? Why not see where it led? Why not end this burning ache in his gut and lower? Maybe if he fucked her he'd finally have a clear head and clean conscience to use her as ruthlessly as she'd used Trey.

And then even those hard thoughts melted away under the warming grace of a woman. Chad's reaction was immediate and physical, totally beyond his control.

Jasmine swayed in front of him, almost, but not quite, within reach, her hips moving slightly from side to side. She tilted her head, her eyes closed, as if listening to some inner instinct that guided the rhythm of her dance moves. As the music's rhythm quickened, so did her pace. Now her feet began to slide on the thick rug as her impossibly long legs, sheathed in the teasing fishnet, sinuously flexed with her flutter steps. While her lower body gyrated, her torso moved, too, but in the opposite direction, arms arching above her head until her body made an S shape so supple he had to touch her to believe. And the fulcrum holding the shape together was covered in a scrap of black lace, the lower part of a woman's body but the apex of a man's desire and aspirations.

He saw long arms reaching for her and looked at them dumbly as he realized they were attached to his own bewitched body. Luckily her eyes were closed again so she didn't see him haul them back to his sides. They felt disassociated, as if they didn't belong there any more than he did. He couldn't tuck his betraying hands into his pockets because the fabric across his crotch was stretched to the limit.

He tried sitting on his hands, but that posture only made his hips thrust forward, right where they wanted to be. Now she was cupping her breasts, hips still moving in the dance, her half-closed eyes appraising him as she seemed to offer them not just to him, but for her own pleasure as well. Her palms kneaded exactly where he wanted to touch. Her cleavage deepened above the corset until she was in danger of spilling out.

When the song crescendoed, she gave a husky laugh and spun on one heel only to end up facing him, arms flung out to the sides, legs firmly planted, head tilted back, long fiery hair brushing the upper part of her spine as she formed a bow about to fly free. The next song began even more softly, giving her an excuse to match it with subtle moves. Her arms reached toward him and undulated, mirroring the slow shifting of her hips from side to side. She seemed to have no bones, no banal earthly limits such as gravity, time, or space. She just was, as elemental as earth, wind, or fire. And he was swept away on every level.

Each nerve in his body was on fire as again he was reaching out to touch her before he caught himself and jerked away. Chad's erection had long since reached its full limit until it grew painful, thrusting imperatively against the confinement of his worn jeans. He was caught in that most atavistic of battles: fight or flight. Get the hell out of here before he was even more humiliated, or accept the living, breathing temptation she offered in a primal battle that was both aggression and surrender.

Which did she want, really? Surely no woman who looked at him like that, eyes at half-mast, licking her lips, body a living, breathing flame topped by fiery auburn hair, could portray such desire if, somewhere, she didn't feel it. As if to prove it, she wriggled between his slack knees, forcing them farther apart, and turned around to brush her supple buttocks, barely covered by a scrap of lace, over his erection.

It was his turn to arch against the couch with the torment, but some stubborn remnant made him draw back the hands that would have reached to her waist to force her curves down harder where he needed contact most. He stuffed his traitorous hands against the couch again, but she saw his torture, and, damn her, she laughed, tilting her head back to brush her long, clean-scented hair against his face and neck. He couldn't help it; a groan escaped his clenched lips. His hands came up of their own accord and reached around her for her breasts.

A husky, triumphant feminine laugh erupted and she danced away. She swayed, her hands gently gliding down all the curves and valleys he longed to explore, staying just out of reach of his long arms.

When she fisted a lock of that hair, so symbolic of the living flame of female passion, and used it to brush her own cleavage, he couldn't stand any more. Leaping to his feet with a growl, he hauled her into his arms. Her laugh of victory was crushed beneath his lips. He buried his hands in her hair and tugged to hold her immobile before the firestorm she'd aroused, her back arched as he forced her lower body into his erection, thrusting into her so she'd feel what she'd done to him.

But she didn't struggle. Instead she kissed him back, her mouth open and inviting. He accepted, his tongue taking her cue and dancing with hers, thrust, retreat, then plea, softly, gently, and finally penitence for his roughness, barely stroking. But her own hands raked through his thick hair, tugging hard, and he realized she didn't want gentleness.

She wanted him. Desperately. Primitively. Almost as badly as he wanted her.

Chad Foster had never been ruled by his baser urges, but for once something was stronger than moral fiber or even the continued nagging fear for his brother: sheer lust. And he couldn't control it, any more than he could control the woman who incited it.

He bent and trailed kisses down the side of her neck to the vee between her breasts, where the wiry corset impeded progress. Breathing as if he'd run a three-minute mile, he straightened to reach behind her back and unlace the corset. While he labored over her feminine fripperies, her task was much easier.

Untuck and unbutton his shirt. Slip it off his shoulders. Nuzzle into his center thatch of dark chest hair. Meanwhile her fingers adjusted his belt buckle.

While she worked, he tweaked and tugged, but seemed to only make the laces tighten. Finally the arousing sound of his own zipper undoing under her deft hands made his next move totally acceptable.

Gripping both sides of the lacing, he gave a violent tug. It ripped, eyeholes popping off. With a garbled "sorry," barely recognizable because he was breathing so heavily, he pulled again and finally the corset parted and dropped to the ground, freeing her to his eyes and hands. He groaned, filling himself, hands, eyes, body, and though he wouldn't admit it, soul, with the scent and taste of Jasmine.

"I'll always love the scent of Jasmine," Trey's voice whispered, but Chad quelled it violently. They'd been building to this moment for weeks, and an hour of reprieve wouldn't much affect his search for Trey.

Or so he told himself.

She stood before him in a scrap of lace across her hips, a garter belt, and fishnet stockings. He'd seen her breasts before, that time at the club, but surrounded by aroused men, he'd felt like a pervert. Now, with the warmth of her supple globes in his hands, in the dim lighting and comfortable privacy of her living room, this intimacy felt not only natural, but inevitable.

He leaned back to see what he touched, running a gentle fingertip around the flushed, aroused nipple. Her aureoles were small and pink, topped by a budding rose contracting as he watched, as if shy at the warmth of his hungry stare. As he watched, her nipple contracted further, pebbling her aureole with goose bumps. She inhaled sharply, going limp in his arms, bowed backward, her face soft and sensual as she tilted her torso up, wordlessly begging him.

Like a woman. Not a stripper.

She wasn't teasing. She was offering the most sublime surrender a woman could give a man, her weight totally supported by his embrace.

He knew what she wanted, and he wanted it, too. He bent his head and fit his mouth over her offering. He didn't suckle; he didn't even kiss. He closed his mouth over the little nubbin, feeling her heavy heartbeat through the contact. He held her nipple there like the precious thing it was to him, and brushed it very gently with his tongue, absorbing her more than caressing. As if in this simple exchange of male-female, the yin and the yang he'd sensed in their kiss at the hospital, they were two partial people binding as one. Never again would one be complete without the other. And he knew in that moment that this was the feeling he'd been missing with his other two girlfriends, a depth and intimacy he'd observed many times between his mother and father.

When she gasped, squirming under his hungry mouth, trying to reach into his underwear, he realized his pants had fallen about his ankles. He propped her up long enough to kick off his pants. She swayed as he switched hands on her shoulders so he could shrug out of his shirt, one arm at a time. Then he lifted her in his arms to take her to the bedroom, but she struggled so violently he almost dropped her. He stopped and set her down. His heart skipping a beat, he wondered if she'd changed her mind, but she only kicked off her high heels.

Then she took his hand. Again he moved toward the bedroom. But she drew him toward her wide leather easy chair instead. He hesitated, feeling awkward. "Here?"

"Here. Now." She shoved him into the chair.

CHAPTER 13

Jasmine's dance had aroused her, too. Never had she felt more free, more right about what she was doing. In the privacy of her home, there were no floodlights, no strangers jacking off beneath tablecloths. She danced instinctively for the man she'd selected, not to fulfill her role as headliner.

She danced to please him.

And oh, she'd succeeded, because he pleased her, too. She knelt with her knees on each side of his thighs, wearing only her stockings and underwear. He caught a full breast as she leaned close, and circled his tongue around the aureole without quite kissing, tempting the rascally little nubbin to a full salute. Her heart was pounding so hard she couldn't hear the soft music anymore. When Jasmine bent and kissed his own little nubbin of a nipple, he gave a soft curse and arched his back into her.

She ran her hands over his chest, leaning back to enjoy the view. He was perfectly muscled, not massive but lithe, a rancher's body built by sweat and toil, not in a gym. A sprinkling of hair coated his perfect pecs, gleaming a bit in the lamplight to match his thick, mussed dark hair. She sank against him, rubbing her breasts from side to side to feel the intoxicating touch of skin to skin.

She felt his hands at the elastic of her panties. It took the last of her resistance to scoot back to the floor and flee to her room for a box, which she brought back with her to the chair. Chad looked at the large box of condoms, then back at her. Something flashed in his eyes she didn't like, but he only took one from the box and tore it open with his teeth.

He reached for his underwear but she put her hands over his to stop him. Kneeling between his spread legs, she slowly, gently, pulled the cotton briefs down his lean hips. Inch by inch, she revealed the essence of his maleness, the masculinity that both started wars and guarded families. When it sprang free, he went to put on the condom, but again she stopped him. She cradled the heavy head in her palms, holding him gently, with a reverence that could not be faked.

He was, quite simply, beautiful. Not abnormally large, but circumcised and perfectly formed. The head was so erect, springing up from the dark nest of his scrotum, that when she ran a gentle fingertip over him she could barely bend the eager flesh. He leaped back into her touch, as if there, he belonged.

In a strangled tone, he teased, "Here, you do it. Mold it, sculpt it, you created it." He caught her hand and brought it around the head of his erect penis.

She sensed he was making light because he was as overwhelmed by the moment as she was, so she responded in kind, happy to let him take the reins for now.

"So I can preserve it for posterity?"

He caught her about the waist and pulled her upward until her soft stomach pressed against him. He rubbed his loins up and down, enticing them both with the connection that would soon be much deeper. "Yes, but erected just for you."

She did what her instincts bade her to do: she kissed him. Running her tongue about the tip, tasting the salty readiness. He bit off a curse and arched his hips upward. She kissed him more deeply and this time when he reached for her panties he would not be denied. He grabbed a hunk of hair to pull her insistent lips away. He ripped her panties down and off, pulled the condom on and lifted her onto his lap.

He paused, trembling with eagerness, but even then he had a care for her feelings. He tested her readiness with a gentle fingertip. She tightened around that shallow touch, pulling him in, and she was almost embarrassed, she was so moist. Lifting her easily with the strength of his arms, he inserted the head and gently began pulling her elastic flesh over his.

She didn't know why, but she didn't want gentle. She wanted raw, unadulterated passion. Some might call it lust, but she didn't care. Instinct ruled her now. She arched her hips down over him, hard, and her hungry femininity took him tip to testicles. The unadulterated sensation was so raw, so intimate, that both of them froze in the act. Their startled eyes met, his gray eyes smoldering, hers so dilated that her pale green irises looked more forest than dappled sunshine.

They sat that way for several seconds, in the most intimate position a woman can know with a man, his erect flesh pulsing with the vibrancy of his male power, deep inside her womb. Somehow, with that simple exchange of glances, as she'd instinctively realized, they hurdled over the impediments of pain and distrust. No matter what came, they would always have this gloriously intimate moment. Then he flexed up inside her as if he couldn't stop himself, and she flexed back with a tiny upward move of her pelvis, pulling him deeper.

The crescendo was inevitable then, their rhythm rocking the chair against the wood floor—and rocking the certainties of their world. He moved up, thrusting deeply, and she moved down on the down stroke. He was as deep inside her as she'd ever felt, but it somehow wasn't enough. She wanted to own him, to brand him, to imprint her being onto his so he'd never forget her.

When his breathing harshened to pants, she knew he was close. She felt him swelling inside her, and she was ready, too, but she had to lift free to complete them the way she wanted to. When she took her soft warmth away, he gave an instinctive, desperate, "No!" but when she pulled his hips forward so she could straddle him with her feet on the floor, he understood and gladly let her adjust him.

In one stroke, she took him in again, the movement now harder because she had leverage. Up, down, again, again, her "Oh god oh god oh god," a rhythmic accompaniment to each downward thrust met by his hips arching upward. She ground her aching flesh against his shaft with each stroke, and the pulsing built to a fusillade of horns, cymbals, and strings, an orchestra of male and female, music only they could hear. With one last clenching of her femininity upon him, she went down as he flew up, her flesh suckling hungrily at his warmth. He gave it and cried out. She felt his pulsing inside her, wishing for a moment that she could feel the splashing sperm, but then the crescendo swept her away, too.

The room swam around her, and sparks danced behind her closed lids. For ten long seconds, she was weightless, her body a bow flying free under the hands that held her at the waist, locking her loins onto his. When the spasms finally abated, she opened lazy eyes and surprised a look in his that would imprint her as indelibly as his penis had. Possession, ownership, destiny, as if he'd known this would happen at her instigation, not his, and most powerfully of all, as if he welcomed it. Incredibly, she felt her cheeks warm, more embarrassed now than when she'd taken him inside.

He gave a soft laugh as she buried her face against the hair on his chest, still sitting on him. "I thought you didn't have sex with men in your place?"

She pulled lightly at his chest hair, not hard enough to hurt but enough to retaliate. "You made me lose my head. But I had to be gentle as you were weak, and all, from the concussion."

He laughed, covering her hand with his. "You're better than bed rest any day." They stayed still a moment longer, but the glow soon faded. He gently moved her aside. The moist slide of him leaving her felt like desolation, but she banned the feeling with a sleepy smile, unwilling to spoil the blissful aftermath.

He went to the bathroom and returned with a towel. He pushed her back in the chair on top of the towel and used a hand towel dipped in warm water to clean her genitals. Gentle strokes. He'd flushed the condom and knelt before her naked. She suddenly felt awkward, wearing only her thigh-high stockings and garter belt, which framed her in a view he obviously enjoyed.

She could only stem the red tide of her blush by teasing him. "So how long has it been, cowboy, since you rode the range?"

His cheeks went a dull red, but he admitted, "Over a year."

She liked him all the better for it.

But when he said, "And you?" she couldn't lie to him.

"A few months. My last boyfriend was an engineer. We were not . . . compatible."

Awkwardness grew between them as he finished his ministrations. Feeling her blush spread, Jasmine stood and hurried into her room for a dressing gown. She took off the stockings and garter belt, hesitating. She wanted, almost as much as she'd wanted sex, to bring him into her bed and snuggle into his arms. She'd violated her one inviolate rule with him, so truly sleeping with him now seemed a minor infraction.

Her skin feeling unbearably sensitive against the brush of silk, she walked back into the living room. He'd put on his underwear and jeans and was shrugging into his shirt. He gave her an uncertain smile. Was he shy?

She said almost inaudibly, "It's silly for you to sleep on the couch now. Would you like to sleep with me? I didn't sleep well earlier so I'm going to lie down."

He considered the offer. Finally he nodded, but when she turned toward her bedroom, added, "But I can't. Not right now. I have to follow up on a lead." He pulled on his boots, adding at the look on her face, "A rain check?"

She nodded. She faked a yawn. "See you later then."

"Later." He walked to the door, but from there he could see inside her room. At that safe distance he added, "Jasmine, you are the most beautiful woman I've ever been with." He exited hastily, locking the door behind him.

Her laugh had a bitter edge. How many was that? She had a feeling the competition wasn't very steep. She climbed into her cold bed, and when she finally dropped off to sleep, her dreams were restless. A ranch house stark against a red Texas sunset, pumpjacks run amok, splashing the pristine land with pollution. And she stood there, knee-deep in grime, but when she tried to wipe the oil away, her hands dripped with blood.

The minute he reached his truck, Chad pulled his duffel bag from behind the seat. As he stared down at his Peacemaker and the recorder synced to the wireless transmitter he'd attached to Kinnard's phone, Chad forced himself to concentrate on the task at hand. He still had Jasmine's scent on his skin, even his hands, but he couldn't think about her now. She was already distraction enough. The ardor she'd given him, pinning him to her chair like a wild filly in heat, was both a blessing and a question.

No doubt she wanted him almost as badly as he wanted her, but it was obvious he was only the latest in a long string of conquests. How easily she'd produced the big box of condoms. He forced the memory away, taking several deep breaths to banish the last warmth of their embrace and bear down on the only evidence he hadn't torn apart six ways from Sunday.

He moved the tiny digital recorder to the middle panel of the seat, where a padded lid covered the deep recess. But before he hit Play, he recapped in his mind what Riley had told him. The evidence Riley had shared with him was flimsy at best. Even using their highly sophisticated databases, they'd found little on Kinnard, either, which in itself was a red flag. Anyone his age who had no digital footprint until ten years ago, when he suddenly appeared with money in California, had gone to a great deal of trouble to erase an earlier identity.

As for the Latino car ring, the one informant the LA gang investigation division had secreted into a gang known to be highly mobile but working in Beverly Hills, had mysteriously disappeared before he could give them solid evidence. Chad recalled the big rigs that had exited the warehouse parking lot shortly before he'd been clonked. He suspected he knew why the gang was mobile, even though when they ran the plates, the construction LLC that owned the trucks seemed innocuous enough.

Though he couldn't prove diddly, the thought tormented him that Trey could have been in one of those trucks while big brother came to the rescue by lying unconscious on the pavement. If Kinnard owned those trucks, he was a master at covering his tracks.

Chad hit Play on the digital recorder and listened. He had several days' worth of recording and thought about fast-forwarding through some of it, but he clamped down on his impatience and listened. He kept a pen poised to record time and date stamps of any interesting clues, but his hand grew tired of holding the pen as the hours passed.

Nothing. Boring meetings about art and artists, office matters, one phone call from the attorney's office to confirm a meeting with Larsen, social gatherings, blah blah blah. Chad was about to switch off the recorder and finish the rest tomorrow when an angry feminine voice left a message. "All right, Thomas, I know you're deliberately not returning my calls and I'm sure you also know there's no answer on that new number you gave me for Trey. If you want me to do your dirty work, quite literally, contact Trey and have him call my new cell phone. No later than tomorrow or I may just decide the money isn't worth it." *Click.* A very definite, angry click.

Chad listed the time and date on his empty pad—yesterday at ten a.m.—switched off the recorder, and leaned back. Who the hell was that? Whoever it was knew Trey and seemed concerned about him. But it wasn't Jasmine . . .

Before he could pinpoint the source of the knot in his gut, his cell phone rang. He answered. "Chad Foster."

"You're . . . Chad Foster?" The voice sounded like that of a young male teen, half scared out of his wits.

"Yes. Who is this?"

"Doesn't matter. Do you know someone who wears a gold nugget necklace engraved with 'Family is all that lasts. Love, Mama'?"

The knot in Chad's stomach became a knife. "Yes . . . where did you find it?"

"On the I-10 toward Riverside. It had a note with it listing this number and a reward of two thousand dollars if you retrieved it. You got the money?"

"I'll get it and meet you in an hour. Where are you?"

"I'm in Riverside. There's a coffee shop right off the east I-10 at exit 445. I'll meet you there tomorrow morning, six a.m." The kid hung up.

The tiredness that had made Chad yawn was gone. He sat straight against the truck seat, looking outside at the darkness. He'd been sitting here for hours listening and now it was late. How the hell was he to raise 2k that quickly? No way to get the funds that fast this time of day, from his retirement fund. He fingered the Peacemaker. If he could find a pawn shop open at—he looked at his watch—ten, he should get at least that for the very valuable, old but pristine gun. But then he'd have no weapon.

Chad sighed heavily, pulled out his cell phone and pressed the button for one of three people in the world he kept on speed dial. He'd be pissed to be bothered at midnight Texas time, but if ever there was an emergency, this was it. Chad hated to ask for help from anyone, especially the man he respected most, but he had no choice. He needed a cooperative witness and would not get it without the money.

Sinclair's voice came on after five rings, rough with sleep. "What is it?"

"Captain, I'm sorry to bother you so late, but I'm in a jam. I have a solid lead that Trey's still alive. I think."

Sinclair's voice became lucid immediately. "What can I do to help?"

Chad explained the situation.

"What zip code you at?"

Chad gave Sinclair the zip.

"OK, I'm going to wire you the money. When I know which outlet, I'll text you the business address and tracking number for the funds. Where are you, anyway?"

Chad hesitated, but he owed his boss, for he still considered him as such, the truth. "Beverly Hills area. Staying for now with the redhead Trey dated for a while. She even came out to Amarillo while I was on assignment, but I don't think any of y'all met her."

"She's helping you look for him?"

"Sorta."

"Isn't she a stripper? I remember Trey talking about her."

"Yes."

Squirming in his seat at the dead silence, Chad was relieved when Sinclair evenly changed the subject.

"Just one more question, Foster: You let the Beverly Hills Police Department know about this reward and where you're going?"

Chad was silent, which was as close as he could come to the truth.

"Dammit, Foster, this could be dangerous, not just for you but for Trey. How do you know it's not a trap? Don't make me call this Riley O'Connor character. It's best if you do it."

Scowling, Chad said, "Okay." He bit back a *How the hell do you know they're involved?* but Sinclair must have heard it in his voice.

"Riley's called me from time to time to give me an update. You might have quit, but even a former Ranger is still representing this department in spirit if not in name. I'll get you the money. At least return the courtesy by obeying the most important police rule."

"Okay! I'll call them for backup, but they're by-the-book lead asses, and odds are they won't even make it in time."

"You have a piece?"

"Granddaddy's Peacemaker." The gun was so old it had never been registered, passing as it did from father to son, but Chad kept it clean and oiled and had fired it occasionally.

Sinclair's tone got rough again, because he knew how Chad treasured the weapon. "Try not to use it, okay? I don't need to remind you how sensitive California law enforcement is to unregistered out-of-state weapons, no matter how old they are."

"Yes, sir." Chad cleared his throat, wondering how to really thank this former boss who still stood behind him despite his reckless departure.

Sinclair seemed to hear Chad's dilemma even across the miles. In his usual fashion, he knew how to diplomatically defuse the situation. "Okay then, well, good luck and keep me posted. And, Foster . . ."

"Yes, sir?" Chad heard the lilt of laughter and braced himself for a barb.

"Be good, and if you can't be good, be careful. If you can't be careful, name it after me." Laughing, he hung up.

Smiling wryly at the witticism he'd heard most of his life, Chad also hung up. But the tease was pointed enough that Chad wondered what Riley had told Sinclair about Jasmine . . . If he only knew how closely he'd called the situation.

While he waited for the text, Chad went back into her apartment and scribbled a message for Jasmine, not wanting to wake her. Or so he told himself. SOMEONE FOUND TREY'S NUGGET NECKLACE WITH A MESSAGE TO CONTACT ME FOR A REWARD. I'M MEETING HIM AT 6 A.M. ON THE EAST I-10 TOWARD RIVERSIDE. MAY NOT GET LOOSE UNTIL THE MORNING. I'LL CALL YOU. He hesitated, then added in bold block letters, AND BE CAREFUL. KEEP YOUR DOORS LOCKED EVEN WHEN YOU'RE DRIVING, BECAUSE YOU'RE BEING FOLLOWED.

When he was done with that, he looked down at his contact list, sighed, and thumbed through to Riley O'Connor's name. He left a detailed message on the cell phone line Riley had given him, and then he locked the door, trying it to be sure it was secure. He went down the street to his truck. He didn't know what he'd find in Riverside, but he had one partner in California he'd trusted with his life before, so he'd best get started now.

He had to wait at the drug store for the clerk to come yawning to the desk, and by the time he had the money, two hours had passed and he still had one more critical errand to run. At this rate he'd barely make it to Riverside in time.

The equestrian center was on the way. The horse trailer might slow him down a bit, but if Trey was really on the outskirts of Riverside, he was being led far away from the big city, where Chester's skill set might come in much more handy than a truck. Chad fired up his engine and turned toward Burbank, yawning. It was almost dawn, and he hadn't slept a wink. His vision was a bit blurry, but all he needed was a huge cup of joe.

Light took over from the darkness, glimmering through the cracks in the truck, awakening Trey from a restless doze. He was so parched, his heart was pounding hard enough to choke him. They'd only given him one bottle of water, which he'd slurped down as they held it to his lips. Trey looked toward the small hole he'd gouged in the rubberized seal around the cab's sleeping area which had a rear access. The seal was meant as insulation and a pad to protect the compartment from weather and noise, but it had grown brittle with age and that flaw might be his salvation.

He'd spent most of the dark hours prowling the trailer. About five hours earlier, his bumbling about the cargo bed had finally yielded what felt like a flashlight. When he turned it on, it was dim, but provided enough light to make out racks and boxes. It didn't take long to find what he needed.

Trey had wadded up the nugget necklace in the blue disposable shop towel he'd found and written on as best he could, using oil and a screw, and carefully fitted another towel over it exactly so the writing wouldn't smear. He wadded up a last towel around the note and necklace, and used a piece of duct tape to protect it, leaving a couple inches of the chain outside the tidy packet in hopes the shiny gold would attract attention. Then he waited, listening to the rhythm of the wheels on the pavement. He'd felt the big vehicle downshift and held his breath. Sure enough, they were slowing.

He'd lost his balance and had to grab the rack as the truck sidled up a ramp, pulled in somewhere, and then stopped. Trey tensed, hoping they didn't check on their unwilling passenger, and breathed a sigh of relief as he heard the gas cap being unscrewed. They'd stopped for gas. There wouldn't be a better time.

Trey had forced the little packet into the tiny opening he'd made, but when he heard voices, he hesitated. He didn't know where the tank was or which side of the truck they were on. If they saw him do this, he was toast. So he waited what seemed like forever, but finally the truck rocked slightly as both the driver and the man on the other side got back into the cab. As the truck began to move out of the lot, Trey pushed his desperate message farther into the hole he'd made. It stuck as the truck gained momentum and he almost panicked, but when he pushed it with the screwdriver he'd found it plopped free. He'd visualized it falling to the side of the highway and prayed whoever found it would want the reward promised more than the nugget.

The necklace was the only identifying item he had left; they'd taken all his ID and his phone. The half-ounce nugget wasn't worth 2k, which was how he'd arrived at the amount for the reward. He only hoped Chad had that much left, assuming he was in LA, as Trey suspected. For sure if they called Chad's cell number, which he'd inked in oil, Chad would instantly recognize the inscription and know he'd left it.

Now, hours later, with no way of knowing if Chad had received his message, Trey sank against the side of the truck, trying to sleep again as the truck rocked on. His eyes were gritty and his throat beyond parched, but he was still too scared to rest. He'd wrapped duct tape around his wrists again as best he could, but it was tough with his hands behind his back. Still, the blood should convince them he'd just loosened the binding. If they caught his ruse this time, it would be his last. Kinnard might not have the balls to kill him, but Montoya seemed to enjoy hurting people and the minute the heat was off, Trey had a feeling he'd be a tumble of bones in a desert grave.

He prayed Chad got his message, because if this didn't work, he was fresh out of inspiration. And while he'd gained a reprieve, he knew eventually Kinnard would have to kill him simply because Trey knew too much about the sorry reputation Kinnard had gone to so much trouble to hide. Not to mention his involvement in stealing cars from his own patrons and swindling farmers and ranchers out of their land . . .

Finally the big rig jerked to a halt over a rough surface. Sitting up, Trey smiled grimly. He must have more of the Foster grit in him than he'd suspected, because he almost looked forward to his next meeting with the son of a bitch. As the cargo door began to roll up, Trey said a quick prayer, using words he'd also never suspected he'd say.

"Keep on a-comin', Chad. Keep on a-comin'."

CHAPTER 14

Fifty miles away from Trey, Chad had parked his dually outside the coffee shop at exit 445, stuck the Peacemaker in his waistband underneath his jacket, and got out. Dawn glimmered in the sky. He checked on Chester, but the stallion was an old hand at riding in trailers and looked almost bored. Chad had his hand on the diner's doorknob when a loud, "Foster, wait!" made him turn.

To his surprise, Riley O'Connor exited an unmarked car with two other uniformed cops. In the sunshine coming up over the buildings, Chad saw one wore a Riverside CA insignia, the other Beverly Hills.

"So you got my message in time." Chad struggled to keep the surprise out of his voice but obviously didn't quite succeed.

The other two cops glared, but apparently Riley was growing accustomed to Chad's behavior. He deadpanned back, "We used our connections to turn all the lights green on the way here. We can do that, you know, seeing we own ten million or so people."

"Yeah, I keep forgetting you guys own Los Angeles, too. Lead on." Chad opened the door with a flourish for the other three to enter the quiet little coffee shop, and followed on their heels. He spotted a nervous kid right away, who kept looking toward the door. He had tattoos on both skinny arms and a pierced nose and eyebrow. Great, the upstanding citizen type, or so Chad's gut reaction butted in. Still, for Trey's sake, he tried to keep an open mind as he walked up to the kid and offered his hand. "Chad Foster."

The kid shrank away. "You didn't say anything about cops."

Chad's hand dropped. "You have the nugget?" He pulled out his wallet and fanned it open, showing all the hundreds he'd picked up before leaving the Western Union outlet Sinclair had given him.

Riley jerked his head at the cops and they sauntered to the counter to order coffee. Riley and Chad sat down in the booth across from the nervous kid. He relaxed a bit, reached into his grungy coat and pulled out a greasy disposable blue shop towel.

Using a napkin from the dispenser on the table, Chad gently worked free the duct tape, which was loose anyway. Sure enough, Trey's gold necklace shone up at him. Chad would have recognized it anywhere. Their mother had given them each one shortly before she died, trying even with her last breath to make peace between the siblings. Chad kept his in the safe at home as he disliked jewelry of any sort; Trey's never left his neck, even in the shower.

"Where did you find this?" Chad asked. He had to clear his throat and try again.

The kid held out a grimy hand. "The money, man."

"I will, I will, but I need as much information as possible to try to track down my brother. He left this necklace, his most prized possession, as a message for me. A plea for help, really. His life is in danger and if I'm to find him I need details. Where exactly did you find this?"

The kid sank back sullenly. "I-10 near the 60 interchange."

"Do you recall the exit number?"

The kid's eyes squinted as if the light hurt them. "No, but it was near an Exxon station because that's where I'd stopped for gas. When I was leaving I saw a piece of the chain shining in my lights on the side of the road. That's all I know." He held out his hand with a pleading look.

Riley had pulled out his phone and was texting notes. In a kind manner, so as not to spook the kid, he got the boy's name, address, and phone number. Chad gave him the money and the kid bolted, almost running out the door.

Riley stared after him. "Going straight to score, I imagine."

"Probably." Chad carefully spread out the napkin, hoping for clues. Along with the grease, there were also bits of grime and in the corner . . . Chad inhaled sharply. "Blood."

Riley bent over the napkin, moving it from side to side with a fork. "What's Trey's blood type?"

"AB negative." Their eyes met. AB negative was a very rare type.

"You have a sample of Trey's DNA anywhere?" Riley asked.

Chad shook his head. "Likely the blood that's there is tainted anyway by all the grease and dirt. But if you can have your lab match the type, that's good enough for me. And proof enough for a judge to get a warrant, especially since this is Trey's necklace."

"To search what?"

"I have a trail of circumstantial evidence a mile long. Kinnard's gallery, of course, his car, his house . . ."

Riley was shaking his head. "Kinnard is friends with most of the judges in Beverly Hills. You still don't have a direct link to him."

Chad slammed his hands against the table. "Dammit, don't cops in Beverly Hills ever use their guts?"

Riley glared. "Yes, for processing food, as nature intended."

Chad debated letting Riley listen to the illegal recording to see if he could identify the woman who'd left a message about Trey, but no doubt Pucker Ass would go through channels and with that namby-pamby captain already pissed off, Chad couldn't chance being thrown in jail. He'd never find Trey in time then. "So you won't try to get a warrant?"

A heavy sigh was answer enough. Chad leaped to his feet. Every muscle in his body was rigid with the effort, but he managed a gravelly, "You'll have the blood typed?"

Riley nodded.

"And if you'd be so kind as to have the surveillance cameras along the I-10 checked for the two big rigs that came out of the warehouse yard as we drove in, I'd appreciate it. We already ran the numbers, but whether they looked clean or not, I'm betting Trey was in one of them and we just missed him."

"Worth a shot. At least we'd have an idea of where they were a few hours ago."

Gesturing to the two cops that it was time to go, Riley went toward the door. After they exited, he held it wide. "Coming?"

Chad stalked out. The patience and politesse he'd used just then to get Riley to cooperate had flat worn him out. His head was aching like a son of a gun and he hadn't eaten since the marathon session with Jasmine. Still, he had to hold it together long enough to check out the Exxon station.

Riley gave him a shrewd look as he sagged against the door of his truck. "Can you see straight? Your vision blurry?"

Chad shook his head. "I just need to eat and haven't slept in over thirty hours, but now's not the time to take a break."

Riley smiled slightly. "I thought you were going to sleep at Jasmine's so she could keep an eye on you."

Chad fiddled with his keys in response, pulling his hat low, hoping Riley couldn't see his reddening cheeks.

If he did, Riley took mercy on him. "I'll drive your truck." Riley held his hand out for the keys.

"Not hardly. You ever driven a horse trailer before?"

"Couple times. Why on earth did you bring Chester anyway?"

"Chester's like a weapon. It's better to have him and not need him than to need him and not have him. He can go places no one else can."

"And if you wreck your truck, how does this help your brother? Or your horse?"

Reluctantly, Chad handed over the keys and hauled himself into the passenger side. Riley fired up the big engine, nodding his approval at the rumble.

Chad was surprised at the adept way he drove the truck out of the small lot, making slow, wide turns to give Chester time to brace himself. But he didn't comment. He was too busy watching the road. "Stay on the access."

After about thirty minutes, Chad saw a familiar sign gleaming up ahead. Riley saw it, too, and pulled into the Exxon lot. The unmarked police car followed.

Chad was out the door before the truck stopped. He used the sampling kit Riley had brought and collected several dirt samples from various places around the entrance. He handed the bagged samples to Riley. "I'm going in to talk to the clerk. Do you have the ability to run a search and see if the Del Mar Corporation has any property in San Bernardino or Riverside counties?"

Riley nodded and went to talk to the two cops. They got back into the unmarked car and used the computer-like console to stab in some letters. As Chad started toward the food mart, Riley returned and caught his arm.

"Let me do the talking for once, okay? This is my investigation after all." When Chad looked at him in his unyielding fashion, Riley said, "I want to save your brother, too. And if Kinnard is guilty of what you say, no one has a bigger interest in seeing him jailed than the Beverly Hills Police Department. Before he does any more damage."

Unlike Pucker Ass, Chad had learned through too many tough investigations and dead ends to trust his gut. Trey was in imminent peril. He could sense it. But he nodded reluctantly and let Riley lead the way in.

As he passed under an overhang high enough for big rigs, Chad noticed the tiny cameras trained at each of the pumps. Gas retailers always installed them now, so they could prosecute deadbeats who tried to sneak off without paying. The question was, would they share? Riley was right. He was better suited for this part of the investigation.

The same morning, after a restless night missing Chad, Jasmine drove toward Roger Larsen's office, unaware that she was tailed several cars back by an expensive but nondescript black Land Rover with dark windows. She wondered where Chad was but figured the best thing she could do now was help the investigation.

As she pulled up outside Larsen's expensive but discreet office, she decided it was a good thing she'd just completed her corporate law class because she knew exactly the document to look for. There were many ways to shield the leadership of a shell entity, but the articles of organization had to be signed legally by the managing member.

She entered the office, relieved to find the receptionist apparently away. She called, "Roger, are you here?"

Larsen walked out of his inner office, a delighted smile on his face. "Jasmine! I'm so happy you stopped by just in time for you to take me for coffee."

Jasmine accepted his quick kiss and gave him her best smile. "I'd love to, Roger, but I have a paper due in a week for my corporate law class. I was wondering if you'd mind if I borrowed a couple of your law books?" When his smile faded she added hastily, "But maybe we could get takeout and you could give me some pointers on how to argue my brief? I love that little Thai restaurant up the street. That is, if I'm not interrupting. It opens early and I'm starving. I love their egg noodle dishes with chicken."

Larsen's smile appeared again. "Sure, I didn't have time for breakfast. What would you like?" He went to put on his jacket, but Jasmine shook her head. "It's hot for this time of year."

He hung the jacket back on the rack inside his office and went to the door. "Back in a jiff." He exited.

The second he was gone, Jasmine snatched a ring of keys out of his pocket, went to his locked files, and looked under the *D*'s. She skimmed through them.

Next she tried the *K*'s. She snatched out the file marked, "Kinnard, Thomas." But there was only a white sheet in it marked, "Removed to confidential files."

She slammed the file closed and searched the office. She looked through his desk, but it only held office supplies. She spied a tiny closet and opened it. Inside was a much heavier vault-type file cabinet with a sturdy lock. She tried all the keys, but none fit the lock. Frustrated, she looked in his desk. Slammed the drawer. No keys. Then she snapped her fingers. She'd heard tiny keys rattling in his pocket more than once. She looked in a hidden, zippered pocket in his suit jacket and pulled out a strange key with an octagonal shaft and head. She tried it in the vault filing cabinet inside the tiny closet. It turned smoothly. She found a file marked "Kinnard, Thomas." It was very thick.

There it was. Her heart sank at this tangible proof of Thomas's involvement in land fraud and probably in Trey's disappearance. She skimmed through a thick stapled pile labeled, "Incorporation Papers, Del Mar Corporation," but she knew Larson would be back any moment, so she didn't have time to read the file. She went to the copier, unstapled the thick sheaf of papers, and inserted them in the sheet feeder.

* * *

Outside, Roger Larsen walked up to his door, whistling. He carried a large takeout bag from the Thai restaurant Jasmine liked, but before he could enter, a hand fell on his arm. He turned, startled, to see one of Thomas's gang members glaring at him. "Why is the *chica* here?"

Roger scowled. "She just needs my help with a legal brief for class."

The hood muttered something that might have been "*pendejo*," but aloud he said, "Check your files, *cabrón*. She's helping the Texan. He's staying at her place. The *jefe* doesn't trust her anymore." He smiled, a gold tooth gleaming to match his heavy gold necklaces. "If we go down, you go down."

In Riverside, Chad kept his mouth shut as Riley questioned the clerk.

"So you haven't noticed any of the eighteen-wheelers that have stopped here in the last eight hours?" Riley's voice was higher than normal with his skepticism.

The bored middle-aged female clerk, a victim of her own ennui, gave him a look universal among quick-stop gas station employees. *If you're not buying something, go away, don't bother me.* "You got any idea how many eighteen-wheelers stop here in a day?"

Riley flashed his badge a second time, but this display of authority had no more effect on her than the first time. "We need to see the surveillance footage, then. This is important, a man's life is in danger—"

"Then you got a warrant, right?"

Riley sighed. "Let me talk to the manager."

"I am the manager."

"Then let me talk to the owner."

"Corporate store. Lunchtime. Besides, they take days to get back to me about this kind of thing. Come back this weekend."

Finally, Riley's by-the-book temperament was fraying a bit at the edges. "If a crime is committed because you wouldn't help us, you could be held—"

Chad caught Riley's arm to shut him up before he got the word *obstruction* out. He tilted his hat back and turned on the Texas charm.

"We're right sorry to bother you, ma'am, but the missing person is my brother, and I'm a Texas Ranger about to lose my badge if I don't find the little peckerwood and get him home so I can get back to my job."

Now, she looked impressed. "A real Ranger? Like Tonto and everything?"

Barely, Chad managed not to roll his eyes. "Yes. I even have my horse with me. Would you like to see him?"

She nodded eagerly. Motioning to another clerk to cover the register, she followed them outside. Riley had parked the rig on a grassy sward beside the parking lot, and Chester, scenting the newly mowed grass, was pawing at the trailer bed in his eagerness to get outside. He stood patiently as Chad haltered him, backed out more patiently than usual, and immediately began cropping the grass, ignoring the woman who tentatively stroked his neck.

"He's beautiful. I've always wanted a horse."

"Stand back and I'll show you how he rears on command." Chad waited until she and Riley were at a safe distance, then raised his right hand high in the air, a command Chester had known since he was a foal. Whether he'd obey was another matter.

Chester took a last ripping tear at the grass, but when Chad patted his withers and raised his hand more authoritatively, the quarter horse obediently reared, his front legs pawing at the air. The clerk's eyes got wide, and when Chester came back down, he must have sensed her awe because he began prancing in place without command. The clerk clapped.

Chad whispered into a sensitive, flickering ear, "Show off. Good job." He led Chester back into the trailer, used the tie-down, and then shut and locked the tailgate.

He went up to the woman and removed his hat, turning it in a circle in his hands as he talked. Less Texas twang this time, but even more sincere. "This is how it is. Our parents died when I was barely out of my teens, and I mostly raised my brother since he was a youngster. He and I haven't always seen eye to eye because he's the artistic type, and I'm, well . . ."

"My grandmother was from Texas. She used to talk funny, too. She told me my dad was a ring-tailed tooter when he was little."

Chad nodded. "Yes, something like that. Anyway, we argued, and he came out here to be with a girl but disappeared before I could find him. I'm pretty sure if we don't find him in the next twenty-four hours, well . . ."

The clerk nodded. "You'll never forgive yourself."

Even more adamantly, Chad nodded. "We promise not to tell anyone we saw the footage. We understand it's against company policy and if we had more time we'd bring a warrant."

Chad waited. Behind the clerk, Riley gave Chad a thumbs-up. Chad just kept twirling his hat. Maybe there was something to this patience gig after all.

The clerk sighed. "Okay, come on in back, but if you tell anyone, I could lose my job."

As it turned out, the convenience store had the latest surveillance equipment, which not only recorded each vehicle arriving and departing with a time stamp, it had a search function for an individual plate. Riley typed in the first of the two numbers they'd logged that night at the warehouse in South El Monte. Nothing. But the second one . . . The footage automatically flickered and stopped on a nondescript navy blue big rig, but they both recognized it.

The two men who jumped down from the cab didn't look familiar to either of them, but they were definitely of the right age, gender, and look to be part of the South Side gang. As they let the five-minute footage play, they watched closely. When the men came back, one rapped on the side of the trailer and laughed coarsely. Then they got back in and drove off—east.

Chad frowned. "Isn't that toward Palm Springs?"

"Yes. You record it?"

Chad had filmed the footage as best he could with his cell phone, holding it up to the small TV screen, but it had been dark when it was recorded. "Yes. Can we put out an APB?"

"With what probable cause? This is Riverside."

"The Riverside cops—"

"Returned to duty when we struck out at the diner. They have their own cases."

Chad stared at the frozen frame of the big rig. "Trey's in that truck. I know it . . ."

"We saw no sign of Trey, and this vehicle came up clean, registered to an LLC duly recorded by the State of California when we ran the plates."

Chad pounded his fist down on the small table so hard the monitor jumped. "Goddammit, my brother is on that truck!"

Riley sighed. "Let me talk to the captain. Maybe he'll call the CHP."

Immediately Chad sat down and looked at the footage again. He slowed the digital speed and watched everything in slow motion. Once, twice . . . what was that? He forwarded frame by frame as the truck drove out of the lot, lurching over the rough edge of the pavement. Chad squinted, pausing the footage. What was that? Something flying out of the cab area, nowhere near the tires. Wishing the parking lot light were brighter, Chad used the close-up function on the recorder to blow up the cab section as the truck drove out of the lot.

There it was, blurry but recognizable. The little wad of paper towels and the faintest glimmer of gold, falling from the cab section as the truck exited the station. The packet fell out of the frame, but when Chad panned back, he could see it must have landed roughly in the same area where the kid had said he'd found it.

Riley came back in. "CHP is shorthanded with all the budget cuts. Without something tangible, the captain said—"

Chad zoomed back on the packet, removing it from his pocket as he froze the frame. He held it up for Riley to compare, indicating the time stamp, about eight hours ago, as he moved forward frame by frame, showing Trey's tiny SOS gleaming for one precious second in the light. It was a spot-on match for the packet he held. "How about a piece of solid-gold proof?"

It was after lunch when Jasmine walked inside her apartment, happy with the papers secreted in her huge shoulder bag. She had the outline of a decent brief, too. Roger had seemed less upbeat when he came back with the takeout, but she'd been careful to leave things as she'd found them. He'd wandered his office, even opening the small closet door, as they talked through her legal argument, opening and closing his desk drawers only to give her a highlighter. He'd paused once at his copier, staring down at something.

Only then did she realize his copier had a page counter. Her heart sank as that hadn't occurred to her earlier, but surely he didn't track his copies that closely. His smile seemed a bit fixed when he turned toward her, but she circled one of the cases she was referencing in her notes and asked a question. He answered calmly and she dismissed her concern that he knew she'd been snooping.

Now, in her apartment, she pulled the organization papers from her bag and read them carefully. There it was in black-and-white: Thomas Kinnard, managing member through a chain of several LLCs. When she was sure she held the most incriminating evidence linking him to the Del Mar Corporation, she hesitated, wondering if she should leave the docs out or give them immediately to Chad. But since she didn't know where he was, it was probably smarter to show them to Riley first; she knew Riley would go through the proper evidence management.

She went to the map on her wall and lifted the edge. Behind it was a small safe where she kept her spare cash. Strippers dealt mainly in cash, and she hadn't trusted banks since she'd learned in law school all the shenanigans they used to siphon off other people's money. She put the incorporation papers inside and locked the safe, carefully smoothing the map back in place.

Now she only had to share the news with Chad. She couldn't wait to see the look on his face. But would he be strong enough and honest enough to admit it when he was wrong? And where was he, anyway?

Hours later after she'd bathed and decided to nap before her shift, Jasmine sat up in bed yawning, automatically reaching for Chad, hoping he'd returned, but his side was cold. She was alone. She was sure he was off working his leads after their dalliance. For a second, she had to battle back tears, knowing that despite the explosive sexual chemistry between them, she'd always be only a dalliance to him. But she couldn't think about that now. She tilted her head, listening.

What had awakened her? She rubbed her eyes and quickly stepped into a skirt and blouse, listening tensely. There, the sound of books being tossed to the floor. Her heart skipped a beat. She went to her closet to get the baseball bat she kept for self-defense and tiptoed to her door. She opened it a crack and peeked outside. Three men, efficiently searching her living room and not even trying to be quiet, which didn't bode well for her. Her car was outside; they had to know she was here. She'd glimpsed the broken lock in the front door.

She closed the door, desperately wondering what to do. Her cell phone was next to the bed, but she had a feeling it was far too late to call 911, and no telling where Chad was. She'd taken self-defense classes and thought she could handle maybe one man, perhaps two, but certainly not three.

Quietly, knowing it wouldn't deter them long, she latched the flimsy bedroom door lock and went to the second-story window. It dropped onto an awning that she hoped would take her weight. Slipping the cell phone and her small wallet into her skirt pocket, she was struggling with the stubborn window latch when her door crashed inward under one kick. She raised the bat for leverage and spread her feet for stability.

When Montoya entered behind the first man, she was glad she had the bat, but with a sinking feeling, she knew it probably wouldn't do her much good. This guy was bad news. "You. Did Thomas send you?"

"*Hola, chica*," came the deep Latino voice she'd heard a few times before. "Where's your boyfriend?"

The other two guys approached, pinning her in from opposite sides. Jasmine swung the bat, connecting with an outstretched hand, but it was a glancing blow. As the man flinched away, howling, he held his hand against his chest and snicked open a switchblade with his free hand, but Montoya shook his head.

The other guy grabbed the bat with both hands and when she struggled to hold on, kicking and biting, he slapped her. Her head snapped around and her grip loosened. He snatched the bat away and flung it against her dresser. It broke the mirror. They pulled her, still struggling, into the living room. She looked around and saw they'd just begun to toss her place. She didn't have much of value outside the vault, which luckily they hadn't found, but then she saw Chad's clothes were scattered and his extra pair of boots had been flung on opposite sides of the room. The ringleader shook her slightly. "Where's the Ranger?"

"I don't know," she answered honestly. "Why should I? He's not my boyfriend."

"No?" That cold black stare appraised the rumpled sheets on the bed, which were visible through the open bedroom door. "How is it they say in Texas? All hat and no cattle." The leader grabbed his crotch. "I've seen you dance. I'm a bull, *puta*. You will see."

And just as she drew breath to scream, Jasmine felt her lips smashed into her teeth by a brutal hand. She was dragged, still kicking and her cries for help garbled against a tough palm, toward the door, where the third guy taped her mouth with duct tape.

CHAPTER 15

Chad paced the parking lot, waiting for the APB to yield a sighting of the navy big rig. Their title search had revealed two locations owned by the same LLC that had registered the truck. Nothing under the name of the Del Mar Corporation, which didn't surprise Chad. Only problem was, the two warehouses were in opposite directions, one in a remote area farther out the I-10 near a town called Indio, and the other north toward Las Vegas.

Both were over an hour from their present location near Riverside, and since they had such a small force, Riley didn't want them to split up. Sound police prudence, but every minute dragged by like a year for Chad. He looked at his watch. Jasmine had to be wondering where he was by now, but her cell had gone straight to voice mail when he tried to call her. He didn't know why he felt obligated to give her an update as to his whereabouts, told himself it was plain old Texas courtesy since she'd put him up. He left her another message and hung up. Riley's knowing smile irritated the hell out of him, but he only turned away to check on Chester for the fourth time.

Finally the police radio crackled. "Indio police report navy 2005 GMC eighteen-wheeler sighted on Route 125 approaching the suspect warehouse."

Chad and Riley were in his truck before the dispatch was finished. Riley responded using Chad's radio, which they'd tuned to the CHP frequency. "Advise Indio police to monitor possible hostile situation but wait for backup. We're on our way."

Jasmine lay, her hands bound behind her, in the rear trunk of a black Land Rover she'd glimpsed before they stuck a black hood over her head. She'd quit struggling because that only made her bonds hurt more. Instead, with a few calming, deep breaths, she tried to reason through why she'd been taken. Why did Thomas suddenly view her as a threat?

He continued to lie about Trey and was likely involved in the car theft ring they'd stumbled on in South El Monte. And she'd seen him in close conversation with the very guy who'd kidnapped her. Plus Chad had warned her she'd been followed, and she had no stalkers that she knew of, which left one conclusion: Thomas had been a master tactician all along, finagling her and Mary into identical tattoos, probably leaving her card in Texas for Chad to find, having Mary seduce Trey into selling his land so he would return to California to be with her. All part of Thomas's plan to lure the brothers away from the Foster homestead so he could drill.

And somehow Trey had figured out what was going on, so Thomas had decided to get him out of the way. But his machinations couldn't account for the passion of two redheads who'd fallen for the Foster brothers . . .

Jasmine squeezed her eyes tightly shut to quell her tears. While she could trace the chain of events to a logical conclusion, Chad would never believe she'd been used just as he had. Even after the explosive sex between them, or more accurately, because of their volcanic chemistry, he still considered her damaged goods, someone who used her allure to manipulate men for money. He'd never believe she'd tried all along to help him find Trey, not unless he came face to face with Mary and realized there were two redheads.

As the car jounced over rough roads, Jasmine braced herself for the coming confrontation. Somehow she knew they were taking her to Thomas, no doubt miles away from Beverly Hills. And somehow she had to convince him she was still on his side so he'd let her go. If only she could help Chad find Trey, she'd go willingly back to Texas with him. Once he saw her standing beside Mary, everything would click into place. She could kick off her stilettos along with her stripper lifestyle. She'd saved a lot of money, enough, if she was careful, to transfer to SMU or UT law school and finish her degree, and Texas was a much cheaper place to live.

And Texas? She waited for the usual knee-jerk revulsion, but it didn't come. She thought of the endless prairies, the desolate deserts, the piney woods near Houston, and the sparkling sands of Port Aransas and South Padre. The men who still opened doors for women, the helpfulness of other drivers if she was stuck with a flat, and the soft cadence of the Texas drawl even in the best drawing rooms.

She was going home.

But first she had to escape. She began working her neck from side to side, trying to loosen the hood, but when the car stopped, she went still.

The trunk opened and she was dragged roughly out to uneven pavement.

Jasmine blinked in the bright light as the hood was jerked off her head. Her eyes took a while to adjust, but finally she made out rows of shelving packed with can after can of paint. Forklifts sat idle, several holding large boxes also marked *Paint*. She didn't know what she'd expected of Kinnard's base of operations, but something less prosaic than paint.

"Hello, Jasmine."

She spun, and sure enough, there was the man himself. His Armani was a bit wrinkled and a five o'clock shadow shaded his face, but his smile was as smooth as ever.

"Why did you bring me here, Thomas? Let me loose."

"Why couldn't you mind your own business? I want to know where you put the incorporation papers you copied."

Jasmine pretended confusion. "What papers?"

"Larsen may be led by his dick, but I'm not. Approximately twenty copies were made on his machine while he was getting your requested takeout. Coincidentally enough, that's the count of the Del Mar organization papers." When Jasmine opened her mouth again, he took an angry stride forward. "Don't bother lying. You're very bad at it."

Jasmine leaned against a shelf, crossing one ankle over the other. "And you're very good at it."

Kinnard shrugged. "Occupational hazard . . . now tell me where the copies are."

Jasmine stayed still and carefully appraised her surroundings. The warehouse was long and low, and if there was another exit other than the roll-up door they'd shut behind them, she couldn't see it. Almost at the end, she saw the huge outline of a big rig parked deep inside the warehouse. The three men who'd brought her here had been joined by three others, all wearing the colors of the South Side gang. They fanned out on either side of her, and she couldn't escape the feeling that she was being hunted by a pack of wolves.

She looked back at the alpha male. *Keep him talking. Delay.* "Why are you doing this, Thomas? You have plenty of money." She hesitated, then admitted, "I saw the articles about you and Gerald Foster. Your vendetta against the Fosters is flat wrong. Trey and Chad were just kids then—"

"I thought you were snooping around. That's why I had you followed. You searched my desk, didn't you? Did you tell Foster about the articles?"

"No." At his look of disbelief she said more insistently, "No, not to protect you, to protect him. We needed more proof and I was afraid what he'd do. I only found fragments, anyway."

"That's because your friend Trey took them. He was going to give them to his brother, so he forced my hand."

Sighing heavily, Thomas looked at Montoya, and back at her. "You really are a lovely young woman. It would be a pity to . . . change that. For the last time, tell me where the copies are."

Jasmine spread her arms wide against the shelf, as if bracing herself. All the while, her fingers were reaching for the paint scraper she'd spied. It wasn't much, but it was better than nothing. "Where is Trey? If you hurt him, or me for that matter, Chad will kill you."

"He's a lawman, like his daddy. He won't dare move against me without evidence." He nodded at a gang member. "And if you won't tell me where the copies are, there's only one way to keep the slate clean."

With flicking switchblades, two gang members moved toward her. But with her supple dancer's grace, she dodged to the side as one reached for her, the knife bared. She stuck a booted foot behind his ankle as she half whirled away from him, striking at his hand with the V-shaped paint stripper. He howled and dropped the knife, stumbling over her outthrust boot, falling to the floor. The other grabbed her shoulder to hold her still. The knife moved so close to her throat it nicked her, but using the momentum of her lower body, she pulled her second assailant with her, backward into the shelf. It teetered, and several cans of paint fell on top of them. She lifted an arm to shield her head, feeling a glancing blow that numbed her shoulder, but the gang member took the full brunt of a can on the top of his head. He fell in a heap against the shelf, disturbing more cans that rocked in place but stayed put.

Jasmine danced away—to face four more angry gang members. She was poised on her toes to run for the entrance.

A police megaphone roared outside, "This is the Indio Police Department and the California Highway Patrol. Come out with your hands up. You're surrounded."

Jasmine screamed at the top of her lungs, "Help! I'm being held by—" A manicured hand covered her mouth before she could get out the name. Jasmine bit Thomas, but for once he did his own dirty work. He wrapped a long arm about her midriff and viciously jerked upward, winding her. Duct tape went over her mouth and she was still struggling to breathe when she was tossed up into the rear trailer of the eighteen-wheeler. Two of the gang members went with her. She felt the rig start up, its engine roaring as it was gunned straight toward the rear of the warehouse. They left the gate partly open, so she could see a little bit.

She hadn't noticed a door there . . . With a crashing, high-pitched whine of metal, the eighteen-wheeler made its own door through the flimsy metal siding and jounced over rough terrain, up a dirt path, away from the police cars circling the front, lights flashing. It all happened too fast, but she'd bet the money in her safe that Thomas was not in this vehicle, that he'd get away.

Breathing deeply through her nose, Jasmine cleared her brain enough to see in the dim light inside the trailer. She held on for dear life to a shelf, auto parts rattling behind a tarp but securely lashed down, and looked toward the rear door. Did she dare try to jump out as the truck moved? She looked at the two gang members. They'd pulled pistols and seemed calm. One eyed her in a way that terrified her more than the gun.

She'd have to jump over him to make it to the door. They hadn't had time to tie her hands so she was able to pull the duct tape away from her mouth, not that anyone would hear her scream over all the racket. She wondered if Chad was part of the law enforcement encircling them. She suspected so. She hoped so.

She was debating moving toward the cab to see if she could get out that way when a moan to her left alerted her. She blinked, and saw what she'd thought was a pile of tarps moving slightly. She had to move toward them on her hands and knees as the truck was seesawing so violently. Tentatively, she pulled aside the tarps as another moan sounded, this one louder.

The tarps moved and formed into a man, sitting up and bracing himself against the truck. "Trey," Jasmine whispered in a mix of despair and relief. At least he was still alive, though he'd been beaten mercilessly by the look of him.

She sank down next to him, pulling him into her arms. He groaned, wincing away from her, and she realized he'd been beaten about the ribs and stomach, too. "I think Chad's outside, trying to rescue us," was all she could think to say to comfort him.

"How'd you end up on Kinnard's shit list?" His voice was so hoarse she had to strain to hear him over the roar of the engine.

"I've been helping Chad look for you. I . . . copied some important papers that link Thomas to the Del Mar Corporation. He was going to kill me, I think."

"Yes." He slumped against the side of the truck, his teeth now chattering, and Jasmine realized some of his wounds must have become infected, because some of the cuts on his arms were red and puffy, oozing pus.

"And Mary? Where is she?"

"I . . . think she's in Texas.

"Drilling on our land."

It was a statement. She couldn't argue with him. She said again,

"Chad will come." As if it were a mantra. She had no illusions about how badly hurt Trey might be.

He looked at her through his swollen eyelids, a ghost of the old Trey twinkle shining even in the dimness. "You love him, don't you?"

Jasmine had been avoiding that truth, but faced with Trey's bruised, battered, but still kind, still caring countenance, she couldn't lie. She managed a nod.

Trey sighed. "Well, I'm glad one of us gets a redhead."

The words had scarcely left his mouth before a pistol butt slammed him in the mouth. Blood spewed from his cracked lips as he sank sideways, unconscious. "*¡Basta!*" hissed one of the gang members. "The two of you, or I'll kill you both now."

When Jasmine shrank away, the gang member scooted back to his post beside the door. Jasmine pulled Trey into her arms to support his limp head, knowing she wouldn't even try to escape now. She couldn't leave him behind. She ran a gentle hand over his head, feeling dried blood and lumps through the dirty blond strands. "Chad will be here soon," she whispered to reassure both of them.

The words had scarcely left her lips when she heard a very distinctive sound even over the straining big-rig engine and jouncing tires. Hoofbeats. A horse. Approaching from the rear. Fast.

Outside, Chad bent low over Chester's neck, expecting bullets any minute now. The bad guys couldn't see him well in the dust trail the eighteen-wheeler stirred up on the unpaved track winding up into the mountains, but they'd still try. *Ping!* A shot ricocheted off a rock beside the road, wide right. Chad moved in more closely behind the rear of the truck.

Far behind, he heard Riley driving his four-wheel drive, minus the horse trailer, but even that vehicle wasn't as nimble over this terrain as Chester. The cop cars, built for speed and maneuverability, had fallen way back. Chad wondered where in hell these idiots thought they were going up this rough dirt track, but then they'd had few options.

By the time they'd all realized the truck had made its own secondary exit, the big rig was a ways up the trail. It was so big it could carve its own path through the scrub, and its tough tires spewed rocks as if they were sand.

Chad had taken one look at the winding trail leading upward and quickly saddled Chester.

"What the hell do you think you're doing, Foster?" Riley asked.

"I'm not losing Trey again, no matter what." Chad leaped onto Chester, dug his heels into his flanks, and almost lost his seat as the stallion bolted forward. Chester was in fine fettle, tired of all the standing, and eager to run.

Riley was left literally eating dust as he hurried to unhook the trailer and use Chad's truck to follow.

Now Chad moved to the right side of the track, keeping pace with the truck, reaching for the door release. Trey was in there. He had to be. His gloved hand almost connected with the latch, but at a curve in the path the truck spat rocks back at Chester. The stallion automatically veered away, back to the middle of the track.

Chad hesitated, afraid to use his Peacemaker to shoot out the tires, but he had no idea what was going on inside that trailer. What if the kidnappers decided to cut their losses and toss Trey out? He had to stop this rig.

Reaching behind his back to pull out his pistol, Chad used one hand to steady Chester into a smooth lope so he would be stable enough to aim. *Whump!* One rear tire flattened as the bullet pierced its tough hide. *Whoosh!* Another lost air on the same side. The truck lurched, its right rear axle grinding against gravel.

This time Chad was able to unlatch the rear door as the truck ground to a stop. He'd barely begun raising it before gunshots spit at him, but he was expecting that and leaped off Chester to the side ledge of the big rig, his booted toes barely finding purchase. He waited for the hail of bullets to die so they'd have to reload.

However, the guys in the cab weren't going quietly. Fire erupted from that direction, too. Chad flattened himself and fired back, but his four remaining shots didn't last long.

Meanwhile, Riley had almost reached them, and one of the Indio cops was literally riding shotgun. He fired several times toward the cab and the returning fire stopped, giving Chad time to raise the rear door enough to swing inside. He took one quick look, but had no time for shock at the sight of Jasmine. Jasmine holding someone with dirty blond hair.

He'd had no time to reload, but he hoped they hadn't either. His buck knife bared, he kicked a pistol away from one hood, and engaged the other. The switchblade his opponent wielded was wicked but no match for his sturdy hunting knife. The other hood picked up a crowbar and approached.

Jasmine used a long leg to sweep his feet from under him. He toppled, hitting his head against an engine block. He went limp.

Chad forced the gangbanger's knife hand away from his midsection, lifted a knee and whacked the guy's wrist against his leg several times. Wincing, the guy dropped his knife. And then the other cops were there, the two perps from the cab already cuffed, pushed in front of them.

Scarcely aware of the other cops, Chad was focused on one thing: the way Jasmine carefully cradled Trey. She bit her lip and shook her head slightly as she looked up at him, tears in her eyes. Gently, Chad turned his brother's head away from her shoulder so he could see it. He looked unconscious and his face was a mass of swelling and bruising. As Chad watched, he spit up blood. Chad felt Riley hovering.

"Goddammit, get a rescue chopper in here, Riley." But Riley had already leaped back outside to pick up the radio.

As gently as they could, they laid Trey flat. Chad took the first aid kit from Riley and peeled Trey's shirt away. Trey's ribs were a crisscross of bruises and one was obviously broken. It looked like he'd been beaten with a tire iron. Chad found little to bandage; most of the damage was internal.

Then Trey groaned. His lashes fluttered and he looked up, those blue-sky eyes smiling even in his pain. "I knew you'd come," he whispered, his voice so hoarse Chad scarcely recognized it. "You got my message?"

Unable to talk over the lump in his throat, Chad nodded.

"They found the hole I cut near the cab and beat me really bad that last time. You still have it?"

Chad pulled the nugget from his pocket and handed it to Trey. He wanted to say a million things, how sorry he was at the way he'd acted, it was time to go home, they'd figure out what to do about the taxes without selling the land, how much he loved his brother. He could only watch helplessly as the grayness he'd felt since leaving Amarillo consumed his world, the last circle of light ringing his brother's peaceful face.

"I'm . . . sorry, Chad. Sorry I came out here, sorry you gave up your job to find me."

Chad covered his hand. "I'm sorry, too, little brother. But we'll get you out of here, just hang on."

The few words seeming to exhaust him, Trey clutched the necklace in his fist. Then he looked at Jasmine. He caught her hand and put the necklace in it. Then he caught his brother's hand, tugging at the glove. Chad removed it and did what Trey wanted—he caught Jasmine's hand in his. In this way they both held the Foster legacy of love in their clasped hands.

Trey's eyes fluttered closed.

"Trey," Chad said. When there was no answer, Chad yelled, "Where the hell is that goddamn chopper?" He began performing CPR on his brother, even knowing it was too late.

Trey's face was as peaceful as he'd ever seen it. . . .

CHAPTER 16

More emergency responder vehicles had arrived, but Chad didn't stir from his brother's side. When a technician jumped into the truck to help lift a stretcher inside, he recoiled at the look Chad gave him and jumped back out.

Chad tipped his hat low so Jasmine couldn't see his face, but she saw his lean jaw flexing. She had no idea what to say to comfort him because tears were streaming down her own face. Trey had been one of the kindest people she'd ever known. And she didn't know why, but she felt guilty. True, it was Mary who'd actually drawn Trey to LA, but she'd been complicit, a pawn in Kinnard's elaborate chess game, to better herself financially and fund her law school ambitions. And she'd used her looks on Chad just as he'd always said, though for a far more basic reason than he realized: She wanted him. For more than a day, or night.

Forever. But he'd never trusted her. Would he hate her now?

The rescue copter whirred overhead and landed some distance away, on the only flat ground. Chad stayed put, his head bowed, holding Trey's lifeless hand.

When two more technicians peeked inside, she tentatively touched Chad's shoulder. "Chad, they need to take him back to the hospital."

He flung her hand off, and still without looking at her, leaped out of the truck and glared at an emergency technician. "I'm his next of kin. You don't touch him without my written permission."

The technician stammered, "Ah, yes—sir, tha-that's standard practice—"

Riley looked up from a conference with Indio, Riverside, and CHP law enforcement. He moved aside and clasped Chad's arm sympathetically. When Chad flinched away he only said, "Kinnard's slipped through us somehow. We figure he must have had his own chopper waiting up in the mountains, that's why he came here to this isolated location. We're trying to track any registration numbers now, but nothing's come up yet. Montoya's gone, too, and his gang members never rat on him, so we've got a lot of work ahead of us."

Chad said emotionlessly, "Where's Chester?"

Riley nodded toward a stand of trees where Chester was munching a clump of grass as his lead was held by a police officer.

"You searched the warehouse yet?" Chad asked Riley.

"In progress."

"I want to be there. Can someone take me back? Someone can ride Chester back to the trailer—"

"I will." Both men turned to see Jasmine standing there, listening. Chad opened his mouth as if to object, but he shrugged and turned back to Riley.

For the first time ever, Riley looked as if he didn't know quite what to say. "I thought you might want to, uh, accompany the chopper—"

"No. I can't do Trey any good that way," Chad snarled. "See he's . . . taken care of until I can get there. But first I'm going to see that Kinnard's brought in, even if it kills me, too." Chad turned on his heel toward a waiting patrol car, pulling an old pearl-handled pistol from his waistband and loading it with bullets from his pocket.

Riley saw the weapon, but shook his head when the CHP sergeant made a move toward Chad. "I'll finish up here and join you at the warehouse," Riley called after Chad. The patrolman drove off, Chad in the passenger seat. As he passed Jasmine and Chester, Chad didn't even turn his head to look at them.

Worried about Chad, Jasmine hiked her skirt to her thighs and climbed on Chester. He stood docile as her slight weight settled in the saddle, not even mad she'd pulled him from his grazing. She kneed him gently and he moved forward, wending his way through various vehicles. When they were clear, she encouraged him to a brisk trot, something driving her to get back to the warehouse as soon as possible, but the dirt track was too rough for a gallop. She couldn't risk hurting Chester.

When she arrived at the warehouse thirty minutes later, she saw Chad holding something, staring down at it intently. Evidence boxes were being loaded into the back of a van and a crime scene investigator walked up to Chad as Jasmine tied Chester to a tree and approached.

"We have to add that to the inventory," the investigator said. "You can review the evidence later."

Chad reluctantly handed it over, tearing off his gloves. When the investigator was out of earshot, he caught her arm and hauled her close, but there was nothing lover-like in his touch as he lowered his head and whispered fiercely, "You lying bitch. I'm going to take you back to Amarillo to face justice, Texas style. It's not fraud anymore, babe. It's accessory to murder." He stalked away to load Chester into the trailer, which had been linked to his truck, adding, "And stay the fuck away from my horse." He got in the cab and drove away, dirt splatting at her so that she had to move aside. She saw Chester stumble inside the truck and knew how careful Chad was, typically, when he was hauling the stallion.

But this behavior wasn't typical . . .

She stared after him. When Riley got out of another vehicle and approached, she bit back tears. "I know he's upset, and I don't blame him for that, but I got myself kidnapped for him. I was trying so hard to help him find Trey . . ." Her voice trailed off as Riley held up a long plastic sheath. Inside was a contract headed simply, "For Services Rendered, Jasmine Routh, consultant, shall supply the following services to the Del Mar Corporation." It went on to list a legal-sounding scope of work that mentioned the Foster brothers by name.

She'd never seen it before but she recognized Roger's fine hand, the bastard. She held out a hand for it, but Riley shook his head and dropped it back on top of the stack in the evidence box. Jasmine said evenly, "I can tell you I never signed a contract like that. This is more of Kinnard's false evidence trail. Can't you see he's doing all he can, including implicating me, to keep Chad away from Texas?" When Riley just looked at her, she sighed. "Luckily I can prove I've been doing all I can to accumulate evidence against the Del Mar Corporation. And I can prove Thomas Kinnard is the principal. Can you take me back to my place?"

Sometime later, at the Los Angeles Equestrian Center, Chad tried to focus on brushing Chester, but the normally soothing motions couldn't block the memories that came in a torrent now. Happy memories of Trey before they got so crossways. But none of them were solid enough to blank out the trauma of his brother's bruised, puffy face, relaxed in death.

Chad leaned his forehead on Chester's shining withers, but even the scent of horse couldn't comfort him. He knew he needed to go on to the morgue and sign the papers authorizing the autopsy. He knew he needed to face Jasmine and make her admit her collusion in luring Trey out here. Maybe then the bile of self-disgust wouldn't make him want to vomit. Above all, he knew he needed to drag her back with him to Texas whether she wanted to go or not. Only there, where his neighbors could ID her as Trey's floozy, and where he had jurisdiction, would she be punished as she deserved. He was the outsider here and he'd already seen the Beverly Hills style of justice.

Slow and maybe.

She deserved now and certain.

Now Trey was dead, no jury in West Texas would let her off scot-free, especially with her name on that contract with the same Del Mar Corporation that had finagled so many out of their mineral rights. That document gave him legal basis to take her back, even without a subpoena.

But for the moment, he was helpless under a black cloud of grief stronger even than the one that had enveloped him when his mama died. Trey had been his last remaining family, and the way he'd tried to bless Chad into a relationship with his girlfriend, as if even in death he wanted his brother to be happy, only made Chad feel worse. And then the horrible thought he'd been avoiding sucker punched him in the gut: Would Trey have been so generous if he'd known

Chad had been screwing his girlfriend while he'd been beaten almost to death?

Broken at last, Chad fell to his knees and wept. Chester nuzzled at his hair, whuffing his sympathy, but Chad didn't even feel it.

Inside her apartment, Jasmine made sure Riley saw the mess everywhere. "If I'm partnered with Thomas, why did he send his hoods to kidnap me and search my place for the most important piece of evidence linking him to the Del Mar Corporation?"

"Is that why you were at the warehouse? They'd kidnapped you?"

"Yes, and I think were about to kill me. Look." Jasmine turned a bright light onto her face and showed him the barest tape residue around her mouth. "Left over from the duct tape." Riley ran a gentle finger along the residue and then did it again as if he liked the feel of her, so she pulled away.

She walked to the map on the wall and tore it down. "Thomas falsified that contract as he's falsified so many documents. I'm no angel"—she began typing her combination into the revealed digital safe—"I do manipulate men for money, but almost from the day I met him, I've done all I can to help Chad find Trey." She reached inside the cavity and pulled out the sheaf of papers, leaving her neat stacks of hundreds banded inside. "Now I'm going to do all I can to bring to justice the man who's responsible for Trey's death. And who's wrecked so many lives." Including hers, if Chad never forgave her for Trey . . . but she didn't say this, at least not to Riley.

Riley flipped through the papers quickly and froze on the last page. "According to Foster, law enforcement agencies in five states have been looking for this signature page."

"Are they strippers who know how to manipulate Kinnard's attorney?"

Riley's grin was genuine and stretched his tired face. "Yes, well, I'm sure you also know this may not hold up to a legal challenge because of the way you acquired it."

"I'm not an attorney or a police officer, and given the Del Mar Corporation has been trying to imply I'm working for them, which I'm not, I think most jurors would agree I have a right to defend myself. And I've been assisting in your investigation, haven't I, as a concerned citizen?"

Riley was already on his cell phone. "Get an evidence team over here right away." He hung up and carefully stacked the copies on the coffee table. "You can positively ID Montoya and his guys as the men who kidnapped you?"

"Yes, if you can put him in a lineup."

Riley stared at the bronze of the bronco rider. "Are you going to see Foster?"

"If he'll see me." She recalled the way Chad had refused to even look at her when she rode past him, but she had to try. She couldn't leave him to face his grief alone, though until she cleared her name, she'd probably make him feel worse, not better.

She wished for the umpteenth time she had Mary's new cell phone number. Mary was the only one who could settle all of this.

In Amarillo, Mary sat in her rental car and stared at the door marked Texas Department of Public Safety. And in smaller print, Land Fraud, Rustling Investigations. The office of Texas Rangers Company C was inside, and she knew Chad Foster had worked there until he quit to go tearing after Trey. She also knew that if she walked through that door, she'd not only lose the financial stability she'd worked so hard for, she might ultimately lose her life, even if she didn't go to prison.

Thomas Kinnard didn't take kindly to informers.

She could probably get Jasmine to help negotiate immunity for her if she agreed to testify against Thomas. But no matter how she weighed the consequences, the alternative was more terrible: Trey had disappeared, and if she didn't go forward, now, it might be too late for him.

Mary drove away, resolved to return with all the pertinent documentation: the surveys, the geological, even her own contract with Thomas. But first she had to dismiss the workers at the rig and shut it down . . .

A couple of hours later, his expression impassive but for the pinkish cast to his eyes, Chad entered the hospital where they'd taken

Trey. As usual, he hadn't been able to find anywhere to park because none of the public spaces in the hospital lot had been big enough to accommodate his dually. So he was double-parked near the entrance, but he couldn't put this particular duty off.

However, when they showed him Trey's body to get a positive ID, Chad's knees threatened to buckle again. He thought of the clinical brutality of an autopsy, which he'd seen more than once: the splitting of the chest for removal of the organs, the weighing of the brain, the corny jokes the medical examiner's team often cracked just to keep their sanity . . .

Chad tossed the pen down without signing the autopsy approval form. "No. I just want to purchase a wooden coffin to take him home in. An autopsy is pointless. We know he was beaten to death, probably with a tire iron. Trey . . . hated hospitals." Chad held up his hand when the morgue technician began to protest. He slapped down a credit card. "Run this. Just pack him in ice, insulate him as well as you can, and I'll come pick him up tomorrow morning." He turned and walked off. Since he had no intention of staying in California to pursue the case, it didn't matter if Trey was autopsied anyway. The legal evidence in Texas would be Kinnard and Jasmine.

Time for an even more unpleasant duty . . . time to go see Jasmine. Chad wished he never had to lay eyes on the bitch again, but she was the best, the only link really, to Thomas Kinnard. One way or another, when he dusted the California dirt from his boots tomorrow, she'd be in that truck with him.

Chad walked outside, on autopilot as his brain was already forging ahead to the likely charges against Jasmine once he got her to Amarillo. He almost stumbled against the tiny vehicle before he saw it. One of those little three-wheeled carts operated by the parking gestapo. Parked alongside his dually while an officious little guy in a uniform scribbled a ticket.

Chad literally saw red. He'd been here less than a month and he'd accumulated four parking tickets and had had to retrieve his truck three times from a tow yard; the cost of this ticket would likely be astronomical. Still, he kept his tone polite. Patient. Or tried to . . . "What's the problem, Officer?"

"Can't you read all the No Parking signs? You're blocking traffic at a public installation where emergency vehicles must have ingress and egress." The parking Nazi ripped the ticket off and handed it to Chad. "Texas plates don't give you the right to take your half in the middle. I've given you three separate citations. You're lucky I didn't have you towed. Would have been within my rights to do so."

Chad fingered through the copies, but his gaze was so blurry he couldn't even read them. He merely got in his truck before he followed his impulse to level the Nazi. But when he moved to pull away, he saw that the little vehicle, parked at an angle behind him, had him blocked.

Chad rolled his window down, but the parking Nazi was speaking animatedly into his cell phone, ignoring him. Chad ground his teeth, but that only gave him an aching jaw. He glanced in his side mirror and saw if he reversed just right . . .

All his frustrations boiled over at once: the fruitless search for Trey, finding him too late, the way Jasmine emasculated him, the way Kinnard had out maneuvered him and escaped a law enforcement dragnet of copters and three different agencies . . . and two days without sleep to cap it off. His disembodied hand reached out for the gearshift and thrust it into reverse.

Chad backed up, the satisfying crunch of metal angel music to his ears as his huge bumper crumpled the side of the little cart. He looked outside his window to be sure the parking Nazi was clear. He was safely standing under the entrance awning, his mouth agape as the hand holding his phone sagged down.

Satisfied the little prick was watching, Chad pulled forward for better leverage and backed up again. This time the flattened side of the cart was no match for the size of Chad's huge tires. The dually barely jolted as the cart fell beneath the four-wheel-drive's rear wheels.

Chad revved his engine and moved forward, the crunch of crumpling metal drawing out his first smile in over a day. He yelled out the window, "I got me here the most powerful passenger truck diesel engine in the world today. You got to ask yourself a question—'Do you feel lucky?' Well, do you, punk?" And he backed over the cart again. One more time for good measure; then he got out to appraise his handiwork. Not a scrape on his own paint or a dent in the tailgate.

"You like Hot Wheels?" Chad asked conversationally. "Me too. Just for you, the new Fosterized Demolition Derby model. Enjoy." Chad tipped his hat and moved to get back in the truck, only to find his exit out of the lot blocked by several security vehicles with flashing lights. Full-size this time. A police car zoomed into the entrance, siren blaring.

The parking Nazi wore his own grim smile, pocketing his phone. "Let's see what the judge has to say, Dirty Harry."

Chad didn't resist as the police officers pulled his arms behind him and cuffed him. And for the moment at least, the residual glow from the sight of the Demolition Derby Hot Wheels car pancaked under his truck was enough to keep him happy even when they hustled him into a Beverly Hills police car.

Wouldn't Riley be happy to see him?

CHAPTER 17

A weary Riley was wrapping up with the evidence guys at Jasmine's apartment when his cell phone rang. He answered, and then held the phone away from his ear as a high, very proper voice blasted him. "I'm going to insist the judge set his bail at twenty thousand dollars at least. This asinine, puerile behavior will not be tolerated by anyone in a joint investigation with us, Texas Ranger or not. Is that clear, Officer O'Connor?"

"Yes, Captain Barnes." Why the hell had the chief let Barnes take over as head of the investigation? Riley suspected he knew the answer: Barnes had asked. Because he wanted to keep an eye on Chad Foster. When Barnes was calm again, Riley asked, "What did Foster do to get arrested?" He listened to another earful. When he hung up his cell phone, Riley was torn between laughing and groaning.

Jasmine caught his arm. "Is Chad in trouble?"

"You could say that. He's in jail." He explained quickly.

Jasmine's tired eyes filled with tears and she had to look away. "He lost it because of Trey."

Riley wasn't so sure, but he only shrugged. "Doesn't change the charges of destruction of public property and endangering an officer."

Jasmine made a move toward her safe, but then stopped and looked over her shoulder at Riley. "They won't let him out until bail is set, will they?"

"No. He appears before the judge tomorrow at nine a.m."

As evidence guys carried out the boxes, Jasmine plopped down on her couch as if she no longer had the strength to stand. "Maybe a night in jail will clarify things for him."

"Maybe." Riley was doubtful.

She caught his tone, but she didn't argue. "I'll go bail him out in the morning."

Riley gave her a look. "Not a good idea, Jasmine. He's a huge flight risk; no way he'll stay here now with Trey gone."

"I'll pay the fine the judge levies against him."

Riley whistled. "It will be in the thousands."

She waved a hand to indicate her lack of concern, and walked him to the door.

He said, "I'll appear in court with him. Maybe that will help."

As he hovered on the doorstep, she reached up to kiss him on the cheek. "Thanks, Riley. When Chad comes back to himself, he'll thank you, too."

Riley muttered something that sounded suspiciously like "not hardly" as he walked down the steps.

Early the next day Texas time, fifteen hundred miles away, Mary got out of the car, hefted the briefcase containing her contract with Thomas and her geological surveys showing where and how they'd decided to drill on the Foster homestead, and walked up the staircase to the DPS office door. With every step, she felt the burden of guilt lift.

Inside, Sinclair was reviewing the files on the Del Mar land fraud case with Corey. "I'll say this for the bastard, he's slick as owl shit when it comes to writing ambivalent legal documents."

"Yeah, Chad mentioned he met some smooth-ass Beverly Hills lawyer type."

"Get his name. We'll run a background on him. Call Chad. I want to know what happened with the reward money I loaned him anyway."

Corey eyed his boss as if hesitating, but Sinclair must have seen the question in his eyes. "Spit it out."

"I thought you accepted his resignation? Why are you helping him?"

Sinclair retorted, "Why are you?" At Corey's dull flush, he relented. "I'm not blind, Cooper. I didn't have to pull your cell phone records to see how often you've been in communication with Foster since he supposedly quit. I've been stretching the rules trying to help him because I'd feel exactly the same way if it was my brother, but I can only do so much unless he comes back and takes up his job again."

"So you'll revoke his resignation if he does?"

Sinclair's gaze strayed to the shredder in the copier room. He shrugged. "Don't quote me on this, but what resignation?"

Sighing his relief, Corey dialed Chad's cell phone number.

Inside an evidence locker in Beverly Hills, Chad's phone vibrated weakly, and then went dead.

Corey hung up a few seconds later. "It just rings. I'll try him later. But one thing I'm pretty sure about . . ." Corey hesitated, obviously not wanting to make his former partner look bad.

Sinclair encouraged him. "Go ahead. I know Chad's tearing LA apart with his bare hands. He's staying with some redheaded stripper or something, so his standards have obviously lowered a notch."

The words were barely out of his mouth when a receptionist ushered a voluptuous, tall redhead into the office. She waved a hand toward the seating area outside Sinclair's door. The redhead started forward, looking determined. Her purse slipped off her shoulder, disarranging her V-neck blouse and revealing a discreet but lovely butterfly tattoo on the curve of her breast. Sinclair's executive assistant met her and offered coffee.

Sinclair nodded as Corey exclaimed, "That's the same tattoo Chad had me try to track down. Oh my God . . ." Corey shook his head.

He and Sinclair burst out at the same time, "Chad's got the wrong redhead!"

Sinclair looked at Corey. "And he likes her, doesn't he? Even though she's a stripper?"

Corey nodded grimly.

Sinclair's smile stretched from ear to ear. "This will be fun."

Totally unaware of the turmoil his actions were causing in Texas, Chad was awakened from a dead sleep by the opening of his cell. He rubbed his eyes and sat up on the comfortable cot. He hadn't been surprised to learn that even jail cells in Beverly Hills were clean and plush, as far as such things went.

The uniformed officer who let him out gave him a sour look. "Your bail's been made."

Chad was flummoxed. The judge, under Captain Barnes's urging, had set Chad's bail at twenty-five thousand. That was pocket change to Sinclair, but not to Chad, and he cringed at the thought of asking for a loan of such magnitude. Half hoping the judge would relent after Riley talked to him, Chad had decided to cool his heels—and his temper—for a day or two. He had done the crime after all, so as cops said, he might as well do some time. But his brother would be buried in only one place. The place he belonged.

Since he hadn't contacted anyone in Texas, who on earth out here had that kind of money? He was no closer to an answer after he retrieved his belongings and signed his exit papers. However, as he read the release agreement, he realized Riley had brokered a deal for him with the DA: They made him sign an affidavit stating he'd be back for his trial but had pressing family business to deal with in Texas. They were allowing him to leave California.

As he walked out into the lovely California sunshine, Chad blinked, dreading his next move. He almost wished he could go back to that cot that was more comfortable than his sleeping bag, but the memory of holding his brother's lifeless hand steeled him. Time to face Jasmine. Do his best to talk her into going to Texas with him. If she refused . . . Chad pulled his cell phone out of the bag, not surprised to find it dead; he'd left his charger at Jasmine's. He shoved the phone back.

By the time he went through all the red tape required to retrieve his truck, it was early afternoon. When he got to her place, Chad hesitated. He still had a key, but he didn't think it was right to use it under the circumstances, so he knocked on the door. No answer. He knocked louder. It was too early for her to be at work and her car was in the small lot.

He was turning away when a muffled scream out back chilled his blood. He leaped down the stairs in two strides. He ran behind the building in time to see Jasmine being forced toward a sedan with darkened windows, its engine running. The guy who dragged her had a hand over her mouth. He couldn't see the face under a hoodie but he recognized that burly frame. Montoya!

Montoya was too busy trying to subdue a struggling Jasmine to see him. She kicked backward with her booted foot and Montoya winced but only tightened his grip. Chad felt for the knife in his boot before he realized he hadn't sheathed it after getting his stuff back at the station. His pistol was in the truck, yet he only had seconds to act. Montoya had brutally dragged Jasmine close enough to the car to open the trunk with his clicker. He tossed her inside, and the one scream she had time for before he closed the trunk was muffled as he shut the lid. He moved toward the driver's door but he never made it.

In a linebacker-style blitz, Chad tackled him.

They went down, Montoya on the bottom, but he'd obviously had more back-alley fights than Chad. And he still had a knife. He bared it along with gritted teeth. A diamond in one front tooth sparkled in the sunlight as he clenched the eight-inch blade's handle and jabbed upward toward Chad's ribs.

Chad saw it coming and jackknifed sideways, but the knife still passed so close it snagged his shirt. It was so sharp the chambray work shirt shredded in a jagged tear, but the blade was slowed for a second, and that was all Chad needed. Rearing back, Chad raised his fist and brought it down with all his fury and grief right into Montoya's grimace. Chad felt his fingers slice open from the diamond as his fist raked across, but he didn't care because he also felt Montoya's front teeth go back into his mouth at the impact of the blow.

Howling, Montoya released the knife and it clattered to the asphalt. He held his arms up to protect himself, squirming in pain from his broken teeth, but Chad had no mercy. He punched again, this time at Montoya's nose. Montoya tried to throw back a punch, but his blow was upward and he was in so much pain, his fist didn't have much impact on Chad's lean jaw. Barely feeling it, Chad punched again, feeling the satisfying crunch of bone. Montoya went limp.

Hearing Jasmine's muffled screams and bangs on the inside of the trunk, Chad jerked free a clothesline someone had strung from the side fence and used it to hogtie the limp gangbanger. Then he felt in Montoya's pants for the keys, and clicked open the trunk.

Jasmine sat up, squinting, both fists raised, but then she saw who it was and sank back. "Thank God. You're out."

He helped her onto the pavement. "Yeah. Someone paid my bail, still don't know who. You all right?"

"I'm OK. He didn't have time to do much damage." She opened her mouth as if to add something, but closed it when she saw Montoya, barely recognizable with all the blood on his face. He was still out. She smiled a bit when she saw the neat way he was trussed, like a steer at a rodeo.

"He say anything about Kinnard?" Chad asked.

"No, but I'm pretty sure Thomas sent him after me. I'm a liability now. So is Mary. We're probably the only ones who know how deeply he's involved in oil and gas deals. He's even discussed them with us."

He started to ask the obvious question—Who is Mary?—but she was still frazzled from her ordeal and he had to get to a phone and call Riley. Kicking the knife well out of Montoya's reach, he followed her up the stairs and picked up her landline. She went into her room, and he heard the water running.

While he waited for Riley to answer, he looked around. Everything was neat as a pin. It usually was, but this time things looked . . . different. The books were gone, as were the bronzes and the map. He was surprised to see a small safe, open and empty. He wondered what she had of such value as to need one, but then Riley's voice mail came on.

He left a message on Riley's cell phone about Montoya and then called the main station number, explaining he needed a medic and arresting officers dispatched ASAP to Jasmine's address. He hung up, going toward her room. "Jasmine, I have to go back out and stay with Montoya. I called the police . . ." He trailed off in shock as he looked around her room. She had boxes and suitcases everywhere. And there, on top of the bed, was an open satchel with stacks of cash on top.

He looked from the cash back to her. "Going somewhere?" He glanced at all the baggage. "Or should I say, are you running somewhere? Was that little scene with Montoya for my benefit? You've been working with Kinnard all along, haven't you?"

A dull, angry flush colored her cheeks. "You have no right to say that to me after I paid your bail."

He blinked. "Why would you do that?" He glanced back at the banded piles of hundreds. "And where would you get that kind of cash?"

An angry zip was his only answer as she closed her satchel and slipped the strap over her shoulder. "Think what you damn well please. You always do anyway."

Chad pushed back his hat, wishing he'd been more tactful. Now she was pissed and would never agree to go to Texas with him. He was debating what to do about that when a knock came at the door.

Jasmine stalked past him and opened it. She stepped back. "Hi, Riley."

Riley glanced between the two of them, sensing the tension in the air, but he only looked at Chad. "You got Montoya?"

Chad led him down the back steps. Montoya was groggy but awake enough to struggle at his bonds. However, Chad had tied him securely, wrists lashed behind him to his ankles.

Riley's lips quirked as he saw Chad's handiwork, but he only said, "Good job, but did you have to break his nose?"

"Yes. He's lucky that's all I did. He was trying to kidnap Jasmine."

"For the second time."

Chad tilted his head as he weighed that information. "So she says. How do you know she wasn't in that rig with Trey because Kinnard told her to watch him? She has been one gorgeous red herring from day one."

Riley stared at him as several cops hustled Montoya away, one reading him his rights as he went. "How you could think so badly of her after she risked her life to help you is beyond me. Not to mention paid your bail and negotiated terms with the DA that allow you to leave so you don't get into more trouble. Also, did you know she got the incorporation papers showing Kinnard's signature as principal of the Del Mar Corporation? That was enough for the DA with all the evidence the task force has been accumulating against the corporation. We've requested a warrant to bring Kinnard back for questioning. He flew to Amarillo this morning. Unfortunately, we didn't find the booking in time to stop him."

For once, Chad was speechless, but typically, not for long. "That's all great, glad she's helped, but answer me this—if she's so innocent, why is she all packed and ready to run the minute Kinnard leaves town?"

Before he could voice the retort obviously trembling on his tongue, Riley had to answer his cell phone. "Yes, Captain Barnes, we got Montoya." He stepped away from Chad to talk privately.

Chad was relieved at the "we" as he walked back up the steps. Barnes had zero tolerance for Chad's methods, and Chad knew the man considered him more of a vigilante than a lawman. So the more Riley took credit, the better. He just hoped they could somehow put enough pressure on Montoya to make him spill his guts.

Only problem was, if they'd issued a warrant to bring Kinnard back to California, he had very little time to build a Texas case.

When he got upstairs, he saw Jasmine had lugged several suitcases to the front steps. With his automatic Texas male courtesy, he took a heavy box from her arms and set it out on the front stoop. "I'm happy to give you a ride; I'll even move your stuff for you in my truck. You going to a new, bigger place?" He removed her key from his pocket and handed it to her.

Still inside shoving boxes toward the door, she tossed it down on the sofa table.

"I rented this place furnished, so I don't have that much to move. I'm sure you have paperwork to fill out, so go on. You don't owe me anything for the bail. Consider it a gift and my way of expressing my regret at what happened to Trey." When his expression darkened, she finished curtly, "As long as you make your trial date, I'll get it back anyway." She turned toward her bedroom but not before he saw suspicious moisture in her eyes.

"Jasmine, Riley told me you helped negotiate with the DA for my release to Texas—"

"So? I know you need to get back to Texas with Trey."

"And he said you got the Del Mar incorporation papers? How'd you pull that off? We've had agents in five states looking for them—"

"Does Thomas's attorney have the hots for them? As you never let me forget, men find me desirable." She tilted her chin up at him, daring him to judge. "And if I was still helping Thomas, why on earth would I hand over the most incriminating document against him?"

Good question. His gut roiled so much he had to burp or vomit. He'd never been so confused in his entire life. She'd done a lot to help him, but the image of Trey, bloodied and limp, would not leave him. At this point he didn't know what to believe.

Even if she'd switched tactics after he'd met her, by her own admission she was a master man-shark, and she'd done all she could to lure his brother away from home. Had she not done that, Trey would still be cursing him in Texas. Still, there was only one way to prove her loyalties . . . "Then come with me."

"To Texas?"

He nodded.

"Why?"

He hesitated, but there had been enough lies between them, even if most of them had been on her side. "To turn evidence against Kinnard so we can try him there, not here. They finally tracked him down on a flight to Amarillo. He went out to finish his land deal, and then I'd bet Chester he's gonna flee. So we don't have much time. "

"Then what?"

For an instant, atypically for him, the *could be* overcame the *was* . . . happy thoughts drifted through his mind. The two of them riding together to the canyon rim, stark against the gray sky, like Trey's painting, except he wouldn't be alone anymore. Jasmine, her belly rounded with his child, cooking not for him but with him, in the homestead's old-fashioned kitchen, their wedding bands shiny and new. It's what Trey would want for him. It's what he'd glimpsed for a day when she took care of him after his concussion.

He brought himself back to her guarded face. Fairy tales were not his stock in trade. He was a realist. He remembered her sinuous grace and sexual power writhing around that pole at the club, and then gyrating with wild abandon on him in that huge easy chair he was trying to avoid looking at now. The big box of condoms. This woman was not wife-and-mother material, at least not for someone as conservative as a Texas Ranger. As his daddy had, and his granddaddy before him, he was expected to project good morals as an example to Texans, both those in the law enforcement profession and outside of it.

With a bitter little smile at his long silence, she turned away. "I get your drift. Good-bye, cowboy. Hope you love those gray days. You'll build a strong case without my cooperation; you're good at that."

Chad took two long strides and blocked her path. "Please, Jasmine, I'm sorry. I don't know what's going on with you and Kinnard, truly. Maybe you are innocent as you say. I know you've done a lot to atone for anything you might have done in the past—"

"Atone?" Her voice rose in pitch, and he saw the flush of anger build in her cheeks again, banishing the lingering sadness in her eyes.

He rushed on. "I only know that without your help it will be much harder for me to get enough evidence to convict him."

"And that's the only reason you want me to go with you?"

It was his turn to flush. How did he answer that? He wasn't sure of anything else, but he wanted her; and if they'd met under other circumstances and she'd had a real job, he'd probably be on bended knee before her now. But he couldn't take her to Texas on a lie. They'd met that way, and it had been disastrous. "For now, yes."

The satchel slipped off her shoulder, but she didn't seem to feel it. "And where would I stay?"

"The department has a fund for witnesses in major cases, and I'm sure the Feds would pay for a hotel—"

She turned away, scooping up her bag. "Not interested. If you need me to testify at a later date, depending on the circumstances I'll consider it. However, at this point the only compelling evidence against Kinnard is here in California, so that seems unlikely."

No shit, Sherlock. She knew the legalities, and he had to respect her for that. "Not if he's apprehended in Texas and you help us build a case."

"I'll leave my new contact information with Riley. Good-bye, Chad. Please go."

He tried to see her face, but she'd turned away, marched into her room and closed the door on him, literally shutting him out.

* * *

In a quieter Amarillo, Mary folded her legs primly in the chair next to the captain's desk as Sinclair continued to drill her. "I'm within my rights as a geologist to conduct studies on Trey's half of the land—"

"Yes, well, the Del Mar contract terms are questionable, at best," Sinclair shot back. "The FBI task force investigating land swindles here in the Panhandle, with our office's cooperation, subpoenaed the title company for a copy of the contract Trey signed. It was almost identical to several this Del Mar Corporation finagled over the last year with other landowners. They've all agreed on one thing: None have seen a dime in revenue despite the fact that pumpjacks are moving up and down like seesaws. Seems this Del Mar Corporation negotiates lower royalty rates than industry norms, and when they kick in it's with huge exemptions. The contract even includes some working interest when it should be land royalty straight off the top. Working interests are often used to dilute investment returns, as I'm sure you know, but they're very difficult to fight in court."

Mary leaned forward. "Look, I didn't come here to debate contract law with you. I sent home all the rig crew working the Foster parcel yesterday. You can decide later if you want to charge me. For now I'd remind you I came forward voluntarily because of my concern for Trey Foster's safety. Do you want to indict Thomas Kinnard for land fraud or don't you?"

Sinclair rubbed his somewhat puffy but still keen blue eyes. Mary realized he looked tired and wondered what else he was juggling.

"Of course. Have you ever met Chad Foster, Trey's brother?"

Mary shook her head. "No, but Trey's talked about him."

"Is there another redhead in California who looks like you that perhaps Kinnard introduced Chad to?"

Oh . . . That was it. Now everything made sense. Mary leaned back in her chair, closing her eyes briefly. Kinnard had outfoxed them all by using Jasmine as her surrogate to keep Chad away from the homestead. She'd sensed the ruse, which was why she'd warned Jasmine to get rid of the tattoo. Mary opened her eyes and looked squarely at Sinclair. "Yes. Jasmine Routh. Let me guess. This Chad Foster is mad at Jasmine, thinking she's me."

The rueful look on his face was answer enough.

Mary's concern for Trey only deepened. She'd known Kinnard would go to almost any length to complete his land deal, but with Chad Foster out there on his tail, Kinnard would be doubly dangerous if he felt cornered. Mary's eyes stung with tears, but she managed to stay calm. "Can you call Chad and see if he's had any luck finding Trey? And maybe set him straight about me and Jasmine? She's a good friend of mine, but she's done nothing wrong."

"We've tried him half the day, but now his phone is going straight to voice mail." Sinclair looked at his desk, at a document with a Beverly Hills Police Department seal. "I do have another number to try. Would you excuse me for a moment?" He ushered her to the waiting room, and then used his landline to dial Riley's cell number.

In Beverly Hills, Chad was downstairs talking to Riley. At Jasmine's cold dismissal, he'd collected the few things he'd left at her place, including his phone charger, but he hadn't had time to charge his phone. He made a mental note to call Sinclair on a pay phone. He had to let his boss know Trey was gone, and that he was trying to bring their best witness back with him. "She's not cooperating."

"Funny, she's very cooperative with me."

Chad scowled. "Horseshit, Riley. She's running away and you're not doing a damn thing to stop her."

"Why should I? She's done nothing illegal. In fact she's been a big help to the department." Riley's cell phone rang. He glanced at the caller ID but stuck the phone back in his pocket with a slight smile as he looked at Chad. "Have you called in to Sinclair lately?"

"My phone's dead and Jasmine kicked me out, so I haven't been able to charge it. I have to get to the hospital to pick up Trey's body anyway. Then I'm packing Chester up and heading out. I'll call Sinclair on a pay phone before I go. I want to get to Amarillo to help apprehend the son of a bitch. I'll be in touch." Chad turned on his heel, ignoring Riley's "Wait!"

As his dually rumbled away, Riley sighed and called Sinclair back. He hated being the bearer of bad news, but the Rangers had to know Trey was dead and Kinnard was in Amarillo by now. Not to mention that their golden boy was acting downright loco, as they'd say in Texas . . .

In Amarillo, Sinclair frowned as he listened to Riley. The news about Trey was bad enough, but now he learned that one of the best Rangers he'd ever worked with had gone nuts and destroyed a parking officer's mini vehicle. For Chad to be that angry, he had to be at the end of his rope. Sinclair knew how much he'd loved his brother. "And this Jasmine is the girl he's been staying with?" He listened. "She paid his bail and even negotiated permission for him to leave the state and he's still blaming her? Typical balls-to-the-wall MO for him. Can't blame her for not wanting to come with him under the circumstances. You sure you can't reach him?"

He listened, nodding. "Okay, as soon as he gets back to the equestrian center, be sure he calls me and I'll set him straight about her. We'll expect him here in the next twenty-four hours or so. Knowing him, he'll drive straight through." Sinclair hesitated and then said sincerely, "Thanks, Riley. I've never worked with your department before, but I can't thank you enough for your leniency and cooperation toward a fellow officer. All the good things I've heard over the years about the Beverly Hills Police Department are obviously true. I'm sure Foster will be thanking you, too, when he learns the whole truth. Keep me apprised. I'll start a team to check out all the hotels in Amarillo. We'll find Kinnard. We may have to flip a coin over who gets to try the bastard. Trey might have been killed there, but he was a Texan through and through, and I know how Chad will feel about this." Sinclair hung up.

He leaned his lean hips on his desk, debating what to do now. He went outside his office to the next room and told Corey what was going on, putting him in charge of the team that would search for Kinnard. Then he went to the waiting room to see Mary. What he was going to propose was dangerous, but she'd offered to help and this was the best way.

In Burbank, Chad barely took time to toss his things, willy-nilly, into the back of his truck, though he was more careful with Chester.

He had to be because the stallion was sharing his trailer with a long wooden box. His entire packing took about fifteen minutes, and then he was on his way. Because he was in a hurry and it was rush hour, he took a few side streets to avoid a freeway, unaware an unmarked car, lights flashing, pulled into the equestrian center lot five minutes after he departed. Riley jumped out.

But when Chad wound his way past the blockage and reached the intersection with I-10 that split between east and west, he hesitated. He'd wanted to go east and keep going east since he got here, but somehow the dually stopped all on its own, engine rumbling. It wasn't that far to Jasmine's. The primitive urge to take her with him was overwhelming. He tried to picture Kinnard before a Texas jury, but the images of her laughing, making love to him on soft prairie grass, were stronger. She was a Texas girl, and he'd sensed her longing for the land of her birth, no matter what she said.

No matter the right or wrong of it, no matter how he'd met her, no matter if she'd been Kinnard's patsy or his accomplice, he wanted her. No, beyond that, he needed her. She made him laugh, she made him cry, but most of all, she colored his gray days with a brilliant palette of possibility. Trey had recognized it immediately and given his blessing.

If he left her now, they might never see one another again.

That disembodied hand appeared in his vision again. It turned the truck west, toward Beverly Hills.

CHAPTER 18

In Amarillo, Sinclair eyed Mary's calm face, wondering how to tell her about Trey. He hated this part of the job. Delaying, he said, "So you think Kinnard will go out to the drilling rig?"

"Yes, and he'll be angry with me for ending the drilling."

"Angry enough to let something slip?"

"Maybe. He's always talked to both me and Jasmine about his deals, but why are you asking me this now? I told you, we need to contact the California Highway Patrol and get them to look for Trey!"

Sinclair sighed and moved in front of her to take her hands and pull her to her feet.

She started to jerk away, shocked at his unexpected move, but then she went very still as her big blue eyes fixed on his sorrowful expression. "It's Trey, isn't it?"

"I'm so sorry, I just found out. He passed a couple days ago. Chad's bringing him home."

"Oh God, no . . . This is all my fault." Mary covered her face with her hands, her slim shoulders shaking as she wept.

Sinclair patted her shoulder, feeling helpless, but he didn't know her well enough to pull her into his arms. Anyway, nothing he could say or do could possibly make up for the loss. If he'd doubted the depth of her feelings for Trey, he didn't any longer.

When her sobs subsided to sniffles, he offered her a Kleenex from the box on his credenza.

She dabbed her eyes and blew her nose. When she looked at him again, her mellow blue eyes were igneous rocks. "I'll give you any information you want, sign any confession. I want to help catch Thomas. Just tell me what to do."

In Beverly Hills, Chad had to park his rig in front of Jasmine's place, blocking the small lot. He was relieved her car was still there. He pulled the handcuffs from his pocket. He'd gotten them at a security supply store when he'd first arrived, hoping to use them on the men who took Trey, but so far the local police had taken care of the niceties. He certainly didn't want to have to use them on Jasmine, but she was a stubborn woman. She'd already refused to accompany him, but for both professional and personal reasons, his mind was made up.

He walked up the steps and saw the boxes he'd moved earlier, still on her stoop. Thinking he'd help her make the right choice, he carried them down to his truck and put them in the truck bed, wondering what he'd say to coax her into the truck with him.

A short time earlier, inside her place, Jasmine had sat in the chair where they'd made love, wishing she felt some residual warmth. What did she do now? She'd given notice at the club, the gallery had been closed, supposedly for renovations, and her best friend was in Texas already. She'd picked up the latest copy of her transcripts and canceled the few classes she'd begun this semester, intending to transfer her credits when she got back home.

Home . . . That was a word she hadn't used in a long time. Maybe because she always associated home with family, and since she and her father were estranged, she hadn't had one of those in years. Until she'd met Chad. That one day with him at her place had proved Trey's instincts were right. They were good for one another. Compatible in so many ways that mattered. If only Chad could see Mary, he'd realize how wrong he'd been. He'd forgive Jasmine for whatever misguided actions she'd unknowingly taken that might have helped Thomas in his scam. And she'd forgive him for being so judgmental when she'd actually risked her life to collect evidence against her former benefactor.

There was nothing keeping her here. She'd packed everything, hoping, no, determined, to go back to Texas with him. She'd been so sure that after the passion they'd shared, all the evidence he knew she'd collected on Thomas, even paying his bail, Chad would finally soften toward her. He'd realize she deserved at least a fair hearing while they worked on establishing some kind of relationship.

Instead, by his own admission, Chad intended to stick her in a hotel and keep things strictly business. That passionate coupling that had been so meaningful to her had meant no more to him than a lap dance with a happy ending. She'd always be damaged goods to him, even when he realized the truth about Mary. Tears flooded her eyes again, but she angrily wiped them away. She didn't need him. She didn't need anyone. At the age of sixteen, she'd run away from all she knew to a future she was determined to forge herself. And so she had, and so she would, again.

At least the roller coaster ride with Chad had made her see the mistakes she was making in her life.

She'd been increasingly dissatisfied with LA's shallow, frantic lifestyle for a long time. After the way Trey had been brutalized, she truly did want to help catch Thomas, and Chad was right about one thing: She could best do that from Texas. Riley knew how to reach her and had promised to keep her posted on the investigations from both jurisdictions.

Which left only one destination, the same choice she'd made years ago, but in reverse. Jasmine stood, wrapping the long strap of her satchel over her shoulder, and reached for her cell phone to call the airline. She debated calling her father first, but instinctively she knew it would be best to surprise him. She had to see the look on his face when he saw her again, with no time for artifice. Only then would she know if he still loved her.

When the reservation agent came on, she asked, "Can you tell me when your next direct flight to Houston is scheduled?"

After she booked her flight, she went into her room and moved the rest of her luggage into the tiny entry. She'd have to come back for her car, or hire someone to drive it to her because she had to get out of here in case Thomas sent someone else after her. She didn't want to make that long, lonely drive by herself.

When she heard steps outside on the front stairs, she froze. The bat. Where was the bat? She'd turned toward her bedroom when a firm knock came, along with a voice she recognized. "It's Chad, Jasmine. Can we talk? I don't have much time. Chester gets restless if I stop too long."

Just hearing his voice took some of the starch out of her spine. She debated not answering, as it would be even harder to tell him good-bye again, but reluctantly she opened the door, keeping the chain on as she worked to stay expressionless. "What do you want?"

In that endearing way she'd noticed when they first met, he took his hat off and twisted it in his hands, as he did when he was searching for exactly the right thing to say.

"Where are you going, Jasmine?"

"None of your business. Why have you come back?"

"I left something. Can I come in?"

Refusing to unhook the chain, Jasmine looked around at the boxes and empty shelves, stepping back from the door to skeptically peer over her shoulder. "What did you leave?"

The splintering of the door frame as he kicked the door open, unseating the chain, brought her surging forward, but she wasn't quick enough. By the time she tried to press her weight on the door to hold it closed, his strong hands pushed it open, forcing her to stumble backward. At that point she had two choices, the same choices he'd given her almost from the beginning: fight or flight.

She darted behind the couch. "You have no right to do that, especially after I put you up. I would've gotten all my deposit back and now—"

"I'll reimburse you. I don't like leaving things behind."

"You're lying, you didn't leave anything!"

"Yes, I did." He circled the couch. "You."

They played the circle-the-couch dodge game, their tempers soaring with each blocked move. "I'm not going with you!" Jasmine finally screeched, so angry she scratched his reaching hand. "All I am to you is a witness for the prosecution, even after I risked my life to help you find Trey, even after I paid your bail, even after—" She broke off, but when she looked at the leisure chair and back at him, his eyes darkened.

He responded, "How do you think it made me feel to have Trey bless us? That's all the proof I needed of how much he loved you—"

"You idiot, doesn't it occur to you he didn't want you to be alone and thought I might be good for you?" She wanted to tell him, *Please, you don't even have to love me; just admit you were wrong about me. Give me some hope and I'll follow you home where I belong*. But she didn't like his tone or the look on his face. In fact, she so didn't like it, she glanced at the door, wondering if she should run. But she was too late.

He dove over the couch and tackled her, his hand red but not bleeding from the scratches she'd inflicted, knocking both of them to the floor behind the couch. For a moment, his weight pressed her into the carpet and they matched, torso to torso, hips to hips. She felt the immediate reaction at his loins. Everything in her wanted to respond, but she'd lived her life by feeling, and had little to show for it.

It was time to think. She'd done all she knew to make him see her as more than a stripper, with little success. He wasn't ripping her guts apart anymore.

"I'm not going," she said dully, turning her face aside from his smoldering gray eyes, so she didn't see steely resolve melding in the coals.

He pulled a tie-back off one of the curtains. In an incongruous, very gentlemanly way, he gently lifted her head, fanning out her hair—and tied the scrap of material around her head, muffling her mouth.

Then, pulling handcuffs from his back pocket, he cuffed her hands behind her back, latching her in a sitting position to the old-fashioned built-in gas stove. She was so stunned that at first she didn't struggle, but when he began collecting her things to carry them down the stairs, she roused herself enough to kick at the heavy stove. She only hurt her booted toe.

Livid didn't cover the way Jasmine felt. How dare he do this to her? Tears of rage blinded her, but she was buffaloed, as they said in Texas, as helpless as a hobbled heifer. Oh, but wait until she got loose . . .

It didn't take him long to take all her boxes and suitcases downstairs. The satchel, she noted, he'd left for last. He'd seen all the cash on top, so she supposed she should be glad when he uncuffed her and slung the purse around her shoulder. At least he wasn't taking her money, not that she thought he ever would.

Hardly mollified, when he hauled her to her feet, she took a swing at him with her fist. He jerked his head to the side so her fist barely scraped his cheekbone. Even that contact with his bones hurt her enough to make her gasp behind the gag, but he only lifted her over his shoulder as if she were a bag of feed and turned for the stairs.

"You want it the hard way? You got it, babe." He latched one arm around her knees like a vise to hold her still so she couldn't kick. When she pounded on his broad back, he smacked her upturned rear end hard enough to sting. "Be still, or we'll both fall down the steps."

"I don't give a damn as long as it breaks your neck," she mumbled through the gag, but he ignored that, too.

Jasmine heard the horse trailer door open, and the next thing she knew she was inside the trailer, standing on her feet two tie-downs away from Chester. Chad was cuffing her to the railing closest to the door, but she was still too far away to reach the door latch. He tossed her satchel against the side wall.

Breathing as evenly as if he'd taken a stroll, he paused. "You gonna be good? Promise not to scream? I'd prefer not to be arrested when I'm finally dusting this place off my spurs."

Her incandescent green eyes, damp with rage, were all the answer he needed. Using the same rope he used on Chester and his cattle, Chad tied her waist loosely to the tie-down above her head, giving her support for the lurching of the trailer. "I'll let you inside the truck once you've calmed down, but I want to get outside town first."

He briefly checked on Chester. The stallion whuffed at him in a way that seemed to question Chad's behavior, and one mellow brown eye fixed on Jasmine. Chad patted him awkwardly. "I know what I'm doing."

Chester whickered a soft, mocking response to that.

Pausing only to tape fly paper over the rear window, hiding his hog-tied prisoner from any curious eyes, Chad jumped down and closed the gate.

A minute later, they were rumbling away and the only home Jasmine had known for the last six years was receding into the distance. Then they turned the corner, and it was gone. Through the side slits in the trailer, Jasmine saw a lowering afternoon sun burnishing the tall buildings with a promising glow. Jasmine was in no mood to be optimistic. The truck lurched over bad pavement, and Jasmine had to brace her feet. Her boot knocked against something, making a wooden *thunk!*

She looked down for the first time. She choked back a scream. A wooden casket occupied the space she and Chester weren't using. Trey . . .

Tears came then, tears that should have relieved her choked emotions but didn't. She'd made up her mind to go home to Texas, but Chad didn't know that. He had absolutely no right to haul her around literally like cattle. She wasn't sure which was worse, being treated like a harlot or baggage . . . While she fumed, inside the satchel her cell phone buzzed with a new voice mail, but she didn't hear it.

As Chad navigated rush-hour traffic to put as much distance as he could between himself and LA, Riley gave up trying to reach either Jasmine or Chad on their phones. Instead, as they left the equestrian center he'd told the patrolman who was driving to go to Jasmine's place. Riley eyed the door as he hurried up the steps; it looked half open.

When he reached the landing he realized why—the jamb was splintered and at the bottom of the door panel was the imprint of a booted foot. Not exactly gangbanger footwear. Riley's heart sank as he pushed open the door to find a vacant apartment and a door chain on the floor. The by-the-book cop actually used an expletive Captain Barnes would have exhorted against. "Fuck me." He looked around guiltily, wondering if someone had overheard him using the *F* word while he was on duty.

Resigned, Riley pulled out his cell phone and speed dialed the California Highway Patrol. He'd done all he could to keep the stubborn son of a bitch out of jail, but this was too flagrant . . .

At about the same time in Amarillo, Mary stood in her room looking down at her cell phone screen. She had six missed calls from

Thomas and two voice mails. She'd been afraid to call him back because she knew he'd hear the venom in her tone and suspect what she was about to do. Instead, she'd texted him that she'd meet him late tomorrow afternoon at the drill site and explain why it was inactive. She'd had problems with the rig crew, she'd lied, and they needed to come up with a new schedule.

Then she sat at her window and watched the sun go down, feeling the loss of warmth and every hope she'd had for the future go with it. She should head downstairs and get something to eat, but she wasn't hungry.

Sinclair had explained the process to her, but she was still a bit nervous. Wearing the wire wouldn't be hard, but finding just the right words without rousing Thomas's suspicions would be a challenge. He always could talk rings around her, or anyone she knew, for that matter.

But as she stared into the growing dark, she realized she didn't really care if he realized she was wearing a recording device. She looked down at the small pistol she'd purchased soon after arriving in Texas, when she'd realized the deal was coming apart.

"Come on, Thomas, get tough," she whispered into the darkness. She hadn't told Sinclair she had a gun because she knew how he'd react. Still, big shot Texas Ranger or not, he was a typical cop and didn't care if he endangered her as long as he nailed his man. She cooperated because for once her interests were aligned with the law.

Legal or not, one way or another, Thomas Kinnard would pay for killing Trey.

While Mary was vowing retribution, on the I-10 East, Chad pulled onto the shoulder beneath growing shadows. A setting sun peered over sere mountains and lazily whirring Palm Springs wind turbines. It was a Monday, so thankfully traffic was heading out of the Coachella Valley, not in, so eastbound I-10 traffic was light.

Taking a deep breath to steel himself to her fury, Chad unlatched the trailer and peered inside. Jasmine glared at him but looked none the worse for wear. Warily, Chad stepped inside the trailer and gently pulled the gag down from her mouth. It sagged around her neck. "I'm sorry, Jasmine, but you left me no choice. We're outside LA now, if you're ready to come inside the truck."

"You mean go peaceful-like while you bushwhack me?" She kicked his shin.

Wincing, he moved back out of range. "You don't belong in California. You've all but admitted it."

"You have no right to decide where I belong, you redneck Ranger. No, I forget, ex Ranger, you couldn't even do that right. . . . No one's bossed me around since I was sixteen—"

He couldn't help it; he shut her up the way he'd been longing to ever since they rolled around together on her carpet. He kissed her. She stiffened, and for a moment he wondered if he should back up or get a knee in his groin, but she exhaled into his mouth, tasting of peppermints, and sagged against him, kissing him back. He untied her waist, unlatched the cuffs and pulled her into his arms, cuffs and all. It was awkward at first, but she pulled his head down and lifted her wrists behind his head, linking them together literally with bonds of steel. She not only accepted his deepening of their kiss, she welcomed it with an open mouth and shyly inviting tongue.

For an instant, while he could still think, he realized she was no more experienced at French-kissing than he was, Even when they'd made love, their kissing had been elemental, rough, not tender or experienced. A burst of mental elation accented the physical contact. In this way, at least, they could learn together. But then he didn't care about anything except getting closer to her, skin to skin. He tugged her tucked shirt free of the waist of her jeans and inched one hand up her soft, warm abdomen to softer, warmer flesh covered in a scrap of lace. He covered the globe with a tender palm, and then worked a finger inside to stroke the nipple, which tightened instantly under his touch.

She lifted a knee toward his groin, but not to hit. She stroked, slowly and lusciously, at the growing length in his jeans. He groaned into her mouth, removing his hand from under her shirt to cup her head in his hands and tilt her head sideways to better fit her for the deep thrust of his tongue. He'd never known this intimacy before with any woman, feeling the limits of flesh because he couldn't get close enough, reach far enough. He wanted to meld with her, to own her, to keep her forever safe in the embrace of his arms . . . She belonged to him, stripper or not. He'd convince her to quit that soon enough; getting her home to Texas was the first step.

They were both too occupied to notice lights flashing in the growing gloom, but then the rumble of a motorcycle pulled alongside them and stopped. Chad lifted his head, blinking into the twilight in time to see a familiar form approaching the rear of the trailer. His uniform was slightly wrinkled for a change, and when he lifted his helmet visor, Riley O'Connor was as serious as Chad had ever seen him.

Gently, Chad pulled Jasmine's twined arms from around his neck. She blinked into the bright headlight as Chad jumped out of the trailer. "She's fine, Riley. I'd never hurt her."

Riley looked grimly from the ropes dangling on the rail in front of Jasmine, to the gag still loose around her throat and the handcuffs. "Yes, well, you can explain that to the judge. I don't care what she does for a living, she's still from my precinct and kidnapping is somewhat frowned upon in Beverly Hills."

Chad frowned. "You don't have any jurisdiction here, Riley."

"No, but they do." Riley jerked a thumb over his shoulder. Jasmine stepped down to the pavement, using her cuffed hands to remove the gag and toss it to the ground while they watched two California Highway Patrol cruisers stop behind them, lights flashing.

Four patrolmen got out of the vehicles, approaching aggressively. Chad had time for only one pleading look at Jasmine. He dropped the cuff key into Jasmine's shirt pocket before he was spread-eagled against the cab of his truck while they frisked him.

For a moment, a pleased smile flickered about Jasmine's lips as she watched him get his comeuppance, until one of the patrolmen gibed at Chad, "You'll be real popular in lock up, Ranger Roy. Your first felony?"

Her smile faded. She exchanged a glance with Riley. He looked away, shrugging as if to say it was out of his hands.

Chad didn't help matters as they let him turn around so they could cuff him. He sneered at the patrolman approaching with cuffs and shot back, "At least I don't have to wear those plug-ugly hats."

They were a bit rougher than necessary as one cop held Chad's arms while the other one began placing cuffs around his wrists.

A distinctive metallic click sounded. All five cops looked over at Jasmine.

Her own cuffs dangled open while she held up the key so it shone in Riley's headlight. "You've got it all wrong, guys. You can't kidnap a willing victim." She beamed that slow, sensual, stripper stage smile at Chad. "Told you you'd like the handcuffs, darling. Just wait until we try the leather halter . . ." The very tip of her tongue rimmed her lips.

Openmouthed, all six men stared at her. Including Chad.

For the moment, Jasmine was the only one capable of movement, it seemed. She twisted out of her cuffs, sticking them in her back pocket, and then with a *May I?* look at the cop holding the still open cuffs on Chad, she pulled them off his wrists and returned them. His mouth still agape and eyes wide, the patrolman limply accepted them.

Jasmine pushed Chad toward the truck. "We've wasted enough taxpayer dollars for one day." Coming back to life, Chad for once obeyed and swung up in the cab, still watching her through the window, wide-eyed, as if he were viewing a play.

Jasmine turned back toward the patrolmen. "I'm not a kidnap victim, gentlemen. If you look, you'll see my bags in the back of the truck. And I think Riley will confirm we were kissing when he drove up." She looked inquiringly at Riley.

He collected his wits and gave a reluctant nod somewhat spoiled by a glare at Chad. He looked back at Jasmine with an *I know what you're doing* scowl, but she only smiled seductively and strolled toward the passenger side of the truck. As she rounded the hood, she paused.

"Thanks so much for the concern, guys, but as you can see, I'm not spindled, folded, or mutilated. I'm here of my own free will. Riley, I'll be in touch." And she got into the truck.

"Can I go?" Chad asked through his rolled-down window.

Shaking his head as if he suspected he'd been snookered, the patrolman shrugged. "Go."

And the dually rumbled away. The minute they were out of view, Jasmine took the cuffs out of her back pocket and tossed them into the rear seat hard enough to gouge the fabric. "That's about the sixth time you owe me, asshole, for saving your butt from the fire."

As he merged with eastbound traffic, Chad glanced at her with a very masculine smile. "True. But I'm more intrigued by something you said."

When she scowled at him, her sensual mouth now set mulishly, he teased, "When can we try out this leather halter?"

CHAPTER 19

Early the next afternoon, at the DPS office in Amarillo, Mary stood still while Sinclair taped the tiny transmitter to her collarbone beneath her undershirt. "These things used to be so bulky it was hard to disguise them, but not anymore."

Corey went into Sinclair's office, shut the door, and radioed to Mary, "Testing, testing, can you hear me, Mary?"

The wireless listening bud in Mary's ear was so tiny it couldn't be seen through her lush red hair, but she nodded and said back, bending her head slightly toward the transmitter under her shirt, "Loud and clear. You can hear me?"

"Copy that," Corey agreed. He came back out of the office and gave her a thumbs-up.

Sinclair helped Mary button her shirt over the transmitter, and then walked around her, eyeing her critically. "Can't see a thing. But don't bend your head when you talk— it's not necessary and it might alert him. This is the latest hardware. We got it from the Defense Department." He stopped in front of her and put his hands lightly on her shoulders. "Are you sure you want to do this? It's not too late to back out. We'll find another way to convict him. The Beverly Hills Police Department and the California Highway Patrol are on the case, too. He has nowhere to run."

"You don't know Thomas. He's like a rat. He can squeeze himself into the most improbable places and lie low until the rest of us have given up. Then he'll come out and rule the world." Mary shrugged away from Sinclair's light grip, her voice dull. "I know him and I think I can get him to brag about what he's done to tie up all the mineral rights he needed for the Dorado field. Still, he never would have gotten this far if I hadn't caved to his persuasions. Trey would still be alive."

"You don't know that. No one made Trey sign that contract. You weren't even there, from what I understand." Sinclair's bright blue gaze exchanged a worried look with Corey, and then he said lightly, "But just in case, one of us will follow you at a distance, no more than a half mile away. All you need to do is ask for help, and we'll be there."

"Have you reached Chad Foster yet?"

Sinclair sighed. "No, and he hasn't called in, but he should be back any time if he drove straight through. Riley O'Connor gave me an update." Sinclair chuckled. "I guess redheads really do live up to their reputation."

The dullness sharpened in her eyes. "Jasmine's with him?"

Sinclair nodded. "Sounds like Chad was determined to get his woman, one way or the other, and almost got himself arrested, but she bailed him out. For the second time. According to Riley she paid twenty-five thousand in bail money to get him out of the lockup after he crunched a parking attendant's car with his truck."

Mary smiled sadly. "Sounds like Jasmine. Has anyone told Chad about me?"

"Her phone's going to voice mail, too. They haven't called in because we haven't been in communication with them since they left California." Sinclair's smile faded. "Trust me, Chad will be set straight, and soon. I don't care what his state of mind is since he lost Trey. There's no excuse for this behavior in a Texas Ranger. Even if I do reassign him, he may be on probation for a while."

At that moment, Chad was passing through the desert that stretched between New Mexico and Texas. He'd driven straight through and he was dead tired. He hadn't trusted Jasmine behind the wheel while he slept. His state of mind was, at best, chaotic.

Jasmine had barely said a word since they'd left Palm Springs. He'd tried to tell her about his land, why he loved it so. She'd listened, nodding, but didn't offer any encouragement when he tried to draw her in. Around Phoenix he switched tactics, talking about the new Texas that was moving away from a ranching, oil, and gas economy to high-tech endeavors. "I don't know if you track what's going on in Texas in the news, but people and businesses are moving to Texas on a daily basis, many of them, frankly, coming from California. Dallas is a telecom hub, Austin is gaining fame as Silicon Hills, and even in West Texas, Midland is close to nabbing a private space exploration company."

He'd glanced at her, hoping to see some residual pride in her home state. He was desperate to keep her there, even after all this was over.

She yawned. "What are you, head of the Texas tourism bureau? Maybe I'd be a bit more enthusiastic if I'd come with you willingly. Why don't you let me get my cell phone and maybe we can talk."

He smiled wryly. "I'd rather make it across the state line at least, before you bring in the cavalry."

"Still don't trust me, huh? If I wanted you arrested, all I had to do back in Palm Springs was keep quiet instead of defending you."

Chad frowned. True enough. Dammit, would he ever understand this infuriating woman? If she'd decided to cooperate, why the cold shoulder now? He cocked his head as he eyed her from his side of the cab.

A satisfied little smile curved her lips. "You remind me of Chester when you look at me with your head cocked like that. I think he understands me better than you do."

He took a deep breath to quell the retort he longed to make. He'd swerved a bit out of his lane during their exchange, and by the time he'd rectified that, she'd leaned her head on the window, moved as far away from him as she could get, and nodded off.

Finally, right after they crossed the Texas border, her silence took its toll on him. He was about to fall asleep despite his usual tricks to stay alert. After a full two days without sleep, he knew he needed at least a nap if he was to be clearheaded enough to appeal his case to Sinclair and explain why he'd brought back an unwilling but key witness—without getting himself arrested. Sinclair wasn't by-the-book like Riley, but he was very strict with his men when it came to actually breaking the law.

He pulled off the road into a cutout for a bank of mail boxes, looking around carefully. There was nowhere for her to run, but just in case, he locked the cabin doors and put her door lock on driver control.

"I have to sleep," he said curtly when she gave him an inquiring look. He lifted the moveable console between them and sprawled his long legs over the floorboard into her part of the truck. He ignored her protest, arranged himself as comfortably as he could against the driver-side door, tipped his hat over his face, and was asleep within seconds.

Jasmine had been mostly pretending to sleep to avoid talking to him, but his deep, even breathing and occasional little snore told her it was safe to study him. Gently, she removed his hat, which was about to fall in his lap anyway.

In sleep, all that arrogant Texan was dormant. He was still not handsome, but so endearingly male and much younger looking. With all the angular planes of his face relaxed, he was somehow harmless. Safe. And since she'd never actually slept with him, despite her residual anger at his snatch and grab, the urge to curl against him was overpowering. It might be her one and only chance to experience that unique bonding experience.

Carefully, so as not to awaken him, she draped herself over his chest, letting her legs dangle down next to his so she didn't have her full weight on him. Turning her cheek against the strong beat of his heart, she took a deep breath of his scent. That too was purely male, a mix of sweat, leather, and spicy deodorant, which he'd used over the last few days to keep himself reasonably decent since he'd had no way to shower.

With the scent of Chad lulling her, and the steady, reliable thrum of his heart, she slept.

A couple of hours later, Chad started awake. For an instant he panicked because he felt constrained by a warm weight against him.

Then he realized it was Jasmine, curled against him like the sex kitten he'd always likened her to. His legs were asleep, but for a long moment he stayed still, drinking her in.

Her glorious red mane was tousled and her makeup had long since rubbed away. A smudge of mascara darkened one eyelid, but to him, she was beautiful. She'd always be beautiful, even when gray fingered her hair and wrinkles fanned out from those mysterious green eyes. . . .

Her eyes fluttered open before he had time to shield his thoughts. She blinked up at him, the lucent green going dark as her pupils expanded.

He tried a tentative smile, and for an instant, she smiled back. No artifice, no sex kitten, just the happy smile of a woman glad to be in his arms. He pulled her closer, bending his head, but her shirt had loosened and he could glimpse the tattoo. It had begun to fade, but he couldn't hide the visceral kick to his gut as he stared at the symbol of everything that kept them apart.

She looked where he looked. Then the moment was gone. She reached over him. There was a click and then she'd scrambled back to her side of the truck, her face averted.

He opened his mouth to apologize, but she was already out the door and rounding the truck. He knew she was going for her cell phone and this time he didn't try to stop her. He got out of the truck and trailed her to the rear of the trailer, where she'd shouldered her satchel and was untethering Chester. She led the stallion out of the trailer and began walking him up and down. After he'd loosened his limbs a bit, she gave him an oat protein bar she pulled from her capacious bag.

Chad's stomach rumbled. "You got another one of those?"

She ignored him, giving Chester a second bar and cooing to him.

Chad felt like an idiot being jealous of a horse, but he complained, "You treat him better than you do me."

"He's nicer than you. And he smells better, too."

While she was occupied with Chester, Chad surreptitiously smelled each of his armpits. Rank. Embarrassed, he stepped up into the trailer to check on the ice in the coffin where Trey lay. They'd put it in insulated bags so it was still pretty solid, but he knew he had to cover the rest of the distance without stopping. For an instant, he looked down at his brother's peaceful face. Tears burned his eyes, and the need for retribution ate at him like acid. He was glad he'd kidnapped Jasmine. Even if she proved to be uninvolved in Kinnard's scheme, she couldn't deny the fact that she was the reason Trey had left Texas.

But the volatile emotions only distracted him and he was about to need all his focus. So he gently shut the coffin lid, spread Chester's horse blankets on top to further protect the ice, and turned back outside.

After allowing Chester about fifteen minutes to crop at the grass, Chad took the lead from Jasmine and led his horse back toward the trailer. Chester planted his feet, snorting.

Chad whacked his rear end. "Up, boy. You know the drill." Chester stamped a rear foot, narrowly missing Chad's boot. He stayed put.

Jasmine took the lead from Chad, patted Chester's neck and whispered into his ear. His ear flickered. He gave a soft whicker and obediently walked right into the trailer. Ignoring Chad, she tied him down, patting him a last time.

Furious, Chad stomped back to the driver's seat and fired up the engine. Damn the woman. Whether directly or indirectly, she'd invaded every aspect of his life: his career, his land, his family, and now she wanted his horse, too?

Jasmine was barely settled, with her belt buckled, before he gunned back onto the highway so fast gravel spit from the rear tires.

"Careful, you'll make him stumble!" Jasmine chided him.

"Woman, if you'd worry a little less about my horse and more about what you're going to say to my boss, we'd both be better off."

"You can't wait to get rid of me, can you?" She turned her head to look out at the barren desert, but not before he saw the beginning of a tear in her eye.

Feeling guilty, he shut up, but hell, she riled him. Physically, emotionally, even spiritually when he awoke to find her nestled against him. One minute she spat at him like a wildcat, and the next she was curled against him with utter contentment. He tipped his hat back to rub his aching forehead.

Ignoring him again, she pulled her cell phone out of her bag and hit the voice mail button. She listened, her face going even grimmer, if possible.

He glanced at her. "Bad news?"

She clicked off after several messages. "Riley was checking on me. And I had a message from your boss. Ross Sinclair."

Chad stiffened. "What did he say?"

"He said if I'm with you to please have you call in ASAP."

"Can I borrow your phone? Mine's dead, has been since I left your place and I haven't been anywhere to charge it."

She offered it without another word. As he listened to Sinclair's office phone ring, Chad tried to marshal the right words. He was half relieved when he got Sinclair's voice mail. "Captain, I'm only a few hours out. I have to stop at the homestead to deliver Trey's body and get Chester into his pasture, but then I'll come straight to the office. I have with me the, ah, witness I told you about. I think with a little persuasion she'll agree to testify against Kinnard if we can catch him. See you soon. I'll fill in all the details then." He handed the phone back to Jasmine, surprised when she turned it off.

"The battery's almost dead," she said. "I'll call Riley later."

Chad let it lie, though he wondered if there was more on that phone message than she was telling him.

In Amarillo, Sinclair listened to his voice mail less than thirty minutes later. As soon as he heard Chad's message, he tried his cell. Straight to voice mail again. Then he tried Jasmine's number. Likewise.

Irritably, Sinclair dropped his cell phone in his pocket and checked his watch. Mary's meeting with Kinnard was in a few hours. Sinclair badly wanted to see Chad's face the first time he laid eyes on her, but if he didn't hurry, she'd already be off on her mission. Sinclair still felt uneasy about using her like this, despite her insistence, and so he made an unusual but typically decisive decision. Going to the weapons storage compartment, he unlocked it with his personal key and pulled out a bulletproof vest and pistol, along with a shotgun, just in case.

* * *

As they approached the red canyons of home, silence ruled in the truck as it had for a long time. Chad glanced for the umpteenth time at Jasmine. She still sat as far away from him as she could, buffing her nails, which should have been worn down to nubs by now.

He knew if he was to make peace with her before all the crap hit the fan, it had to be now. Tomorrow would either dawn a new day for them or be the end of any hope of a relationship. He hesitated, the words burning in the back of his throat, especially with Trey's dead body in the back, but the softer side of him, instilled by his loving mother, pleaded with him. She'd never wanted either of them to be alone, and she would not have been judgmental about Jasmine, as their father would have. Most compelling, Trey had certainly given his blessing, almost literally with his last breath. *I love the scent of jasmine.* His words whispered in Chad's memory. *I love the scent of Jasmine, too, little brother*, Chad whispered back to him in his head.

As the colorful red and purple strata near Palo Duro Canyon came into view, Chad's joy at being back where he belonged made the crow he had to eat a bit tastier. He took a deep breath. The words came out much easier than he would have expected. "Ignore me all you want, but it's reckoning time. For both of us."

She stiffened slightly but still didn't look at him. The buffing went faster.

"Tomorrow you'll either be in custody or staying in Amarillo's nicest hotel, courtesy of the Feds and the Texas Rangers. I'm sorry I had to bring you back this way, but with a little time, I think you'll see you belong here, just like I do."

The buffing stopped, but she still didn't look at him.

Chad burst out, "If you hate my guts, why did you help me so many times?"

She spoke, her tone icy. "You're right about one thing. It's reckoning time between us. We have a word for it in Texas. Comeuppance. You're about to get yours, cowboy."

"Jasmine, I . . . that is . . . goddammit, you keep me addlepated or horny as hell. I can barely think when I'm around you. But this much I know . . ." He trailed off, turning into the narrow caliche road that led to the homestead. He stayed quiet, forcing her to look at him with guarded green eyes. He slowed to a stop, knowing he probably had one chance to get this right. He flung his hat onto the seat, wanting no shade over his face. For once, they'd see each other clearly, no shadows, no guessing.

"You make me sad when I make you cry. You make me happy when I hear you laugh. You make me see possibilities instead of problems when you wake up in my arms." His voice lowered. "You make me see bright colors instead of shades of gray. Just like Trey wanted for me." His tone lowered almost to a whisper. "He gave us his blessing and that means a lot to me."

The nail file went back into her bottomless satchel. Her head bowed, and he couldn't read her face, though her mouth trembled slightly. "So you believe me finally? That I've never been involved with Thomas, Trey wasn't my boyfriend, that I've tried to help find him from the beginning, and that I may be a stripper but I don't live a stripper lifestyle?"

What did he say to that? He couldn't lie to her, but suddenly, the memory of that young woman's voice came to him on the recording he'd taken from Kinnard's phone. He reached into the backseat for his duffel bag, pulled out the recorder, and put the counter on the correct spot. He hit Play.

She listened to the message, her face going white. When he hit Stop, she nodded. "That's Mary. Trey's girlfriend. I didn't play him, or lure him to California. She did. But she also fell in love with him." She reached into her bag and pulled out her cell phone. It beeped, indicating the battery was very low, as she held it to his ear.

Sinclair's angry voice blasted him. "You stupid son of a bitch. Trey's real girlfriend, Mary, is turning state's witness against Kinnard and she's meeting him tomorrow at four p.m. on your land, wearing a wire. I want you back on duty by then. You caused all this mess, so you're going to help mop it up. You've been a-keepin' on a-comin' after the wrong redhead. This Jasmine girl is innocent. According to Mary, she didn't even know what was going on. Call me as soon as you hear this." And he hung up sharply.

The cell phone fell out of Chad's hand to the seat. Jasmine took it and put it back in her bag. Chad knew he should fire up the truck, deliver Chester and Trey to the homestead, only a couple miles away now, and get to the office lickety-split. It was three, so there wasn't much time.

Instead, he slumped against his seat, feeling two inches high. It took all he had to turn and look at Jasmine. He whispered, "I'm sorry."

Jasmine moved her wrinkled blouse aside to bare her tattoo. "And this?"

Chad hesitated, and that was apparently enough to spoil the tentative truce. The memory of that big box of condoms came back to torment him.

Jasmine turned her face away. "Just do what you have to do and get me into a hotel. I'll always be damaged goods to you, and I can't and won't fight that anymore."

Chad opened his mouth, but then, in the distance on the bluff, he saw a familiar unmarked SUV. Sinclair's vehicle, high above his place. Chad knew instantly Sinclair had brought this Mary to the meeting himself.

Which meant one thing—he was concerned for her safety.

"We'll settle this later, but you have to give me a chance to make things right."

"I don't have to do anything." Jasmine buttoned her blouse to her neck.

Chad fired up the truck and covered the last two miles to his place far faster than he should have. On the way, he turned on his police radio to his old frequency, now that he was within range. He doubted if Sinclair would broadcast very freely given how slippery Kinnard was, but it was worth a shot.

Mostly static and then clear, "Foster, you there?"

"Here, Captain." Chad turned up the volume, careening to a stop in the front driveway near the pasture. "Just got home."

"Call me on that gal's phone."

Jasmine handed over her phone without a word. She got out of the truck and walked around, appraising the run-down old white clapboard house.

While he talked to Sinclair on her phone, Jasmine led Chester out of the trailer. The stallion was tired of his confinement and ready to run. He pulled at his lead. She led him to the water trough.

Chad hung up the phone and handed it back to Jasmine. "It went dead while I was talking. You can charge it inside while you wait for me." He ran to the sagging screen door, opened it, and unlocked the heavy handmade oak front door. He peeked inside, turning on lights, and then turned back to Jasmine.

"It's not much, needs some repair, but it's home."

Jasmine looked inside the open door, back to Chad. He saw her ambivalence and knew it would probably take a while for her to forgive him. He couldn't really blame her.

He tried to take her hands, but she pulled away. He said, his drawl exaggerated by his stifled emotions, "Just give me until tomorrow. I promise I'll make things right. If I don't—you can handcuff me to the trailer and I'll confess to kidnapping you. I'll go quietly if they arrest me."

Chad pulled Chester away from the water trough and got the saddle from the storage compartment inside the trailer. He saddled Chester with the easy efficiency of the born horseman. Then he ducked inside his truck, pulling out his pearl-handled pistol and carefully loading it. He strapped on his holster, took a long swig of water, and then mounted Chester. "I'll be back as soon as I can. Make yourself at home." He kneed Chester up the long drive toward the bluff.

Just before the bend took her out of sight, Chad turned in the saddle to look back. Jasmine still stood in the yard, swaying slightly, as if she wasn't sure what to do.

For now he had no time to think about her or all the stupid mistakes he'd made. He reined Chester up onto the bluff. Only then did he see the small rental car parked some distance away, down the slope toward the huge fracking rig that had been erected since he'd left. He pushed his hat back, scowling, because he understood enough about horizontal drilling to realize this rig probably was angled under their homestead, and this half of the land was his, not Trey's.

He glanced at his watch. Three forty-five. Their new accomplice was waiting near the rig. He saw the gleam of red hair exactly the deep auburn shade of Jasmine's and this first physical proof of how wrong he'd been literally made him sick to his stomach. It also increased his fiery rage at Kinnard and his own stupidity. Like a puppet master, the man had used old Foster values against him and Trey. Chad was so glad Sinclair had gruffly reinstated him during their phone call, or more accurately, never accepted his resignation. No wonder his databases still worked and Riley had cooperated in sharing sensitive files with him . . . but they were on his turf now, quite literally.

Sinclair had parked behind a huge pile of boulders so he couldn't be seen from below. He walked up to meet Chad. "About time you got back."

Chad got down. "Fill me in."

Sinclair did, in his usual economical, logical way, finishing with, "And she's never worn a wire before, so I thought I should supervise, stay close enough where I can help if she gets in trouble."

The words were barely out of his mouth before they saw a rugged Jeep cross the dry arroyo separating Foster land from the next parcel over. It was four-wheel drive, and the man driving it knew how to handle the terrain.

"Not taking any chances, is he? Won't even use the road." Sinclair used binoculars to get a good look at his adversary.

Even at this distance, Chad recognized the iron-gray hair and erect posture of the man behind the wheel. His lips curled in contempt and he wasn't even aware his hand had fallen to his pistol butt until Sinclair gave him that minatory look that always pulled Chad back from being overly ambitious.

"No more vigilante justice this time, Foster. You did enough of that with that gal Jasmine, and I can't cover for you anymore. We do this by the book and the bastard will go away for good, given the amount of fraud and Trey's death."

Chad's teeth ground together. But he only nodded. Still, he clutched the pistol butt as if his hand had a will of its own.

Down below, Mary pasted a smile on her face, though her fists clenched at her sides. In her lifetime, she'd had to suck up to so many men she hated that this meeting should have been easy, but it wasn't.

But then she'd never hated anyone as much as she hated Thomas Kinnard.

Still, when he slowly got out of the Jeep, doing a three-sixty to appraise the terrain all around him, she moved forward to hug him. "Glad you made it okay. How was your flight?"

He shrugged. "Have you heard from Jasmine?"

"Not lately. Why, is there anything wrong?"

"Not really, just curious. Why the hell is this rig idle?" He glared from the expensive pile of massive Tinkertoys, back to her.

"My guys walked off the job, a dispute over their wages since they're not union. I had no authority to give them a raise." Her voice hardened a bit. "And as I told you, I've been so worried about Trey, I was not working efficiently anyway. The cell number you gave me was bad, and despite my repeated messages on your cell and at the office, you've never called me with a new one. Why is that?"

Kinnard looked away from her piercing blue eyes. "Trey and I had a falling out. I think he's changed his number because I can't reach him either."

You lying bastard, Mary thought, but she only said coldly, "If that were the case, he'd have called me with the new number. Something has happened to him."

Kinnard glared at her. "Look, your problems with your boyfriend are your own business, but this rig goes back on line by tomorrow morning or you're off the job. You think you're the only geologist around who will take the generous compensation I'm giving you?"

"It won't mean a hell of a lot to me in jail."

Up in the huge boulders, Chad and Sinclair exchanged a concerned look as they listened, a tiny recorder whirring in Sinclair's SUV. As usual, Kinnard was cagey. Nothing he said tied him to Trey's death, but if Mary continued with her needling, he'd suspect her. They could both see she was starting to lose it.

Chad began inching toward the bluff so he could see. The bastard was slippery as owl shit. But then the tenor of the conversation changed . . .

Below, Mary couldn't hide her fury and pain any longer. "I hope you choke on your own platitudes," she snarled. "You think everyone in the world is dumber than you are. Well, Jasmine got a copy of your organization papers as the managing partner of the Del Mar Corporation. She gave it to the Beverly Hills police and they gave copies to the task force investigating your straw companies."

Kinnard's gaze sharpened on her face. "How do you know that?"

Mary stumbled a bit. "Ah, Jasmine told me."

"You just said you haven't talked to her." Kinnard grabbed her arm. "You're hiding something."

Mary brushed him away. "You disgust me. I disgust me, for ever being taken in by you. Where's Trey?" Her voice was so loud it echoed off the cliffs.

Kinnard did a careful look-see again all around him, but when he spotted nothing, he focused back on Mary. His gaze dropped to her blouse, a heavy, black button-up affair rather warm for the weather. He reached for the top button.

Up above, Chad saw Kinnard's move and cursed. He mounted Chester, kneeing the stallion forward.

"Not yet, Foster." But Sinclair had drawn his own pistol. He, too, moved as close as he could to the path down the bluff without revealing himself.

Mary tried to pull away from Kinnard, but that only ripped her blouse, revealing her tattoo, and, slightly above it, the tiny transmitter. Kinnard slapped her. "You bitch!"

Mary doubled up her fist and struck him back, right square in the nose. "You're alone, no one cares about you, and you're going to prison for the rest of your life for having Trey killed!"

But Kinnard wasn't listening anymore. She was furious, but he was still stronger and taller. He grabbed her and shoved her toward his Jeep, where he pulled a roll of duct tape from the glove box. But he'd barely begun wrapping it around her wrists when a sound caught his attention. Horse hooves rattling on loose rock.

Kinnard looked up to see Chad Foster poised against the cloudless blue sky. He was an Old West symbol of retribution in his hat, jeans, and boots. He wore a gun belt and his spirited quarter horse made short work of the slope. Chester was snorting with eagerness. His coat was shiny in the late afternoon sunshine, copper-red like blood. Once they reached the bottom of the bluff they accelerated into a gallop.

And above Chad, a black SUV sped along the bluff, down the road toward the homestead.

Biting off a curse, Kinnard shoved Mary into the passenger side, her hands wrapped with only one circle of duct tape. He ran around the Jeep, got behind the wheel, and hotfooted it back the way he'd come, down the arroyo. He still had a lead, but it was closing fast.

CHAPTER 20

Chad knew every inch of this landscape. Kinnard would come out on a back road that, with the many twists and turns carved between bluffs in the hilly terrain, would eventually exit onto a blacktop that led toward Amarillo. Chad knew Sinclair had already radioed for backup and relayed the license plate number and description of the vehicle, but Kinnard had outwitted a police dragnet once before. It wouldn't surprise Chad if the man had another helicopter waiting, and the border with Mexico wasn't out of range for a big chopper.

Bending low over Chester's neck as the gap between him and the Jeep widened after Kinnard topped the arroyo and made the adjacent road, Chad kicked Chester slightly. That's all it took. The stallion leaped forward like a rocket, though Chad knew he couldn't keep up this speed very long. Chad eyed the hills above, seeing all the canyons and cliffs in his mind's eye. Since he knew where this dirt road came out, he could cut through the hills, if Chester was up to it. It was a ways.

Chad reached down to feel Chester's withers. No foam as of yet, barely any sweat. After two days in the trailer, Chester was well rested. So Chad veered off the road up into the hills.

Inside the Jeep, Mary struggled with the duct tape binding her wrists in front of her. At least Kinnard hadn't had time to securely fasten them behind her back. He'd jerked the receiver off her chest and made her take the device out of her ear, too, smashing them both. But right now she didn't care whether the Rangers were still listening. This had always been very personal to her. Now it was more than that, because she knew her life was in danger.

She looked at him in utter and complete loathing, with plenty left over for herself. "You are a real piece of work. Have you always been a human bulldozer, destroying people's lives, or did you have to work at it?"

He didn't even glance at her as he backhanded her hard enough to jerk her head back and make her mouth bleed. "Shut up, bitch. I trusted you, gave you huge authority on this job, and you've betrayed me and lost the millions you would have made, because of a hormonal rush for a kid who couldn't pour piss out of a boot with the directions on the heel."

This was the closest he'd come to admitting his role in Trey's death. She should have felt some visceral satisfaction that she'd at least forced that much from him, but everywhere she looked, especially here, she was reminded of Trey. Tears smarted behind her eyes again, and the fury drained out of her, leaving her the way she'd been most of her life: desolate and alone. "What are you going to do with me?" she asked dully. He'd left her purse behind, so she couldn't even reach for her gun. She'd failed at this, just as she'd failed Trey.

He had to concentrate on a challenging series of curves as the track followed the arroyo, but finally he answered, "I have a chopper waiting to fly me to Mexico. I'll decide then, though natural redheads are real popular there. Not to mention valuable. They like tattoos down there, too."

The smile he lobbed sideways at her like a grenade normally would have made her cringe and run for cover. This time, she just sank back against the seat, giving up on trying to work free of her bonds, giving up, period.

He eyed her with genuine curiosity. "You know, I've had people killed, though I didn't give the order for Trey's death. He kept fighting me to get away, even though I was trying to keep him alive to give you time to get the rig up and running smoothly. I figured you could calm him down when you came back to California." He twisted the wheel sharply, knocking her against the passenger door. "Now, I may have to do the dirty work myself. Could get interesting—" He broke off as they both heard the noise at the same time. Hoofbeats. A horse not far away, galloping fast.

Mary smiled through the blood on her mouth. "We agree about one thing. It's about to get real interesting."

Chad was fifty feet behind them and thirty feet above. They were coming up to a long series of S curves and Kinnard would have to slow to navigate them. Urging Chester down a slope, Chad came up only twenty feet behind them now. He was riding too fast to pull his pistol and aim for the rear tires, plus he was worried he might hurt Mary if the Jeep tipped. He kicked Chester harder than he ever had. With a surprised grunt, the stallion bolted forward, finally breathing fast. Chad rode him up, almost to the rear bumper. The Jeep had a hitch and a rear tire cover. If he jumped, he might make it.

He was reaching out when the passenger door opened. To his horror, as they gunned along a raised track above a bluff, Kinnard pushed Mary out of the Jeep without even slowing down. She screamed, and for one flashing instant, Chad saw the duct tape around her wrists so she couldn't brace herself. She tumbled over and over sharp rocks on the edge of the road, cartwheeling over the bluff and out of sight.

Chad cursed a blue streak, wheeled Chester to a stop, pulled his pistol, and fired at the Jeep's rear tires. But Chester had been a rescue mount and he saw Mary fall. Without being commanded, he moved toward the bluff to start down it. Jolted in the saddle at this unexpected movement, Chad missed with his first three bullets, but he pulled Chester to a stop and the fourth one was spot-on.

The left rear tire gave a loud *whoosh* as it deflated, but Kinnard kept going. Chad paused for one quick look down the road, but his backup wasn't in view yet. He knew Sinclair would hear the shots and come as quickly as he could, so he reined Chester down the slope, cursing himself for not taking time to rig himself properly with a first aid kit.

Chad knew he was playing right into Kinnard's hands by stopping to help Mary, but he had to check on her before continuing his pursuit. As soon as he topped the bluff and saw her curled like a rag doll at the bottom of the steep slope, blood pooling around her head, he feared he was too late. Leaping off Chester before he'd stopped, Chad hurried over to her. She was deathly pale and still. He tested her pulse and was relieved to find one, though it was weak.

Despite the warmth of the day, shock was her biggest short-term danger, so he used the only covering he had: Chester's blanket. One side was sweaty but the other side of the thick fabric was dry. Chad wrapped her as much as he could. Then, gently, trying not to move her head, he felt for a wound. The depth of the cut into her skull concerned him greatly. He stood and whistled as loudly as he could. Then he pulled his pistol and gave two rapid-fire shots into the air.

He loaded his revolver again with the full six shots while he waited for what seemed like hours, but finally he heard vehicles blasting up the road toward the bluff. He climbed up the slope, waving his arms on the side of the dirt road. Sinclair, with Corey next to him, pulled to a stop. The heavier truck behind him was laden with equipment, including heavier weaponry, surveillance equipment and . . . Chad's heart leaped.

He smiled at his boss. "Thank you." He led them to the bluff, glad to see they'd brought a medic. Several troopers clambered down to Mary, one carrying a defibrillator.

Confident Mary was in good hands, Chad unchained the ATV from the back of the pickup bed. The backup cars were too far behind to catch Kinnard now, especially since he'd be close to the blacktop by now, where he'd probably commandeer a vehicle. His only hope was going cross-country, following the arroyo, and there was no better mode of transportation than this now that Chester was winded. "Take good care of her, will you? For Trey."

Chad's voice trembled a bit, and he cleared his throat before he said more clearly, "If you make it back before I do, would you please check on Jasmine? No matter what, even if you have to jail her as a suspect, don't let her leave."

Sinclair's knowing smile irritated the hell out of Chad, even under the stressful circumstances, but he got on the ATV, checked that the tank was full, levered it into top gear, and zoomed off so fast Sinclair had to back away from the cloud of dust.

Chad heard Sinclair shout, "Don't kill him!" but pretended not to.

He was exhausted, running on adrenaline now, but the image of Trey's still face would have goaded him out of a coma. Justice, Foster-style, was about to be meted out to this son of a bitch, for the last time . . .

Kinnard's left rear tire had long since shredded away when he finally reached the blacktop leading back to Amarillo. The rim was crumpling now, and it struck sparks when he limped along the road. Finally, in the distance, he saw a car coming. Hiding his pistol beneath his dusty suit jacket, he angled his vehicle across the road, got out and waved his arms. He saw the startled face of someone who looked like a local rancher, for he had a beat-up truck filled with hay and wore a fraying straw hat, as the vehicle approached and slowed.

The crank window lowered. "You okay, mister?"

Before Kinnard could reach the driver-side door, wearing his usual charming smile, they both heard it. It sounded like a motorcycle, but the timbre was a bit deeper. Then Chad Foster burst up the side of the arroyo and bore down on him astride a powerful ATV.

Cursing, Kinnard pulled his pistol and aimed it at the rancher. "Get out."

The rancher reached for the sky and slowly got out. He was tall, lanky, and he was eighty if he was a day. But when the ATV stopped alongside the road, he saw Chad clearly. He smiled, lowered his arms, pulled a toothpick from his hatband and started picking his teeth while he watched the show. He leaned back against the passenger door.

Kinnard brandished the gun at the rancher. "Move. I'm taking your truck."

The next moment, the gun was shot out of his hand. Kinnard cursed, cradling his sprained wrist. He took time for one look at Chad's liquid mercury eyes, shiny even surrounded by layers of dust and tiredness, vivid even beneath his hat, and then Kinnard used his unwounded hand to pull from his jacket pocket a switchblade he'd filched off a South Sider. He grabbed the old man, using him as a shield. He held the knife to a leathery throat. "Drop the gun or I'll slice his gizzard."

Chad kept on a-comin'. He stopped ten feet away and said calmly, "I don't think so. You're already going to be tried for one murder, maybe two if Mary doesn't make it. On the other hand, I'm plumb exhausted. I've already missed several shots today, so maybe I'll miss again. You want to try me?" Chad glanced at the old man. "Howdy, Buster."

The old man responded, "Howdy, Chad." He didn't seem overly concerned at the knife still held to his throat.

Chad sighted down the shiny old pistol, pulling back the hammer with a loud click. "On the other hand, I'd purely love to send you to prison with a shattered kneecap." The rancher was so skinny he didn't make a very good shield, and Kinnard's left leg was fully in Chad's line of sight.

Kinnard's grip loosened slightly. The rancher stomped on Kinnard's foot and dove sideways. Chad leaped for Kinnard's knife hand. Kinnard, his teeth bared in hatred, was fresher. But Chad was meaner . . .

Chad had holstered his pistol so his hands would be free. He used them to slam Kinnard's knife hand against the side of the heavy old truck. Crying out, Kinnard dropped the knife. Chad kicked it away.

Quick as the snake he was, Kinnard grabbed for Chad's gun. He had it out of the holster and was aiming for Chad's ribs when they both heard sirens in the distance. Chad's brutal grip around Kinnard's one good wrist slackened.

That was all Kinnard needed. He kneed Chad in the groin. Chad anticipated it and moved sideways, but his grip on Kinnard's wrist loosened further, allowing Kinnard to fire. The shot passed so close, it singed Chad's shirt. It also ricocheted off the side of the truck, grazing the rancher. He winced and caught his arm.

That was all the motivation Chad needed. Body-slamming Kinnard against the sturdy truck, Chad wrenched his gun away. In one smooth motion, he opened the cylinder and dumped his ammunition in the road, closed it with a click—and then used it butt first on Kinnard. Right cheekbone first, which resulted in a satisfying howl and crunch of bone, and then the left cheekbone. Nose, chin, the gun making a wonderful cudgel, all the more satisfying because it was a Foster legacy. Kinnard's face grew bloody, and he sagged, unconscious, held up only by Chad's weight propping him against the truck.

Chad's arm was caught in midstroke. "Easy, Chad," came Corey's soft voice. Chad blinked, moisture stinging his eyes. He didn't know if it was sprayed blood or tears, but finally he staggered back. Kinnard fell to the ground.

Neither bothered to catch him. After Chad checked on Buster, who showed him that the bullet had barely grazed him, Chad accepted the canteen and red kerchief Corey handed him. Chad took a long swig, poured water on the kerchief, and wiped his face and eyes. "Where's Captain Sinclair?"

"He went back to the office. We airlifted Mary into town."

Chad gave him a concerned look, but Corey shook his head. "It doesn't look good." His serious expression was softened by that impish grin. "He picked up your gal as he passed your homestead. She was walking to town."

Chad closed his eyes. "She's not my gal." *Yet . . .*

"Well, she was madder'n a wet hornet when he wouldn't let her leave. He had to hold her on charges. She was pissed you didn't take her with you."

Chad nodded. Typical. "She hasn't done anything."

"That's not the way the California HP tells it." Corey chuckled.

Great, now he'd be the latest joke around the office, Chad thought glumly. Cops of every stripe were merciless in their ribbing. He visualized a leather harness poised above his desk.

After they revived Kinnard, read him his rights, and took him, dazed but able to walk, into the backseat of a cruiser, Chad tried to marshal his depleted energy. "I'd rather face an army of Kinnards than that pissed-off redhead."

Corey's grin widened. "You can let her cool her heels for a night. She's in an isolated cell, so she's fine."

"Just take me home, Corey," Chad said. "I have to . . . see to Trey. Or get some more ice. And I have to go on the Internet and check Houston information." Chad ignored Corey's curiosity and got into the passenger side of the truck, for once leaving his colleagues to clean up the rest of the mess.

* * *

Twenty-four hours later, a shaved, rested, washed Chad, wearing his newest jeans and work shirt, along with his dress boots, entered the cell block at the DPS holding tank. Sinclair was on his heels, that ever present smile tweaking an otherwise impassive expression.

Chad glared at him, wishing he'd go back to his paperwork. He checked his watch. It was time.

Then Jasmine was there, wearing the same T-shirt and jeans she'd worn all the way from California. Her hair was mussed, but even without a scrap of makeup, she was gorgeous to Chad. He noted that her tattoo had faded even more. The glitter paint was gone, and the bright yellow was more of a cream.

He met her eyes. He knew Sinclair had told her about Mary's passing; his indirect role in that couldn't help matters. For once, he didn't make excuses or ask forgiveness. He just stood there, drinking her in, hoping his eyes could convey the hope for a future with her that he couldn't quite express, at least not with Sinclair so close.

Now was obviously not the time anyway . . .

"How dare you hold me against my will like this?" Jasmine's fury was all the more dangerous given it was delivered in an icy tone. "Is this any way to treat a cooperative witness? I have a good mind to go back to California. You can't hold me without habeas corpus, you have to charge me—"

"I can hold you for looking at me crossways for a few more hours if I want to," Sinclair rejoined. "You're a material witness in a case against a man responsible for millions in fraud damages and two murders we know of."

"You got your man, so let me go," Jasmine ground out, clenching the cell bars as she glared at Chad. "Or so help me I'm going to sue you all for false arrest and illegal incarceration. I lost my best friend, my home and my job helping in this investigation and this is the thanks I get? I have the right to call a lawyer!" Her voice trailed off. Her eyes widened as a new arrival was ushered into the cell block.

Chad stepped aside so the old, silver-haired but still very erect and dignified man could approach Jasmine. "It's about time. My number's still the same." Judge Routh cleared his trembly voice and gave his daughter a pleading look.

Chad gave her an even more pleading look over his shoulder, and then he retreated as the jailer unlocked her cell. But he was happy to see Jasmine fly into her father's arms, crying.

Judge Routh patted her back awkwardly. "I've missed you, child. Let me see you." Jasmine looked up at him with a luminous smile.

That was enough for Chad. At least he'd done one good thing for her, even if she never forgave him. Knowing he'd made his Mama and Trey proud, Chad followed Sinclair back to the offices for more paperwork.

But he couldn't concentrate. He paced up and down, waiting, as it seemed he had for a lifetime, for the woman he knew now was meant for him, no matter how different they were. He stopped, glaring into Corey's and Sinclair's smiling eyes. "What's a man who knows nothing about women doing falling for a woman who knows everything about men?"

"Sounds like a match to me," Corey said. He pulled something from a box on his desk and fixed it to dangle from a light fixture above Chad's desk. Chad scowled, but Corey only twiddled the toy kitten wearing a harness and carrying a whip. It spun in a circle.

"Besides," Corey added, "we all want to see pictures of you in a leather harness."

Sinclair burst out laughing. Chad tossed his hat at Corey, who ducked. Chad continued his pacing.

Sinclair needled, "I have a deer head on my mantel that looks braver than you."

Corey grew serious. "Trey gave you a great gift, Chad. Don't let it go."

"I know that." Chad barely glanced at him, he was so fixated on the door that led to the holding tank. Finally it opened and Judge Routh entered the office. With a grateful handshake and a smile for Chad, he left with a smile at his daughter, who brought up the rear.

Jasmine was carrying her satchel. Chad knew what it contained. She didn't need him for anything at all . . . well . . . he glanced at the kitten over his desk . . . especially now her father was back in her life. His heart in his throat, he waited.

So did Corey and Sinclair.

Jasmine said, "I've signed the release papers, though I still think it was wrong for y'all to put me in jail." As she looked among them, her gaze settled on the toy sex kitten above the desk.

Chad held his breath, expecting her to get angry, but instead, she laughed. She tucked her hand in Chad's arm. "All right, darling, let me see this ranch house of yours so we can see if the beams are sturdy enough."

Chad walked out with her on his arm, his heart about two tons lighter, his colleagues' laughter ringing in his ears.

But this time, he knew only the scent of Jasmine.

Two weeks later, Jasmine and Chad pulled up on the high cliff overlooking the canyon. They'd deliberately waited until dusk. Jasmine jumped off Chester, and Chad stepped down from his new quarter horse, still learning the green young stallion's eccentricities.

Jasmine leaned back against his chest, her arms wrapped around his, where they cradled her. A small but fine-quality diamond engagement ring bedecked her left hand, and the tattoo was gone in the vee of her blouse. She drank in the beauty of the colorful landscape washed now in the red, gold, and purple of sunset. "It's so beautiful here. I understand why you've never wanted to leave."

"Thanks for paying the back taxes, Jasmine. I'll pay you back."

She looked at him, and the love in her eyes was a gift he knew he didn't deserve. "You're right you will. For about, say the next fifty years . . ." She looked back at the view. "It looks just like Trey's painting, except it's in full color."

"No more gray days for me. And I'm not alone." Chad's throat tightened with emotion, so he did what he usually did when he was moved. He made a joke. "A man will give up a lot for a woman, but my horse?"

Jasmine smiled. "He's just like you, darling. He chose me and he wouldn't take no for an answer." And there, on a canyon rim as old as time, they kissed, celebrating yet again a love that would keep them new.

On the rise behind the homestead, a freshly dug grave bore a simple headstone that read, "Trey Foster. Beloved brother. Family is all that lasts."

Two empty black landscape buckets rolled a bit in the wind as the sun sank below the horizon. Lush green foliage and white blossoms fluttered in the breeze behind the headstone, where they would grow and nurture Trey's grave. The identifying plastic spikes in the freshly turned dirt around the plants read "Jasmine."

Meet another one of Colleen Shannon's rugged Texas Rangers in *Sinclair Justice*, available from eKensington next July . . .

CHAPTER 1

The sign said: Amarillo: 50 miles. Beaumont to El Paso: 1046. Welcome to Texas."

Managing not to roll her eyes at the typical Texas braggadocio, Mercy Magdalena Rothschild pressed slightly on the accelerator, impatient to get this interminable trip over with. A new BMW M5 convertible was a great way to cover the miles, but it was still a very long way from Washington D.C. to the booming metropolis of Amarillo, Texas.

'Emm' as her best friends called her, was not looking forward to her destination or to her tasks, but as soon as she saw this job posting she knew she had to apply. For Yancy.

But the fact that she had another mission in coming to this border state besides her new job as Historic Preservation Trust Officer in D.C. never left the back of her mind. An unapproved mission even her parents didn't know about, but one thing she'd learned in her very expensive ten years of higher education: how to do research.

Even of the criminal variety.

Even of the missing persons variety.

But thinking about Yancy and Jennifer would only bring the tears, never at bay very long, back to her tired eyes, and on this long and winding road, she couldn't afford that. Trying to distract herself, she shuffled to that very Beatles tune on the iPhone connected to her sophisticated iDrive in the car's onboard computer system.

The song, one of her favorites, still wasn't distraction enough, even when she sang the lyrics she knew by heart.

She broke off when she reached the part about the road leading to "your door." Yeah, like she'd meet someone in Texas. To say men didn't get her was putting it mildly, but their rejection had a universal ring, as different as all five of them had been.

One of them had even declared plaintively, "You're just weird, you know? And why do you use such big words?"

Because words are the font of knowledge and life, you dullard, learn a few, she'd wanted to say, but had held her tongue until the door closed behind him.

Emm sighed, doubly depressed now. Her eyes burned behind her sunglasses, but the ache had nothing to do with the bright spring sun. Yancy had been missing for six months, nine days—she glanced at her watch—and thirteen hours. Jennifer longer than that. She'd never forget the knock on the door at her tiny efficiency that night almost exactly six months ago.

The D.C. detectives who'd taken the missing persons report had stood there, looking uneasy. "Ma'am, we have news about your sister and her daughter. May we come in?"

In her matchbox living room they'd laid it out to her. The reward she and Yancy had posted for information leading to Yancy's missing daughter Jennifer had, he told her, finally yielded a clue. Yancy had, as usual, been hell bent and determined to follow up on her own. Emm, embroiled in her orals for her PhD, had begged her to wait. Then Yancy had disappeared, too . . . .

Of her own volition, before she even completed her orals, Emm had traveled the D.C. metro area to the low-end bars Yancy favored, handing out and posting flyers for both women. Mother and daughter strikingly resembled one another and Yancy had been a teen mom, so she was only in her late thirties and looked a decade younger.

Finally, three months after Yancy's disappearance, nine months after Jennifer had been taken, one of the flyers yielded a tip. The night cook at a seedy little café in downtown Baltimore was coming off duty at one in the morning, and he'd seen a woman who matched the picture of Yancy being forced into a big black sport truck with Texas plates. Her scream was choked off as she was forced into the front seat between the man who snatched her and the driver. He gave a description of the man who grabbed her but never saw the driver.

When the detectives asked why he hadn't come forward earlier, he gave the usual spiel about being afraid of being deported, but when the señorita—that was you, Ms. Rothschild, they'd told her—had pleaded for information, he overheard and felt guilty. Besides, he wanted the reward to send back to his family in Mexico.

"But what exactly does this mean?" Emm had asked. "Yancy was taken to Texas? What about Jennifer?"

The detectives seemed uneasy. The younger one had looked away, but finally the older detective answered quietly, "We had an urgent message from Yancy asking us to call, saying she had a lead on her daughter's whereabouts. We were working a dual homicide and by the time we called her back, her phone went straight to voice mail."

Emm had wearily rubbed her tired eyes. "So? And I was preparing for my orals so she didn't even call me to tell me she was going after Jennifer. What does that have to do with her being missing, except prove we'll all incompetent, self-absorbed assholes?"

They let that slide. The older detective continued, "We think your sister got too close, that she must have stumbled across the north-eastern source of the human trafficking ring. And they . . . took her too."

Or worse. Emm heard what they didn't say.

"At least that's what we think if the eyewitness is correct. So we combed surveillance footage all over D.C.'s major arteries for a similar truck with Texas plates. We found several matches heading south on the interstate but that's a lot of plates and none of the registered owners match the physical description given by the witness. In the meantime we've informed the Texas authorities and were told there's a high end snatch and grab ring with national reach culminating in West Texas. They bring in the . . . their . . . their . . ." He cleared his throat.

Emm inserted quietly, "I think the term in your nomenclature is merchandise."

He looked relieved and nodded. "Anyway, they bring them from all over the nation through Texas to the border. We still haven't figured out how they smuggle them across. The Texas Rangers are heading the task force along with the Border Patrol. We've given them all the information we have but will still work the case from this end as well."

Emm had to clear her throat because as she asked the question, she dreaded the answer. "What are the . . . .the merchandise . . . used for? Surely Yancy is too old for, for . . ."

He opened his mouth, swallowed, and then looked away.

She closed her eyes, biting her lip to stifle a moan. She was a trivia and science buff. The average American citizen might not be aware that slavery was worse than ever now in the technological age, partly because of the anonymity of the internet, but she knew the statistics. She also knew the vast majority of the kidnapped women, especially someone as beautiful as Yancy, were forced into prostitution. She was almost forty, but looked twenty-five. After being taken more than nine months ago, Jennifer was probably nothing like the vibrant young seventeen-year-old she'd once been. But she was young and adaptable and would have found a way to survive.

But Yancy? Her wild, irrepressible older sister wouldn't tolerate boundaries, or orders. Once on the inside, assuming she'd been taken by the same people, she'd risk her life to find her daughter. And she would not take well to captivity.

"What can I do?" she whispered over the tears she was restraining.

"I know this is difficult, but keep handing out flyers, ask everyone your sister knew if she had any Texas connections, maybe try to find out why she was in that part of Baltimore. We'll let you know if we get any more leads. Let us know immediately if you get any new information, no matter how insignificant." Both men gave her sympathetic smiles and left.

And that had been that, at least for the last three months. As she finished her demanding doctorate, in her spare time Emm had talked to everyone she could think of: classmates, friends, acquaintances, tenants in her sister's apartment building, old bosses, old boyfriends. No one knew why Yancy had been in downtown Baltimore or of anyone who drove a big black Texas truck. The trail ran cold for the detectives too, until finally they were off to another big case and they quit contacting her. Just another missing woman, and since she was Emm's half sister, Yancy wasn't even a Rothschild.

Now, three months later, back on the long lonely road to nowhere, Emm glared around at the sere landscape too tough to yield more than mesquite and cactus. Maybe Yancy was already dead, maybe Emm was on another foolish crusade, as her father had scolded her. Maybe her sister was buried in this wasteland . . .

Emm removed her sunglasses to dash angrily at her eyes, pressing harder on the accelerator.

So far, despite all the pressures she was under, she'd been good, exceeding the speed limit only when she could see for miles or she had another speeder to follow. She looked around, even over her shoulder, and the landscape was so open she could see horizon to horizon. Nothing. She was dying to try this new baby out. She knew the effort her father had expended to give his only natural daughter this hundred thousand plus vehicle, partly his way of voicing his regret that his wife was a self-absorbed alcoholic who had long ago lost interest in her older daughter's fate. As sales manager for a BMW dealer, her father made good money and had been able to get a screaming deal on this car, but the only Rothschild inheritance he had was a silver dollar collection given to him by a remote relative. And the name, all too often, had been more of a burden to Emm than a boon. People assumed she had money and that she was cold and snooty because of her unusual grasp of the English language. Wrong on both counts.

Yancy had even less money since her own father had passed when she was a child, and their social climbing mother was not happy about her willful older daughter, who refused to get a steady job or go to college. But Yancy and Emm had always been close. And Jennifer . . . the tears threatened again as she remembered her beautiful, blond, green-eyed niece. She tried to picture her as she likely was now, a dead look in her eyes, forced into short, tight dresses and hooker make up.

Emm's foot twitched at her unhappy thoughts, pushing down until the speedometer passed the conservative eighty, only five over the limit, the speed she'd tried very hard to maintain since she hit the

Texas state line. She knew the expensive red sports car and her New York plates made her a delectable morsel to the typical Texas highway patrolman's ravenous appetite for revenue.

She looked around again. Clear. Emm would never admit it, but her mouth was dry and she couldn't attribute the slight shaking of her hands to the long trip because she'd deliberately scheduled the last leg at a leisurely pace so she'd be fresh for her meeting. She was properly dressed in a sensible gray suit, sensible shoes, with her hair sensibly tied back, her usual camouflage for field work. She was a woman in a world of men, and she'd learned long ago to downplay her considerable good looks. Especially in a place as conservative as Texas, west Texas, to boot. The most conservative part of Texas, and the last bastion in the increasingly progressive state of the rugged individualist.

Badly needing her usual stress reliever, Emm gave up her battle, What was the big deal, anyway? Speed was her only vice. Not the oral stimulant, never, but the automotive version was almost as addictive. She had the twelve speeding tickets to prove it. Her insurance was astronomical, but nothing invigorated her as much as the wind howling through her hair and the roar of a powerful exhaust cheering her on. This car was meant for speed and she only had about thirty miles left to her destination, so it was now or never. She'd earned her favorite high and the thoughts about Yancy made every nerve in her body jangle with the need for action.

The needle hovered at a mere eighty-five now, ten over the limit. She took a last careful look around but this section of road was too open for a speed trap. The needle on her M5 convertible didn't bobble when she pressed on the gas—in one gentle arc it went from eighty to one hundred in about two seconds. The engine was so smooth, the throaty growl was entirely too civilized. The sleek German machine wasn't even challenged. Feeling one of her hair pins fly free and not caring, Emm pressed harder on the accelerator.

Finally the engine roared back as if to say, "That all you got?"

Laughing, having the best time she'd had since graduation, Emm pressed harder still—110, 120, man this baby could fly.

The wail of the siren was faint at first. She'd glimpsed something black and big and shiny out of the corner of her eye as she streaked past a gate in a long row of white fencing, but she'd discounted it as a rancher's truck. She looked in her rearview mirror and stifled a groan, immediately taking her foot off the gas pedal. A siren wailed and she saw a blue and white light flash from a side of the SUV's roof. The light had obviously been attached only when the driver saw her zip past, so this cop was not a typical highway patrolman.

The neat little speech about how big Texas was, and no, she really didn't know she was going that fast, her Beamer was a new graduation present, went out the window with her deep breath. "Good going, Emm," she said to herself. "No one's more hard nosed than an undercover cop." She pulled to the side of the road, got the registration from the glove box, and took her insurance card and her New York driver's license from her purse.

In her side mirror, she watched the man approach. He was tall, over six feet, with iron gray hair she could just glimpse under his expensive Stetson. Black, of course, to match his black jeans. His shirt was white, a dress shirt crisp with starch, sort of like his spine. His eyes were covered in mirrored shades but there was no mistaking his glacial tone. "If you want to race that fancy little import, I can give you the address of a race track in Lubbock. Do you have any idea how fast you were going and all the lives you endangered, including mine, as I was about to pull out of my driveway, by driving like that?"

"I'm sorry, officer, I was just in a hurry to get to Amarillo. You know, I'm like that bumper sticker: 'I'm not from Texas but I got here as fast as I could.'" He'd stopped at her open window now and perused her documents, glancing between her driver's license photo and her flushed face. Her hair pins had long ago lost the battle, and her brown mane shot through with blond and red highlights was tangled. She took off her sunshades so he could see her eyes. She blinked. "See, blue? Just like it says. I promise I'm not here to commit murder or fraud . . ." So far her attempt at charm was an abysmal failure. His mouth was beautifully shaped, meant for laughing, but she couldn't get it to even twitch. She'd been out of the dating scene too long.

With a curt, "Don't move," he stalked back to his SUV, to run her I.D. She stifled another groan. It had almost taken an act of Congress to get her license back last time, not to mention thousands in fees and a good traffic attorney. Once he saw how many tickets she had. . . . Nevertheless, she was stunned when he returned to her side of the car with a pair of handcuffs.

"Get out of the car, please." He stepped back slightly, appraising her with eyes she knew were arctic behind the shades.

She looked at the start button on her dashboard. She had one of the new ignitions, the kind that started only when the key was in the car. Her foot was on the brake, so she only had to punch the start button and she suspected she could quite literally leave him in the dust.

"Be sensible, Mercy Magdalena," she could hear her Irish grandmother pleading from the grave. This was not a good beginning to her first field investigation, and fleeing an officer of the law would not endear her to her federal employers. She looked at him from the corner of her eye. Besides, she might need some help from the local constabulary in looking for Yancy.

He'd stiffened alertly as if he'd read her mind. His icy politeness softened to a Texas drawl that was somehow more menacing. "Please, do it. Resisting arrest carries a much longer sentence than speeding and I'd purely love to buy your car at the police auction."

Colleen Shannon grew up in West Texas where the skies are as limitless as the tales told by its many colorful residents. Surrounded by oil men, lawyers, and drillers in a community that has produced two presidents and many national leaders and businessmen, Colleen grew up reading and writing stories of every kind. After college when she married and was expecting her first child, she used a scrap computer to write her first romance. She sold it herself in less than a year, and at the age of twenty-six began a new career and never looked back. The strength of her first book led to her nomination by *Romantic Times* as Best New Historical Author. She went on to win or be nominated for many other awards, and her fifteen single title releases have appeared on numerous bestseller lists. She has well over a million books in print.

Her newest release is from Kensington, a romantic suspense, her first published contemporary. It is planned as the first in a series about modern Texas Rangers, another interest of Colleen's because her ancestor, a Texas Ranger, was one of the first people buried in Brown County cemetery. Another of her ancestors was a signatory to the Texas Declaration of Independence.

Made in the USA
Monee, IL
15 February 2022

91299315R10142